KNOWLE
IS
EVERYTHING

Kevin Shurvinton

CHAPTER 1

Ryan felt the warmth of the late afternoon sun radiate gently against his face, he shifted awkwardly in his chair. What state of affairs was he entering into? Deep down he knew something did not add up. Of that he was sure. Ryan gave a short cough trying to clear the lump in his throat, buying himself a precious second or two while he weighed up the facts.

Max sat opposite, staring intently into Ryan's eyes. His face a vision of tranquil contemplation. His body relaxed, confident, composed. But the eyes. They were working. Studying every flicker of body language from Ryan. Ryan knew behind those eyes Max was analyzing, interpretating and considering the answer he would give, before he offered it. Ryan shifted once again in his seat, the hard leather suddenly uncomfortably hot, mild perspiration sticking his shirt to his back.

Max remaining motionless, raised an eyebrow marginally. The subtle gesture prompting an answer. Ryan felt himself automatically react to the gesture, his mouth subconsciously opened, throat muscles tensed, but no words came out. Ryan sat with his mouth half open realizing he had committed to give an answer he wasn't ready to provide. His mind reeled to find a question to ask to buy more time. Infinite questions were in his mind, but nothing came to the forefront to ask. He closed his mouth again.

Eighteen months had passed since Ryan had arrived in the dream factory known globally as Hollywood. It was his destiny. Since he could remember this mecca was his calling, and he had answered the call. He knew the big break would not just come to him. He would have to be persistent and unwavering in his determination. Every biography he had ever read all told the same basic story. If you aim high, be prepared for the knockbacks, lots of them. But if you can keep climbing over the souls of your own broken dreams, eventually you may just reach a desperate hand on the treasure you seek. Eternal failure may lie ahead, but while you're still in the race – there's always a chance.

Ryan was a small-town boy, blessed with incredible looks. A manly face, beset by a strong muscular jawline and perfect symmetrical features, yet at the same time very apparent feminine qualities. Extensive & costly dental work polished off the product that was Ryan. The repayments of which were causing more headaches than finding the rent money each month. His blonde hair shimmered in the rays of sunlight casting into the room. It sat perfectly. It always did. Beyond any insecurities Ryan had born in his time in this colony of perfect entities and shallow personalities, his hair never concerned him.

He had left his home a local celebrity, with attention and kudos on tap. Now he was a nobody, his narcistic being starved of devotion and hungry for limelight. That hurt more than the financial hole he was teetering over. However, the money situation was the factor which was ultimately going to end his search for glory. He had to fix this and buy himself time. Time to find his break, time to find his birthright.

"Well?" Max broke Ryan from his internal rumination. He glanced back at Max's eyes. Still processing fast and hard.

Ryan swallowed hard, He gave another fidget and broke eye contact with Max. This gig was not film, nor television. No stage to own in front of an admiring audience. It was acting but housed in circumstances which made no sense. The motives of the man before him were at best questionable, but what choice did Ryan have? He couldn't face returning home a failure. Accepting the disappointment of some and glee of others. No. He couldn't.

His voice encompassed with reluctance; he warily accepted the invitation.

CHAPTER 2

Zac pondered that night so many years ago which had changed his life forever. The feeling of resentment towards his father elevated from the pit of his stomach. He stopped himself and immediately the sensation was replaced by a mixture of guilt and pity towards the man who was once his hero. The hero of many. But that was before, a different time, a different life. That existence now departed, never to return.

Roy, his father was now sober and rebuilding some resemblance of a life, but this had commenced too late for forgiveness. At best it was a chance of damage limitation for Zac and the other people affected by Roy's decline.

Zac looked at his watch. Damn. Why had he arrived so early? The waiting was causing levels of anxiousness to grow, worst still time to contemplate the pain in his life and the scars burnt into his soul. Focus on why you're here, Zac told himself. He took a sharp intake of breath followed by a sip of coffee and considered what might be discussed in the next hour or so. He surveyed the plush hotel reception, full of expensive fittings and fixtures. Bellboys and receptionist dressed in suits so smart they looked more like CEOs ready to enter the boardroom. This was the selected location where the interview would take place.

Zac, twenty-two years in age had developed into a slim, but athletic young man, although he rarely ventured near athletics tracks these days. His hair was mid-length with a center parting. His skin slightly tanned, with handsome facial features and dark brown eyes. His mother's eyes. The reception was air conditioned cool, nevertheless Zac felt anything but cool. He breathed in deeply once, twice, three times. Zac managed for a short time to empty his mind, his heart rate slowed down and he regained control. He watched the hotel staff as they busied themselves at the far off reception desk.

"Zac?" A voice suddenly bought him out of the haze. Zac looked up with a clumsy expression and nodded. "Maxwell Taylor." The figure in front of Zac introduced. "But just call me Max." He extended a hand and shook the now rising Zac's hand with a firm, but friendly manner.

Zac knew his name well, this was the first time he had the opportunity to see what the man looked like. He suddenly felt honored to be in the company of such a well respected and pioneering computer programmer. It had all started a few weeks ago at home.

Zac was now close to graduating, with honors, from the illustrious MIT. A kudos which he had anticipated would attract offers and attention from all the big tech names throughout the States. He was already applying for a vast number of jobs with a relevance to his degree in computer science and programming. This in itself had been a harsh fall into reality. Prior to Zac commencing the process he had often conversed with the other students in his class about what kind of career they wished to become part of. The household names of companies they desired to work for. They had speculated wildly on the employment package they could command.

The harsh reality of being a new boy on the block had soon hit home. Yes, the degree counted for a lot in terms of a marker, but without the employment experience to back it up, it positioned him, what appeared to be just above worthless, MIT graduate or not. The seniority of positions Zac had fantasized about he now realized were clearly not yet on his radar... Upon approaching a lecturer about the issue, Zac was candidly informed it was with good reason.

"Those kinds of positions either go to someone within the same company, who has worked his or her butt off for the last fifteen years, or if nobody internally is suitable, they would headhunt someone else appropriate from a rival company." The lecturer had educated him. "Put it this way, when you passed your driving test did it automatically make you a good driver? At the time you probably thought you were, but after a few years behind the wheel I'm sure it has become apparent it was not the case. Compare your driving now to back then."

Zac nodded in agreement.

"Now I guarantee after another ten years of driving you will develop, read the road ahead better and anticipate before it happens. It is the same with this. You start at the bottom, work long and hard and get good. Slowly and I do mean slowly, you will get noticed and if you're determined enough one day you can achieve the leap to those senior positions. However always bear in mind there are many others attempting to do the same."

From that point Zac adjusted his sights to "realistic" and began applying for the particularly mundane positions in computer programming that he could make his with no experience. Melissa had moved in just over six months ago. It was difficult at first sharing his space with someone full time, but he was beginning to feel settled. Melissa's sympathetic understanding of Zac's past helped greatly in the arrangement working. She knew he had issues and he needed time to himself to concentrate on his work. It was the access to this solitary space keeping him calm and reasonable. Her preference to spend more time together was a sacrifice Melissa knew she had to make. When Zac spent countless hours at his computer, she would visit her mother, Sally. Or meet up with friends. After time she understood this was a healthy dynamic. So many of her past friends had met a man and literally disappeared off the face of the earth. Devoting all their free time to their partner, losing contact with everyone around. If they split up, the realization hits. Their whole social life unconnected with their ex-partner had disappeared. Friends have moved on and it is difficult to rebuild.

Zac was Melissa's first real love. She had been the quiet schoolgirl with only close friends. It was only in her late adolescence, the strong noticeably beautiful side of her developed. She was now a young woman with soft delicate features. Her cheeks would often glow red at the slightest embarrassment, a throwback to her timid youth. Melissa was a head turner. She was slim, tall and had long flowing strawberry blond hair. It was an unexpected change for her to leave the status of being the girl who disappeared in a small group of friends, to being the woman who stood out in a large crowd. Although ill at ease to admit it even to herself she knew her status had changed. Deep down it bestowed her a newfound confidence.

She met Zac in a night club at the end of the night. Melissa had noticed him in there looking awkward and out of place. She herself was not having the best of times. The club scene wasn't for her, but friends take you out of your comfort zone and influence you to follow their interests. It was one of her first times and the whole atmosphere was intimidating. She could tell he was in the same situation, dragged in by friends and left to suffer. Melissa scanned the club, her friends, fully intoxicated were on the dance floor teasing the men around them with flirtatious smiles and looks. She looked again at the lost young man and made a decision. She could not believe her own bravery, embarking on an act completely alien to her. Picking up her drink, she walked straight up to him.

It turned out to be a good decision. Within months they were deeply in love and moving in together. Melissa felt happier than she could ever remember. She held a real optimism their relationship would only go from strength to strength. The only looming issue concerning her was when Zac graduated. The near certainty they might have to move away for his job. Leaving her mother, to whom she was very close, more so after Jim, her father had ran off with a work colleague, was going to be difficult. Her father had given no warning to what he was intending to do. Sally had not even suspected an affair, let alone Jim leaving her. One day she and Melissa came home from a day out shopping to find a letter on the coffee table. All his clothes and personal effects were gone and so was he. It hit both of them like a ton of bricks. Her mother's world had been devastated by the event and Melissa, while managing her own grief had to nurse her mother through a nervous breakdown.

Six months later, on Melissa's sixteenth birthday he had tried to establish contact with her again, but she couldn't forgive him for what had happened. If he had been a man and spoken to Sally face to face. Admitted to her he had met someone else and wanted to be with her. Then eventually Melissa may have considered trying to salvage a relationship out of the whole mess. Leaving a cowardly letter was a step too far.

Now a few years on Sally was strong enough to cope, she hadn't met anyone significant since, but had a wide, varied social life and a strong friend base. Leaving her to move away with Zac wasn't the issue it might have been, but Melissa would have to be careful not to shock her Mother. She would need plenty of notice to get used to the idea. She had already begun dropping hints about her possible future. They would miss each other terribly, but as long as Sally could cope without her, she knew her life was with Zac. Leaving her friends wasn't such a big issue. They would be missed, but Melissa's newfound self-assurance would help her building up new friends after relocating. The same went for her career. She had worked her way up to duty manager of a local jewelry store. Although it would be a compromise on Melissa's part to leave her job after so quickly elevating herself through sheer hard work and determination, she hoped it might throw open new options to her. It was fair to say Melissa was not exactly popular for her fast track through the positions of the business and the resentment from her colleagues was making her job twice as challenging. A fresh start, maybe even a middle manager in a new store might be just the ticket. The jewelry store she worked for was a national chain so Melissa hoped she could simply transfer to one within the area of their possible new location.

"I have a room in the hotel. We'll hold the interview there if that's ok?" Maxwell offered. Zac nodded in agreement. Max led him to a grand looking elevator with highly polished golden doors. As they opened Zac was surprised to see an elevator attendant operating it. He thought the days when people did such jobs had long since disappeared. God knows what it would cost to stay here, he thought to himself. They stepped into the lift and without asking, the attendant pressed the button for floor five. Zac shot Maxwell a sideways look. He looked relaxed; Zac was not relaxed. The silence was making the tension worse. Zac wanted to say something but couldn't. As they reached floor five and the doors opened finally allowing Zac to step out. He felt a wave of relief fall over him. It was a short walk down the hall to the hotel room.

Zac was expecting to enter a normal hotel room, with just a bed, a restroom and a television. They stepped into a plush spacious hotel suite with a large lounge area, a grand table dominating the room directly in the center, large comfortable looking couches surrounded the feature. The carpet was thick and soft under his feet. Noticeable even through his shoes. A large plasma screen television hung from the wall and doors opposite led to a balcony with a fantastic view of the city. Not a bed in sight, instead several doors leading off from the room. This was not a hotel room Zac had ever experienced before. It was million miles from the sad dingy motel rooms that was his world.

"Have a seat." Max gestured with his hand to the couches. Zac smiled and sat down trying not to look as if he were amazed by the grandness of the room. "Coffee?" He asked sitting down opposite him, placing a tray on the table containing a freshly brewed pot, and cups on it.

"Yes, thank you." Max poured the coffee and then sat back into the couch.

"How aware are you of my work?" Zac immediately thought back to the morning he first read the letter. He was sat at the Kitchen diner, nursing a cup of coffee, still trying to wake up when Melissa came out the bedroom. She was wearing stripy pajamas, her hair tied back into a ponytail. Zac in his dressing gown looked up and smiled to greet her. His usually immaculate hair was ruffled and messed.

"Good morning darling." Zac offered "want a coffee?"

"Yes please." Melissa returned, walking towards the front door. She crept out to the mailboxes. It was an apartment of six, but the mailboxes were situated by their front door, so she often chanced going out into the communal corridor, not properly dressed to retrieve any correspondence. She re-entered the apartment more awake than a few seconds previous. "You've got some mail Zac." She proudly announced as she excitedly threw the letters at him. This in turn perked Zac up.

"Let's hope our luck is in." He beamed. Zac was feeling somewhat buoyant. He had attended two different interviews in the previous week. The jobs were bottom feeder positions but with multinational tech companies. After two positive interviews he had a good feeling. Surely one, if not both would come back with a job offer? He was going to be an MIT grad for Christ's sake. He ripped open the first envelope, unfolded the letter and scanned through it.

"Any good?" Melissa enquired.

"Damn it. It's from E-Life. Thank you for taking the time to meet us." He read out loud. "We enjoyed having your company for the interview, however unfortunately you have been unsuccessful in your application of programming assistant. We will hold your information on file, and should a similar opportunity arise, we will contact you again." Zac screwed the letter up, tossing it in the bin and gave Melissa a dejected look.

"Well at least their keeping you on file." She offered optimistically, if a little naïve.

"Yeah, sure they will." Zac replied, disbelieving the pledge. He opened the next envelope. "Shit." He threw the letter on the counter. "That's Elite Internet Solutions and another no." Melissa opened her mouth to say something but decided against it. She offered Zac a sympathetic smile, but he wasn't looking. Zac picked up the next envelope and despondently opened it. He scanned through the content. Then scanned again. Then he started to read it properly. Within a few seconds Zac's expression changed. Melissa noticed the sudden look of concentration on his face.

"Well?" she asked impatiently.

"Just one second." Zac replied not taking his eyes off the letter. Once completed Zac allowed himself a second or two to consider the content, then looked up at Melissa "I doubt you've heard of Max Taylor, have you?"

"No?" Melissa sat beside him trying to look at the letter herself, frustrated by waiting for the contents to be revealed to her. Zac turned the letter away from her and smiled. "Come on, please." she begged.

"Max Taylor is a psychiatrist who last year, released a software program called "Self Diagnose". As the title suggests it offers a diagnosis of mental health problems. It basically takes you through a diagnosis process linking its questions to previous answers. It's based around mental health and questions you about any psychological problems you might have. We covered it at MIT as its thought to contain some of the most complex algorithms ever devised. Through the process as the name suggests it provides you with a diagnosis. I know that lots of doctors and psychologists are up in arms about it, patients trying to tell them what was wrong with themselves. It offers some basic steps to take once diagnosed, but then instructed people with a condition to get professional help. It's more about the analysis than the treatment. The studies we looked at in class all concluded it was incredibly accurate. There were a lot of comments that it was more likely to provide a correct diagnosis first time than most medical professionals. Naturally this caused a bit of a stir in the medical community.

"And?"

'Well, the letter is a job interview from Max even though I didn't even apply to him. It says he's writing the next edition that will not only diagnose the problem but treat it as well."

"It sounds a bit controversial to me." Melissa offered.

"Yes." Zac paused briefly while he considered this. "But he wants someone to work closely alongside him to develop it. What a challenge that would be, a step closer to a type of artificial intelligence. Still, something no one has ever achieved." Zac stated confidently.

"Wow." Melissa thought to herself for a minute. "Do you think it's possible to do, to make it work realistically?"

"I don't know. I really don't." Zac looked back down at the letter. This was the manner of job he thought he could only dream of getting, but here he was reading a letter approaching him. "But I'm willing to find out for that amount of money." He returned the letter toward Melissa. Her jaw dropped open at the wage, $12,000 a month, plus bonuses for successful completion of specific modules to be negotiated at the interview. Melissa stared in amazement at the figure.

"How the hell can he afford a wage like that?"

"He's minted after the first version, it sold worldwide. I dunno why he's offering this to a lowly like me? Says I've got to phone him to arrange a meeting." Melissa leaned across and grabbed the letter out of his hand, gave it a kiss and carefully placed it on the table. They both embraced each other.

Zac explained to Max his knowledge of the previous release. He talked about the case study at MIT considering the complexity in the algorithms. Max immediately looked impressed by Zac's answer.

"That's great. I completed a lot of the programming myself. I farmed out certain aspects to remote programmers. Only I know how it all works together. A few trusted professionals assisted with the more complex parts, but no one has the full picture.' Max explained. "It was a very intense couple of years, I don't mind admitting that I struggled with it, but it's all worth it when you have the finished product." Max paused and took a large sip of coffee. "As I briefly explained in my letter, I now want to write a program for a virtual psychiatrist. Not only diagnosing mental health problems, but also counselling the user, providing real treatment for their condition to a standard you'd pay thousands for. I know that it's an ambitious ask. It has to work without glitches and be consistent to be credible." Max paused and arched his hand around his jaw line stroking his toned and moisturized face. "It would be an achievement in itself to get this program up and running, working some of the time. However, to maintain my brand and ensure it's a viable product, it needs to perform much better than some of the time." Zac nodded in agreement, his mind working fast. "A program like this is dangerous. We have to take responsibility for how it affects the people who purchase it. I certainly wouldn't want to fuel the inevitable protesting and disapproval from my medial colleagues. I'll get some anyway, but that's a good thing, free advertising. Controversy always increases sales." He finished with a smile. Zac politely chuckled in agreement understanding the irony of the statement. "So, before we get down to discussing the more technical details, tell me about yourself."

Zac talked about his time at MIT and Melissa. He didn't mention Roy or his deceased mother. After the technical side of the interview was complete, Zac asked where Max was based.

"Glad you asked, that Zac." Max enthusiastically replied. "Well to be honest, I'm going to need you to relocate I'm afraid."

"I had anticipated it." Zac countered positively.

"Good. Well, if I took you on, I would actually like you to come and live in my house." Zac raised his eyebrows. "Now don't worry, I own a beautiful mansion, all state of the art. Melissa would be welcome to stay as well. There is plenty of space. You'd have your own private quarters with a double bedroom, a private bathroom, living room and kitchen. All rent free of course." Zac felt himself breathe a sigh of relief. "It's situated in the northern part of New York State, it's quite remote though. About ten miles to the nearest small town. How does it sound?"

"It sounds great. I would need time to think about it and discuss it with Melissa."

"Sure." Max said with a wise smile. "I wouldn't expect you

to accept this minute if I offered you the position. I promise you though she would love the place. Great views, an ultra-modern design, a ridiculously large roll top bath..."

"You got her at the bath." Zac joked, knowing Melissa would give anything for that particular luxury.

CHAPTER 3

Four weeks later Zac and Melissa landed at LaGuardia airport. Both were feeling a mixture of emotions, as if pioneers on an expedition to find new and undiscovered lands. Zac was swayed with trepidation, more than he had expected, but with Melissa at his side he knew he was not making the leap alone.

Melissa below her excitement thought only for her mother. Since they agreed to go, she had dreaded abandoning Sally. Melissa kept thinking back to telling her mother they were leaving and going in weeks. Sally had given nothing but encouragement. To the casual observer it would appear she had no problem at all with her daughter moving on. It did not fool Melissa. She knew underneath the bravado and goodwill; her mother was anguished with the understandable abandonment and the inevitable loneliness it would bring. She had spent as much time with Sally as possible until the move. Not sure if it was helping or making it worse. Several times Melissa had offered to stay, if she wanted her to. Her mother had laughed it off "I don't need you cramping my style" she always jokingly replied.

As they walked off the airplane to the baggage claim Melissa tried to dismiss the thoughts formed in her mind's eye, haunting her, Sally sat by herself, crying in her own loneliness and despair, but it remained. They picked up their luggage and met the prearranged driver. The luxurious private car whisked them off, on the way to their final destination.

The drive was almost two hours. Melissa tried to hide her worries, but Zac could detect her underlying negativity. He wasn't feeling much better himself. That was until after not seeing another car or house for about five miles the driver rounded the corner and turned onto a private road revealing a beautiful huge glass and steel structure flowing out of the hillside. They both stared in awe. The building had no corners, only long sweeping curves of glass protruding out of one side of the waning hillside bending out into the open proudly, seeming almost impossible before the never-ending curve returned back into the barren rock the other side. The long sweeping arch of glass appeared to be an unbroken, floorless and from their viewpoint no support was visible underneath. This provided the impression of the building simply floating out of the hillside. The effect materialized as truly impossible, as if the building should simply break away from the cliff face, collapsing into the ground below.

As the car approached, massive pillars set far back underneath the structure came into view. Clearly these were responsible for creating the illusion. Zac and Melissa took a long look at each other, both amazed. The driveway led between the pillars to a large underground garage. Zac surveyed the collection of European dream cars surrounding him open mouthed. In one corner a charcoal grey Aston Martin DB9 sat in perfect elegance. In another a white Porsche 911 Turbo. Behind that an orange Mclaren Speedtail. They parked alongside a very ordinary by comparison, silver BMW X5.

"How much money does he have?" Zac whispered to himself. The driver slowed to a stop and turned off the engine.

"Please wait here." he said stepping from the vehicle. The man walked over to an intercom by a pair of elevator doors. He spoke into it for a short while then returned to the car. He gestured for them to vacate the vehicle while he opened the trunk to recover their luggage. As Zac stepped out the elevator door began to slide apart. He leant forward trying to peer into the open gap, but it was empty. So instead Zac dusted himself off and stretched his legs after the long journey. The driver quickly carried the suitcases into the elevator.

"Please enter the elevator." He instructed returning to his vehicle. Zac tipped the driver and waited for Melissa to join him, offering his hand. Holding hands, they stepped into the elevator and looked for a button to press. There was no visible button, but as soon as they were in, the elevator doors shut. Smoothly it automatically accelerated into the house.

The doors reopened to reveal the smart and affluent in appearance, Max Taylor.

"Welcome." Max stepped forward giving Zac an excited handshake, before embracing him and giving Zac a pat on the back. The casual friendliness took Zac by surprise, but it felt good. Max stepped back and turned to Melissa. "And you must be Melissa?" He shook her hand and moved closer to give her a polite kiss on the cheek. She immediately felt warmed by his welcome.

"Are you tired? How was your journey?" Max asked. Zac and Melissa looked at each other and gave a mutual sigh.

"Yeah, it was long, but we had no problems." Zac answered. Melissa nodded in agreement.

"Your house is amazing." she said.

"Thanks, I hope you like the inside as much. Come on, leave your bags there and I'll give you the tour." Zac let his eyes wander around the entrance room. The elevator shaft was positioned proud of the back wall cut into the hillside. Two doors sat symmetrical of each other on both side walls with a pair of grand looking sliding doors immediately in front. Finished in cream with an oak wood floor the room had a balanced blend of old and modern contemporary about it. Zac was already impressed.

Max led the way to the door on Zac's right. It opened into a huge kitchen diner. On the far side began the glass wall displaying a breath-taking view of the remote landscape. Max noticed Zac's open-mouthed gawping at the view.

"If you think that's good, wait until you see the great room." Max stepped further into the room. The kitchen was a mixture of shiny black modern doors and granite work surfaces presented in clean elegant lines. In the dining area sat an oversized solid oak table with twelve chairs surrounding it. Beyond, nearer to the window two less formal couches sat inspecting the view for themselves.

"This is my kitchen and dining room, but you're both free to use this room as you please."

Max then stepped back into the foyer area. He led them across the room to the door on the opposite side. They stepped into what appeared a futuristic IT room. Several state of the art computer stations resided amongst ultramodern long sweeping desks. Four seductive deep leather computer chairs accompanied each of the workstations. Adjustable metallic blinds isolated the room from the fantastically distracting views through the radius of glass behind them. The room was lit in a pleasant soft blue, not harsh like the fluorescent hell of regular office lighting.

"This is the office. I like to keep the view out. When we're working in here, I don't want distractions. We have a lot of work to cover over the next couple of years. I kept the room comfortable so we can spend large amounts of time in here, but also designed it so we stay focused." Max's voice was a little more serious and sterner than before. Zac and Melissa nodded silently taking in as much as they could. "One thing I would like to get straight while I'm on the subject, this room after now is out of bounds to you Melissa." She looked a little taken aback. "Nothing personal, but like I said, no distractions while at work. With you both living and working here, we need boundaries."

"It makes sense." Zac replied. Melissa knew she had to agree.

"Anyway, onto the great room." Max ushered them back out, the soft lightness returning to his voice. He masterfully strode to the giant double doors. Gripping both handles with an exaggerated heave prized the doors apart. They glided smoothly and silently, allowing the momentum to carry them, disappearing into the wall, until they gently slowed to halt on their dampened stops.

Zac walked into an awe-inspiring stylish and sophisticated space, filled with large leather couches. The largest plasma screen he had ever seen. A bar area fully stocked with an array of different liqueurs. The whole room was an oversized oval. Through the massive panoramic window, a perfect view of a large clear expanse of water. Zac hadn't noticed the lake on their arrival as small hills around this side of the lake obscured his view. From up here the slight was magical. Sunlight rippled playfully across the cool blue, sparkling, hypnotizing his eyes. As he looked closer birds could be seen gliding gracefully though the cold air, waiting, then diving purposefully into the depths, hunting the plentiful life from within. Max fell silent, giving them both time to take in the whole reason for the seemly impossible location and design of his house.

"My god." Melissa loudly whispered.

"I can sit and watch this view forever." Max finally said. "I just wish I could find the time to do it." They all laughed. "Feel free again to use this room as much as you want. It needs to be used more." Zac walked up to the glass and peered out. Eventually he forced his eyes away from the visual oasis and looked down at the ground in front of the house. He was surprised how far above the ground level they were. It seemed much higher than when he first set eyes on the house from the ground.

"Come on then, let's continue the tour." They followed Max out back to the elevator and stepped inside. "Pool." Max spoke loud and clear. The elevator doors closed. They headed down. "Voice activated lift." He explained.

The swimming pool was located below the garage underground. They stepped out into the pool room. Their bewilderment continued. The pool was large enough to be an open to the public baths. A large Jacuzzi sat in the corner of the room. Expensive mosaic tiling littered the walls and floor.

"I'm a passionate swimmer, so I spared no expense in this room."

"It shows." Zac quipped.

"Your house is fantastic." Melissa complemented.

"Our house for now Melissa, he replied. Again, feel free to use this room as much as you like. Right onto the final and top floor." they all stepped back in. "Top floor." He spoke to the elevator and off they climbed.

The doors opened to reveal a long, wide corridor with a large glass skylight spanning the length of the room, all the way to meet the front curved window. The walls painted in a neutral cream color.

Once more two doors stood symmetrically on opposite sides. Max led them to the door on the right-hand side. Inside was another small corridor with several doors, again with cream walls and lit by a skylight.

"Now this is your private quarters. After today I will stay out of here, it's important to have your privacy. He opened the door on the left and bought them into a reasonably sized living room. Again, similar couches to downstairs and a plasma screen, albeit to a more modest scale. A desktop computer sat in the corner. It also enjoyed the large window. The lake was still visible, but off to the side as the angle worked against it. Still a brilliant view, but not in comparison to the stupidly wide and central great room. After examining it quickly Max took them through the end door into a kitchen diner. Maintaining the continuity, it was very similar to downstairs, but all reduced in size. It also benefited from light beaming through at the beginning of the house's wide rap around window.

"I know it's all a bit the same, but hey, I'm a single guy, I didn't have a woman to gives me loads of different ideas." Max joked.

"It looks fine to me." Melissa commented.

The final door in the corridor led into a bedroom, in contrast far more traditional than the rest of the house. It had a quaint English feel to it. Flowery wallpaper, thick rugs on the floor and extenuated by a large four poster bed.

"Wow. I love it." Melissa burst out excitedly. Zac and Max shared a smile as she hurriedly moved about the room unable to hide the emotion on her face.

"I copied this room out of a magazine." He confessed. "I'm guessing it was a good decision."

"Yes definitely." Melissa agreed, just noticing an additional door in the room.

"Melissa, go through the door." Max instructed giving Zac a knowing look. Without a second's hesitation she was gone. For a moment all was silent, soon broken by a short squeak of excitement.

"Zac!" she called. He quickly walked into the room. Inside the theme continued as an English Victorian style bathroom. Melissa was stood over one item, a huge ceramic roll top bath. Zac smiled back at Max. Any guilt she felt for abandoning her mother had disappeared. Replaced by the dream house, a dream house she resided in. The icing on the cake for Melissa was undoubtedly the bath.

"I can take it, we're all happy then?" Max asked. Melissa nodded like a little child, her cheeks flushed and unable to wipe the smile off her face.

"I can honestly say it's beyond our wildest dreams Max, thank you so much." Added Zac. Max gave a contented smile almost to himself. After a short pause his face turned back much more serious, repeating the change in the office.

"One final thing, but it's a big one." Max stopped as if allowing his guests to prepare themselves. "I have to take security of my electronic intellectual property very seriously. The Wi-Fi is secured and only accessible on the computer terminals. It's ring-fenced so there is no access to social media or messenger sites. All the USB points are secured and so is the Bluetooth. I can't risk data leaking out, nor anybody knowing what is happening here."

Zac & Melissa looked at each other, then back at Max.

"We don't really use social media. I don't think it will be too much of problem." Zac hesitantly stated. He looked at Melissa for validation who nodded.

"Good." Max smiled. "Incidentally in this remote location cellphone signal and 4G connection are near impossible. There is a landline in the kitchen which you are free to use."

"I can use it to call my mother?" Melissa asked cautiously.

"Of course, whenever you want Melissa. Use the desktop in your sitting room for the internet, any secure site other than the ones I mentioned are accessible." The pair smiled signaling their agreement. "Thanks for your understanding guys. Just so you know, outside by the lift, the other door is my private quarters. I'm sure you will respect my privacy as well and not go in there."

"Of course, we wouldn't dream of it." Zac answered sincerely.

In the darkness Ryan watched their every move around the house. The monitor lighting his face in a sinister glow. They were now at the end of the tour and Max would be leaving them soon. As Ryan watched he contemplated Max once again. As if the leaves had decayed from lush green to perished brown in a heartbeat, in Ryan's eyes so had Max. This provider of hope, light and opportunity had revealed himself in all his evil and malevolence. Now Ryan viewed Max's victims on the secret network of cameras throughout the house, with fear and pity. Ryan knew at the very start something underlying was present, something dark and corrosive. Now he was trapped into this macabre scheme, understanding attempting to back out provided a consequence he would rather not discover. He was as trapped as they were. Only they did not know it.

CHAPTER 4

"We're so lucky," Zac said packing away his clothes.

"It's not luck, it's your ability," Melissa replied from the bathroom, filling shelves with toiletries. "I'm so proud of you."

"Thanks." Zac beamed inside, growing in confidence. It was rare for Zac to feel good about himself. With all the hardship in his past, demons haunted him. He blamed himself for so many things. Those demons attacked him daily, even hourly, leaving him racked with guilt. Now as an adult he had learned to bury the feelings deep inside, rather than expressing himself with anger and aggression in his adolescence. Any compliment from Melissa, the most important person in his life, helped him to feel more secure in himself. It wouldn't last for long though. The negative emotions would always seep back in.

They had arranged to meet Maxwell in his kitchen-diner after an hour for a welcome meal and drinks. It was a good chance to get to know each other and settle in.

"Let's have a quick bath before dinner together," Melissa spoke excitedly.

"We don't have time for a bath now, that thing will take an hour to fill with water alone," Zac complained.

"Okay," Melissa replied, her voice tinged with disappointment. Zac immediately felt guilty for being so sharp. He walked into the bathroom and gave her a loving cuddle.

"Look, we can have a bath together tonight after the meal and take our time. If we did it now, we would only be rushing," he backtracked.

"Yeah. I know you're right," she reluctantly agreed. "I know I'm being silly, I'm just so excited to have a bath like that, I can't wait to use it."

"Well, I promise to make tonight really special."

Darkness fell over the house as Zac and Melissa made their way down to dinner. Zac apprehensive of just walking into Maxwell's kitchen-diner knocked on the door.

"Come in," his voice called from inside. "You really don't have to knock. Make yourselves at home," he said in a friendly tone whilst simultaneously cooking away in the kitchen. "I've made lasagna with my secret recipe sauce. There's a load so I hope you brought an appetite."

Zac inhaled the exceptionally appetizing aroma deeply. He suddenly realized how hungry he was. "It smells great, and yes I'm famished. I'm really looking forward to the meal."

"Both of you grab yourself a drink. There's beer in the fridge, Zac. Melissa, what would you like?"

Zac headed for the fridge.

"Beer's fine for me too," she answered.

While Maxwell cooked, Zac and Melissa leaned against the kitchen counter and talked to him about the house and the strife he had gone through to get it built, and about the spectacular view he had captured. Zac had instantaneously borne respect for Maxwell back at the initial interview, and as he learned more about him it amplified. The guy was an absolute success in every way. Evidently very wealthy, he had made vast quantities of money from his foresight in computers. He owned a house that anybody would adore, an assortment of cars normally only seen in magazines. Zac guessed he was in his late forties, but he easily appeared young enough to pass for forty. He swam a greater distance in a day than Zac could manage in weeks. To top it off the guy oozed charm and charisma. Zac had belief in Maxwell; admiration he had not felt for many years. The way he had once felt for his father before the death of his mother. He enjoyed the way Maxwell made him feel and was eager to please his new role model.

After the meal and pleasant conversation, inevitably talk turned to the job ahead. How and what Maxwell actually wanted to achieve. It seemed to Melissa they were talking drivel. She couldn't grasp all the technical jargon spouting from them both. After an hour of it she decided to retire back upstairs.

"I'm sorry, but I'm going to have to leave you to it. I'm feeling shattered after the journey and need to sort myself out." She had to interrupt between the fast-flowing discussions and feeling slightly annoyed she had been left out of the conversation for such a long time, not so much by Zac, he was eager to impress, but Maxwell was a psychiatrist, with significant people skills. She had expected him to perceive her isolation and need to interact at this awkward stage.

"Okay, darling. See you in a bit," Zac answered, so wrapped up in the dialogue he had failed to realize her boredom.

"Well, it was great to finally meet you, Melissa. Zac is certainly a lucky man," Maxwell complimented. "Before you go up, I must warn you both that you will probably see my handyman about the place. He's called Alex. A nice guy, keeps the pool running okay, cleans the cars and fixes any household problems. He's about most days." Melissa nodded as Maxwell continued, "She's not here at the moment, but my niece Sarah also stays with me from time to time. I think she likes the use of the house, rather than visiting her uncle."

"Okay, thanks for letting me know. It might have been a shock to bump into a stranger," she answered. "Don't be too long," she whispered to Zac. She rose and gave him a kiss on the cheek.

"I won't," he replied.

"Goodnight, Maxwell."

"Goodnight."

With that she left to fill the bath ready for Zac's return.

CHAPTER 5

Melissa opened her eyes. She hung in the initial transformation from slumber to consciousness. Her sight was blurred, eyelids heavy. She forced them to stay open. After a long vigorous stretch against the backboard of the bed she let out an embellished, overstated yawn. Her weighty eyelids compelled her to give up and let them close, for a few seconds she lost the battle. When they reopened her vision began to focus. Zac was lying on his side next to her, propping his head up with his hand, his elbow wedged into the bed.

"Good morning, my darling," he said softly. "I'm really sorry about last night."

Melissa, still half-asleep could not remember anything for a short period. Suddenly it all came back to her. After going up to their quarters, Melissa had run the bath. She had been looking forward to it and got in to wait for Zac to join her. She remained there for what seemed an eternity, her fingers and toes shriveled, the water had long since turned cool and uncomfortable. She could no longer remain awake. Getting out feeling isolated in her new location, she had got into bed forlorn.

Zac had tried to sneak in without waking her, knowing he had let her down. She had awoken, and discreetly peeked at the clock pretending to be still sound asleep.

"I thought we were going to have a bath together. Why didn't you come up or at least let me know you were staying down?"

Zac sighed. He lifted his free hand and tenderly stroked some stray and wayward hairs off Melissa's face.

"I'm sorry," he said. "I didn't mean to leave you on our first night here. I was just so excited talking to Maxwell about what we were going to do, I guess I forgot myself."

"Look, put it out of your mind now, but just remember I'm on my own here. While you're working on some exciting project, I have nothing to do. So please try to remember that and let's make the most of the time we get together."

"Okay I will. Now give me a kiss." They cuddled and met with their lips. Zac felt better for being forgiven quickly.

"So, I take it you had a good night, last night? What did you get up to?"

"Oh, darling, he's such a great guy. So interesting to talk to. His knowledge of every subject is infinite."

"He made a good first impression then?" Melissa quipped, amplifying the sarcastic tone in her voice. Zac smiled.

"Yes okay. It's just nice he's not a jerk. I'm probably gonna be spending more time with him than you over the next couple of years. It's important we get on."

Melissa pulled the pillow out from under her head and threw it over her face like an ostrich burying its head in the sand. "Don't remind me."

"You'll probably see more of me now than you would if I had taken any other job. At least this way you're not losing me to commuting time," Zac reasoned.

"Yes, but it makes it worse knowing you're so close and out of contact, especially because the office is out of bounds." Something suddenly hit home to Melissa. "What the hell am I going to do while you're working?"

"Well–" Zac tried to think up an astute instant answer, but Melissa had only meant the question to be rhetorical and abruptly cut him off.

"It's not as if I can pop into town, or there's anybody here I can make friends with. We're in the middle of nowhere." Frustration crept into her voice as she began to realize the full implications of the move.

"What about Maxwell's niece? He said she stays here all the time." Zac desperately endeavored to negotiate the escalating crisis.

"But how often is that? How do we know we'll get on together? It's too much to have everything staked on."

"Jesus," Zac snapped heatedly. "I can't help the situation, can I?"

They both lay in an irritated silence for a few minutes. Finally Zac spoke. "There is something else you probably won't like." He shifted around awkwardly. "Maxwell has said he needs as many volunteers as possible to be psychologically analyzed and profiled, to use as background data. To help give the computer program background data..." long pause "...as it were."

"No way, Zac." Melissa's response was prompt and resolute. "With both our parental records? We would come across as bizarre, all messed up."

"I know," Zac agreed. "I hardly want to tell my new boss my dark and chaos-filled past, do I? But he's insistent. I think he's struggling to get the numbers he needs."

Melissa said nothing. She sat forward, bringing her knees up to her chest, wrapping her arms around her legs and resting her head in an ungainly sideways manner on top of her knees. Melissa's sulk pose. Zac knew it well. Almost like a hedgehog curling into a ball to protect itself. When unhappy with a situation and cornered without an obvious escape, Melissa always reverted to this position. Zac opened his mouth to say something but stopped himself. He felt provoked and dismounted the bed, bouncing it, overcompensating every move to illustrate his feelings. Melissa rocked back and forth from the bouncing but did not reposition herself. "Well it's up to you. He wanted to do mine today and yours tomorrow. If you're going to refuse, then you can tell him yourself."

"Okay, I will," she said in a subdued voice, calling his bluff. He stomped off to the bathroom for a shower.

CHAPTER 6

"Okay, before this starts there are a few things you need to know," Maxwell cautiously informed Zac. Maxwell had taken him into the office and sat him in one of the deep leather computer chairs. Zac couldn't believe how comfortable it felt. It didn't help him relax, there was little prospect of that. Zac wondered what Maxwell would make of his past. Would he sack him on the spot and ask him to leave immediately?

Maxwell slumped back into his chair; he rubbed his nose as he spoke. "Although I am asking you to participate for the benefit of the program, it will certainly benefit you to talk to me." He paused for a couple of seconds.

Zac wondered what he meant by that, surely he couldn't know anything of the turmoil in Zac's short life.

Maxwell continued. "In this session think of me purely as a psychiatrist, not as your employer. Anything you say to me will remain completely confidential." Zac nodded, not looking at all reassured. "Anything you mention here will not affect your employment in any way."

"You're sure on that?" He wanted to test the point.

"Yes. I am. I employed you purely for your programming quality and I hope your ability to push the boundaries of what is possible. Not because I wanted you to be a Stepford employee," Maxwell demonstrated sincere potency in his voice. "As for any embarrassing secrets – I have been a practicing psychiatrist for many years and a psychiatric specialist in the later part of my career. Believe me, I really have heard it all."

Zac was taken aback by Maxwell's reaction, but at the same time felt more reassured by what he was hearing. "Okay. It's just... it's a difficult thing for me," Zac conceded. Get a grip, Zac.

"I know. Believe me when I say you'll feel better for talking about personal things. We'll start off having a bit of a chat. Afterwards I will ask you to complete a series of questions and tests. Then after that we'll have another chat."

"Okay." He didn't feel okay.

"I may need to speak to you again, further down the road, if something doesn't tie up with the computer." Maxwell gave his nose another rub. If anything is opened up for you, anything affecting you or that you find disconcerting, then let me know. I can help you to deal with it." He spoke with a candid manner.

"Thanks." Zac knew he had no room to maneuver. In the back of his mind alarm bells were ringing. He had a troublesome sense this would only lead to strife.

"Right, so let us begin," Maxwell declared, picking up a Dictaphone, placing it on a desk between them both.

"I didn't know you were going to record this," Zac's voice was packed full of panic.

"Yes. Don't worry. It's just so I'm not having to be distracted, furiously writing notes while you're speaking. I can concentrate better and write it up later. Of course, I will erase any files afterwards," Maxwell convincingly reassured him. Zac wasn't happy, but Maxwell's rationale seemed legitimate enough.

"Hmm," Zac could not have permitted consent with less enthusiasm.

"First of all, tell me about how you first met Melissa."

"Erm, okay. I met her in a nightclub, when..." Zac stopped himself midstream. He wanted to say more, but the presence of the dictaphone intimidated him. Like being interviewed by a policeman, like being interviewed by his father, before... A recording tape granted no remorse. Any slip of the tongue was documented permanently. Any faux pas were now to be everlasting. He gazed at the offending item. "We just got talking and one thing led to another." By now he was transfixed.

Abruptly Maxwell grabbed the dictaphone, clicked it off and tossed it casually on to the table behind him. He grabbed a notepad and pen beside him.

"You're not comfortable with being recorded, I can tell. It doesn't matter. We'll do this one the old-fashioned way."

After Zac's initial humiliation, he felt a blanket of relief spread over him.

"Now tell me about meeting Melissa."

Zac rapidly felt more relaxed. His new-found admiration for the man opposite alleviated the pressure and he allowed himself to talk, uninhibited and more amenable than for many years.

"Well, like I said, we met in a nightclub. It was the first time I had ever been to one. To be honest, I detested the place. I'm really not into that sort of thing."

"That sort of thing?"

"Yeah, you know. Large groups of drunken volatile rowdy people. An unpredictable situation that I don't feel safe in," Zac rationalized.

"A lot of people feel that way," Maxwell concurred, nodding. "Go on."

"Well, I had gone because it was a college friend's birthday." A smile developed on Zac's face as he recalled the contented memory as if he were viewing a photograph of a much loved, but long time deceased relative, full of nostalgia. "I was stood in the corner, shifting about awkwardly. I wasn't drunk. I might have felt better if I was." Zac leaned back deeper into the chair, permitting the expensive leather to engulf him. "Then suddenly I caught eye contact with this woman." Zac paused and delivered a frown, searching for an improved description. "No, I caught eye contact with a dazzlingly stunning lady."

Maxwell rubbed his chin, listening intently, not taking any notes.

"I looked away in panic, half expecting her to do the same. When I braved another glance, to reassess the situation, I was astounded to see she had not only remained transfixed on me, she was also striding purposefully toward me."

Maxwell gave his chin a doubtful rub and arched an eyebrow in an exceedingly suspicious mannerism. "Sounds like every guy's dream," he stated.

"Yeah. I guess so. Not for myself at the time, I was so aggravated by my surroundings. I was feeling so uncomfortable an advance from anybody seemed threatening. Anyway, I must have looked a real idiot at first. She said hello and explained she also was not at ease in the nightclub. All I could do was nod like a simpleton. She told me she'd noticed I was feeling the same way. I hate to think what I must have looked like for her to notice from across the room. To be honest, most of it was a blur. I hardly said a thing. She talked rapidly, non-stop. I guess it was her way of dealing with the situation."

Maxwell gave a comprehensive nod. Still he didn't write a note.

"The only good thing I managed to say all night was at the end, just before she and her friends left. I held her hand and told her if she met me for a drink somewhere quiet, I would be a different person. She gave me the brightest most magnificent smile, then kissed me softly on the lips. That was the first time I had ever kissed anyone properly. I can still remember it now."

Maxwell nodded again, giving a friendly grin.

"I guess you're thinking I was a bit too old to have my first kiss?"

"Not at all," he reassured.

"I wasn't very good with girls back then." Max looked sympathetically at Zac. "Or now really." Zac added, almost to himself.

They spoke at great length about Melissa, and what she meant to him. Zac was surprised at how prominent and influential she was in his life. It was not until now he fully understood their relationship or his affection for her. How much he loved her. An overwhelming yearning consumed him. They had parted on bad terms. He had let her down last night. Zac wanted nothing more than to take a break and go to Melissa. Illustrate to her what she meant to him – everything, his entire world and then some.

An imminent break did not seem likely. Maxwell had a lot to cover. He needed a large quantity of information. His dark ambitious scheme depended on it.

"Tell me about your parents."

Maxwell had broached the one subject Zac was dreading. He suddenly felt his entire mental and physical being stalling. He knew the question was inevitable. Zac gave Maxwell a vacant expression, while inside he reeled. He hoped Maxwell wouldn't be able to interpret his reaction, attempting to hold the impartial look. Finally, he spoke. "To be honest, I really would rather not bring them into this."

Maxwell gradually slumped back into his seat, and caressed his chin, studying and considering Zac's aspiration to fool Maxwell, which tumbled in vain. He could read Zac like a book. Eventually after what appeared like a ceaseless pause Maxwell held out both his hands face up. Stretching his fingers, to accompany his current facial expression: Well? Maxwell hadn't even said a word, but Zac suffered incredible pressure to cave in.

"It's just I don't have anything to say on that subject."

Maxwell subjected Zac to another prolonged silent hiatus. This time he didn't rub his chin. He sat statue-still, leveling an intense stare at Zac, his face stern. "I understand certain things are personal." His voice was not stern. "But I have to insist we plough on with this. It is essential I have all the information I need for the computer to learn and understand your psychological profile. Please remember this is all completely confidential. I won't judge you on anything, no matter how bad or bizarre. Your employment will be unaffected. And if you've had problems with your parents, talking to me will help you to feel better. I can help you."

"I'm sorry, but it's just not something I'm ready to talk about."

Instantly Maxwell's face reacted, it became threatening. "I'm counting on your profile. Both yours and Melissa's." His voice was unyielding this time. "I haven't got enough volunteers as it is." He wasn't aggressive, but the underlying tone in his voice was compelling enough for Zac to realize he was being backed into a corner. He didn't want to talk about his father or mother, but it seemed the consequences of refusing would be significantly worse. He tried to think fast, considering his options. He could lie about what happened, but if Maxwell were as experienced and as qualified as he portrayed, he surely would recognize Zac's untruths.

"It's not that I'm trying to be difficult," Zac said, trying to buy some time.

"Let me help you," Maxwell repeated as he softened his voice and his eyes in equal amounts.

Zac finally conceded. "What do you want to know?" He felt like a mouse caught by a cat. The mouse could squirm and wriggle as much as it wanted, but it just encouraged the cat to play with it more. The end result was inevitable. Better to just yield and hope for an abrupt death.

"Okay, Zac. Well done." Maxwell didn't flinch. He had known that Zac would be straightforward to break. He had too much riding on this. "First of all, tell me about your mother."

"Well…" Zac noticed his hands' clamminess. Interview mode had resumed. "My mother, Amy, er, died when I was twelve." The words were forced, his voice strained.

"I'm very sorry."

"Thanks."

"Tell me how you remember her."

Zac's mind's eye reflected back. He could remember her well, a loving mother who always had time for him. Watching as a small child as she made the pastry for a pie they would enjoy as a family, the tell-tale flour marks on her face as she kneaded the dough, her long wavy hair tied back off her face, revealing beautiful features that were too often hidden or disguised when her hair was down and in its usual place. Dark brown eyes that seemed especially large, a cute button nose and petit lips, full of color. She had a presence all of her own. Zac recalled she treasured only the things in life with real value. Not a person who surrounded herself with fashionable clothes, meaningless trinkets and expensive gadgets. Her family, Roy and Zac, encased in a loving home was her solitary desire.

"She was such a wonderful woman and mother. I know everybody says how great people were after they're dead, whether they were or not, but my mother genuinely was."

Maxwell offered a kind smile, acknowledging the phenomenon of people only remembering the good points of someone after they have passed on. He didn't speak or write anything down, making sure not to break Zac's momentum.

"I really miss her. She was the hub of our family, it all worked well around her." Zac stopped. Suddenly he had so much to say, he didn't know what to say next. It surprised him. Zac had spent a lifetime stockpiling emotions, suppressing them to the point he didn't realize they existed. Now suddenly with the bolt off the door the emotions flooded through him, like a blast of dynamite breaching a giant dam.

Maxwell recognized the reason for Zac's stall in words and expertly guided him. "How did your mother die?"

"It was an accident, a car accident. Not anybody's fault really." Long pause. "The investigation said it wasn't anybody's fault. Just one of those things, they said. My father drove into the back of another car. They said human error. He wasn't speeding, just lost concentration." Zac felt a sudden nausea rising from his stomach, combined with an overwhelming desire to burst into tears. He fought the urge, and it abated, for now.

"Were you in the car?"

"Uh-huh."

"Were you hurt?"

"Yeah, quite badly."

Maxwell fashioned an anxious face.

"I was in the back. The force of the impact … err, I mean I hit my head hard against the window. They put me in an induced coma. They were worried I would have permanent brain damage. Incredibly I made a full recovery."

"How do you feel about being so badly hurt? Do you feel angry?"

"No, not really. It's not easy to describe. It's kinda ... er ... I'm just glad to be alive. My injuries are not significant to me. The death of my mother superseded everything else."

"Yes. I understand." Max gave Zac a long, drawn out concerned gaze. "Your father lost concentration?" Zac answered as if to defend his father against the question.

"It was my birthday." Zac stopped briefly. "They were taking me to the zoo." The final words were heavy, almost as if the guilt attached weighed them down. "If we weren't on that trip my mother would still be alive."

"Zac that's awful." Maxwell considered his words carefully. "Zac. We'll look at that. We will. The circumstance of the journey or it being your birthday does not make it your fault."

"I know." Zac let out a long sigh. "Like I said before, it was an accident. Everybody agreed."

"Set aside for now the reason for the journey, do you believe it was an accident?"

"Yes."

Maxwell waited, not saying anything. It was the oldest trick in the psychiatrist's handbook. If you think the patient is telling half-truths or holding information back, best to not respond to the answer. Nine times out of ten the patient will embellish on their original answer, usually giving away direct and vital clues to the information they were trying to conceal.

Zac bit. "My father was not responsible for my mother's death. Yes, he caused the car accident, but I certainly don't blame him for her death."

Maxwell's heart skipped a beat inside his chest. His poker-faced expression didn't show anything on the outside, although he sensed an imminent breakthrough. In such sessions the only reactions or sentiment shown were implements to enable him to better scrutinize the mind of his prey. Something had been said, something subtle. The way Zac had worded his last sentence. It opened a new door for Maxwell to probe into.

"You don't blame your father for your mother's death?"

"No."

"Do you blame anybody for the car accident?"

"No."

It was time for the killer blow. "Who is it that *you do* blame for the death of your mother?" It landed with a thump. Kapow.

Zac was taken aback with this camouflaged ambush. His head pounded as he rummaged around for a clear thought. The answer didn't arrive from a lucid notion. It emerged from somewhere else, from his subconscious.

"Me." Bingo, Maxwell thought, confirming everything he had already deduced. For Zac it was an utter revelation. Maxwell played the waiting game again trying to fish out more. It didn't take long. Zac's subconscious was on a roll.

"It was my fault my mother died. I'd placed my camera, a big heavy one, on the rear window shelf of the car. When my pa had the accident, the force launched it into the air. My ma with her seatbelt on would have easily survived, but the damn camera smashed into the back of her head." Now the tears came in floods. "It killed her instantly," he blubbered hysterically.

"And you think you're to blame?"

"Yes," Zac broke from his crying for a second. He leveled his eyes at Maxwell. "If only..." Zac stopped, knowing the point had been made.

"If," Maxwell hesitated to give the word more gravity. "If, Zac, is the biggest word in the dictionary. Humans are far from infallible. We all make mistakes, a lot of them. Some have no consequences, others do. A few have major consequences and can ruin your life."

"If I hadn't put the camera on the back shelf, she would be alive. As simple as that."

"I'm not denying that fact, but because the camera killed her, it doesn't mean it's your fault she's dead."

"Are you saying my father is to blame?"

"No." Maxwell held a few seconds for the word to sink in.

"It's the same as the cause of the accident. You don't blame your father for that, do you?"

"No. It was just an accident."

"That's right. However, he did cause the crash, just something easy to pick apart in hindsight. Your father did not set out to crash the car and almost kill you. I'm guessing he hadn't got behind the wheel high on drink or drugs?" Zac shook his head to confirm. "Well then, at the time, as you said, it was just one of those things. You weren't to know placing your camera on the window shelf was putting your mother's life at risk. If you had known, you wouldn't have put it there. It's easy to blame yourself with the benefit of hindsight. But you didn't have hindsight before the accident. Think of it now without the hindsight, turn your mind back. Back to the car journey, just before it happened."

As painful as it was, Zac cast his thoughts back, remembering the trip so clearly.

"Remember what you knew before it happened. How could you know the risks of placing the camera there? There's no way you could."

For a moment Zac was back in that car on that day. The memory was so clear in his mind it could have happened yesterday. His whole life since had been spent denying that event had ever happened, the mental shutters were down and locked, but now they flung open and every sense within Zac's mind was teleported back. Zac sat in the back seat waiting to leave holding the camera excitedly, his birthday present. His father walking around the car, ironically checking the condition of the tires. Always the cop. His mother still inside the house, completing her final checks. The faucet was off, the oven was off, and god knows what else she had to know was off before permitting herself to leave. Zac could not wait, and all this stalling was frustrating him. Finally, Roy satisfied himself the car was good to go and jumped in. He fastened his seatbelt and adjusted the mirror, he always did. Nobody had moved it since he last drove, but it was habit. Then the wait continued. Once again this was the normal ritual, Roy would always grow noticeably frustrated. This time Zac shared the frustration.

"Come on Amy." Roy muttered under his breath. Another minute passed "What's she doing in there?" The rhetorical question which Roy had to ask before there was any hope of leaving. Eventually she appeared at the doorway. At this point it was a fifty, fifty if she would suddenly remember she had to check something else for the tenth time and go back in the house. Mercifully for both Zac and Rory she locked the door and made her way to the car. A few steps shy of the car door and progression, she turned and walked back to the door. Roy let out a long sigh. She checked it was locked although she had only performed this action seconds earlier. Eventually Amy took the last seat she would ever take.

"Finally." Roy quietly muttered. He started the car and pulled out onto road.

The journey should have been an hour or so, but traffic was heavy. Progress was noticeably slow. The mid-morning temperature was sky rocketing. Roy's air conditioning was not operating correctly, he knew it needed re-gassing but had not found the time to get it done. Zac could sense he was regretting that oversight now, observed him endlessly fiddling with the AC control in some vain attempt to get it working again. Zac was still holding his brand-new camera and suddenly became aware his hands were sweating from holding it tight in the hot car. After some consideration he became concerned the sweat would damage it and decided to put it down. He reached around and placed it carefully on the rear parcel shelf of his father's vehicle. There it sat in complete innocence.

They eventually made it onto the freeway, Zac inwardly praying for some respite in the traffic. It was not to be. What followed was a succession of crawling for five minutes or so, then a brief period where all the vehicles sped up and the anticipation of getting through to the other side. However as abruptly as reprieve would appear, a cascade of taillights would form. They would return to crawling along at walking pace.

Roy was generally a calm and patient man, but he had his limits. Zac could sense they were being tested. He would again fiddle with the AC controls, place his hand over the vent to test the pitiful breeze emitting and quietly mutter something to himself, then crane his head around out of the window to inspect the progress of the traffic. The cycle of this continued for as long as Zac could remember. When the next speed up occurred, Zac was already waiting for it to end. However it sustained, growing in momentum. The cars all around continued to accelerate along with Roy, like a stampede of wild horses. The sudden freedom compelled the collective drivers to dash like it was the Indi 500.

"Roy, slow down." Amy cautioned. It was the last words she would speak. Zac could not remember the car in front braking. He did not recall the almighty crash as their car ploughed directly into the back of the vehicle in front. He could identify the memory of the violent lurch forward. Although he did not actually see it, he could visualize the camera launching itself through the cabin like an asteroid hurling toward an unsuspecting planet. In his mind's eye he witnessed it strike his mother's head without care or remorse. In reality, he had been knocked unconscious a microsecond before the tragic event occurred.

"Could you know those risks Zac?" Maxwell asked again snapping Zac back to the here and now. He could appreciate that Maxwell was making sense, but he was not going to let himself off that guilt hook so easy. It did serve to form debate within his thoughts. "So, you don't think it was my fault?" he asked.

"I know it wasn't. The question is, do you?"

Ryan sat behind a television screen. He munched on sunflower seeds, washed down with a sports drink, apparently offering thirty percent more lasting performance. Ryan doubted that. However, the image exhibited on screen was at the forefront of his thoughts. Zac confessing his most concealed thoughts to Maxwell.

Ryan couldn't help but feel deeply uncomfortable for eavesdropping on such a moment, never mind knowing it was being recording. He was overcome with the sensation of being voyeur, a pervert with a secret camera in a lady's changing room, the realization that a boundary of trust was being grievously abused. You don't have a choice, Ryan, he told himself. You're in too deep now.

"Talk to me about your father," Maxwell asked.

"It's quite complicated really."

Maxwell waited, but Zac did not supplement his answer. "I'm sure it is. After what happened, it must have been a great strain on both of you."

"That's not it. There's a lot more to it than what you think."

Maxwell's eyes widened slightly. He had not intended to reveal reaction this time, but even the most unsurpassed poker player cannot mask a reaction entirely, when the stakes are so high.

"Before the accident my father and I had a very close relationship. He was a cop, a highly respected cop. I really idolized him."

"But the accident changed that?"

"No. Well yes, but not in the way you're thinking. Like I said, I honestly don't blame my father for what happened. But after I woke up from my coma, he wasn't there. My cousin Cathy was the one to tell me my mother had died. I didn't know at that time the camera had killed her, but I was obviously devastated."

Maxwell nodded in agreement feigning a sympathetic look.

"I really needed my pa more than ever, but he wasn't there for me. He never was again." The words fell out of Zac's mouth like lead bullets.

"What happened?"

"My father lost it completely. He had a complete breakdown. I had to live with my cousin for a year. In all that time I hardly saw him. I desperately needed him, but he wasn't there for me. I had both parents taken from me that day."

"But you moved back in with him a year later?"

"Yeah, I moved back with a man named Roy. He was no longer my father. He might have been able to save our relationship if he'd wanted to. As far as I could tell, he was only interested in one thing."

"Which was?"

"The bottle, it's as simple as that. He drank non-stop, night and day."

Inside Maxwell squirmed. That was the flop. "That had to be tough on you? Even more to contend with?"

"Yeah, it was. I was left to fend for myself. I lived with a drunk not a dad."

"I take it he didn't work?"

"That's the problem. Somehow, he kept his job, as a cop. I guess he was admired so much before, nobody had the heart to sack him, especially after losing his wife."

"That happens more often than you'd think."

"I'm sure it does, but you can't carry someone in a job like that. Not someone with a loaded gun."

That was the turn card. "True. Especially with so much authority," Maxwell furthered.

"Yeah, well, it was only a matter of time before somebody got hurt." Zac's voice trailed off.

"What happened?" Maxwell asked, suppressing the emotion in his voice.

"I'm sorry. I can't talk about this. It's too much. I need a break."

"Soon," Maxwell promised, "but for now just try to hang in there." He gave Zac a sharp glance.

"He shot someone," Zac blurted out coldly, a lack of

feeling in his voice. He now realized he was not leaving without revealing what had happened. "A child." Zac's eyes filled with tears. His head down, like a naughty school child being told off by a teacher. "He was nine years old. Jesus, he was only nine." Zac raised his head toward Maxwell, his tear-stained eyes meeting with Maxwell's, pleading for help, pleading for something. The river card.

"It's okay, Zac," Maxwell promised. His eyes had softened. As Zac's beseeching eyes stared into Maxwell's, he detected deep emotion in them.

"My father was drunk on duty and he accidentally shot a child and killed him." The words left a polluted tang in his mouth.

"He was drunk when he shot the child?"

"Yes, he was always drunk."

"Did he get arrested?"

"Yeah, but cops being cops, they covered the whole thing up. Okay he lost his badge, but he didn't serve any time for what he did." Anger now started to creep into his words. "His partner gave a false statement, to get him off. There were no other witnesses, but I don't think they looked very hard. If anybody had revealed the truth, I'm sure he would have gone down for at least manslaughter, if not murder."

"How do you feel about that?"

"I don't know, to be honest. I'm definitely angry. He's my father, I don't want him to rot in jail, but I also feel pissed he got away with it. What about the poor kid? My father's actions cost him his life. That kid had done nothing wrong. What about his parents?"

"Were they present at the time of the shooting?" Maxwell asked.

"Yeah, well the father was. To be honest, I don't know too much about that, such was the extent of the cover-up. All I do know was he understandably went crazy when my father got off. I think he tried to get it into the newspapers. He tried to get the whole thing reinvestigated and bring down all those who helped cover it up. The same thing any of us would do."

"What happened?"

"Like I said, I really don't know too much about it. All I do know is he failed in his attempts to get my father convicted. There were suddenly so many heads on the chopping block the police circled the wagons. I guess I worried he might come after my father for vigilante-style revenge, but as far as I know nothing happened." Zac swallowed hard. He took a moment to study Maxwell's face, wondering what he might do or say next. Would he throw them both out, terminating his employment? Would he phone the police himself and report what Zac had just confessed? Maxwell's face was blank. Emotionless. But the eyes, something flickered in his eyes. Not surprising, Zac guessed. He could not possibly have been expecting Zac to spill the beans on such a heinous event.

"Where is your father now?"

"After losing his job he decided to concentrate on staying constantly drunk. About the only thing he could do well at the time. I went back to live with Cathy. It was such a relief to get out of the situation, get some normality back into my life. Get back to studying. It was then I found my proficiency with computers. After my father lost the house, I lost contact with him, until about a year or so ago. He has managed to get himself back together. He lives in San Francisco, a good few hours drive away from our home town. He's off the drink now and works as a night watchman."

"What happened when he re-established contact?"

"He phoned me out of the blue. I couldn't believe it. I just put the phone down on him. Then he started to send me letters. They said he was sorry and was now okay. He wanted to see me."

"Did you?"

"Yeah, eventually. It was really hard. I wouldn't say we are okay now, but we have a relationship of sorts. Speak to each other on the phone once a month, that kinda thing."

"But you're still really angry with him?"

Zac paused to consider the question. "Yeah, I am. I'm truly

angry."

"Have you told him how you feel?"

"Er, no, not really. He knows. I don't think he needs me to rub his face in the mess he caused. More importantly, he's still really fragile. A scathing attack from me might send him back to the bottle. I really don't want that to happen."

Maxwell nodded. He placed the untouched note pad and pen on the desk.

"Okay, Zac. I think we have reached a good place to take a break. We've got more ground to cover, though. Some for the computer program, but more for yourself. It's important we talk through everything that's happened in your life. I'm certain it will help you in the short term, and definitely in the long run."

Zac nodded. He was rapidly becoming aware of the burden of emotions brimming inside him. "I'll give you an hour, then meet me back here and we'll work through all the psychological tests."

"Are there a lot of tests?" Zac enquired, dreading the answer.

"Loads," Maxwell grinned. "Like you wouldn't believe."

CHAPTER 7

Ryan jumped as Maxwell burst into the room. He felt like a teenager caught smoking by his father. Ryan knew spying on such a sensitive affair was immoral, although he still felt foolish for acting as if caught red-handed. Maxwell had instructed Ryan to watch the session and demonstrated how to operate the vast network of hidden surveillance cameras throughout the house. Then he had instructed him how to save the footage files of use. Ryan would have loved a role playing the superspy, but never wanted to do it for real.

"Ryan. Did you get all that?" Maxwell appeared flustered. He had an anxious and impatient air.

"Yes. I cut the footage and saved the file, just as you said to."

"Okay, thanks. Take a break." Maxwell initiated, physically ushering Ryan out of the room. "Be back no later than forty minutes."

"Er, okay," Ryan replied as he was all but bundled out of the door.

"And for Christ's sake, don't get spotted. Not until I know who you're going to be." With that the door slammed shut leaving a bewildered Ryan stood there answering it.

"Okay boss, sure thing," His voice was ripe with sarcasm. On the other side of the door Maxwell dropped to his knees, shaking and gasping uncontrollably.

Roy sat alone in his apartment. He had just returned from his nightshift watching over a factory just outside the city. Whilst at work he often speculated at what was worth guarding. The stores were full of lengths of mild steel bar and plate, which for their size, weight and awkwardness to steal, were scarcely worth the endeavor. The machined finished components were of no use to anybody but the customers who ordered them. These parts were used in production machinery. Machines that boxed and wrapped mass-produced products. Hardly something the average thief could offload at half price in his local bar. Not like DVD players or car stereos.

The machinery used to produce the components was certainly valuable, but without heavy duty forklifts, mobile cranes, big trucks and a lot of time, it was going nowhere. An ineffective job for an inadequate man, he told himself as he wandered round the darkened factory. Knowing his title of "Chief of Security" would be more precise if called "the just-in-case man."

The one thing his job allowed him was to think and ruminate. With nothing to occupy his mind, the outcome was torturing himself night after night, dwelling over all the things he had done to ruin his life. How he had cost his ever-loving wife hers and how, although he didn't quite manage to kill his son at the same time, he had successfully achieved destroying him mentally for the rest of his life.

Despite this, Roy found the desire to drink minimal at work. He had been a proud man in his former lifetime and was keen to fulfill even such a lowly vocation to his highest capability. But now, sitting at home after distractedly attempting to sleep, and failing, the demons of addiction commenced. They stirred through his mind, grabbing at him like single-minded women, fanatical in a designer boutique sale. The urges were deep-seated with nothing to do or to distract him, except the dreary monotony of daytime television, and endless pointless games on his cellphone. Those internal demonic forces wrestled and strained with his resistance.

Every day he was tempted. Further than tempted. His willpower was pushed and pulled, he was going against the one thing his mind and body urged him to do, like trying to fight the urge to breath. He had been dry over a year now, hoping it would get easier, but it didn't. So many times, more than he cared to remember, Roy had left his apartment and walked to a bar or liquor store, his mind telling him, just one more drink, just one, then everything will be fine. Typically, when he reached the door a click back to reality would hit him, as if the entrance was an invisible line in his mind that once crossed there was no way back. One time when Roy reached the liquor store, he had crossed that line. He found himself buying a whole bottle of vodka, the largest in the store. He fought the desire to open and drink from the bottle right there on the street. Upon arriving home, he opened it and poured himself a sizeable drink. The glass even touched his lips before a hidden strength inside him screamed No! Roy instantly tipped the lethal contents down the sink, binning the empty bottle. Although he wasn't currently so vulnerable to the cravings. He was far from the exit out of these woods.

CHAPTER 8

Zac's head swam. How many tests does he want me to do? He had been laboring over them for three and a half hours. They were back in the office. Maxwell sat quietly, working away behind a computer. Zac was at another desk answering multiple choice and written tests. Every time he completed one Zac foolishly thought, that's it, all done, only for Maxwell to take it and then hand him another.

Eventually they were all concluded. Maxwell finished up by showing Zac a series of black and white images, asking him to say the first thought that came into his head as a response. He noticed Maxwell actually making notes this time about how he answered. Zac could not help but find it perplexing he had not recorded anything from their preliminary session. To be honest, he was more thankful Maxwell had not recorded the whole episode on his Dictaphone.

During his earlier break, Zac's main objective had been to go up to the living quarters and make up with Melissa. All the talking about her, their relationship, and everything else from his preceding life had made him comprehend just what a vital part of it she was.

He told her all about what happened, not anticipating how constructive and optimistic it would leave him. How, although the encounter was painful and distressing, it had a rejuvenating effect, feeling good to exorcize past ghosts. A revelation transpired inside him. He had been living with a form of numbness for years, keeping the volume turned down on his feelings. Even though Maxwell had offered modest feedback, on reflection Zac realized he had been focused into specific directions, manipulated into understanding himself.

Now the battery of testing was complete. Maxwell informed Zac before they finished, he would need him to go through another session, this time a little more biased to what made him tick rather than counseling his personal problems, purely for the sake of the computer program. Zac understood, feeling less defensive after surviving the initial onslaught. Maxwell added a desire to have an hour-long session with Zac once a week to work through the harrowing events in his past life. Now the worst of it all had been admitted, Zac could only feel assured this would be a good thing.

"Let's call it a perk of the job," Maxwell said.

"Are you all done?" Melissa asked as he came in through the door. It was evening. She was in the kitchen chopping vegetables. Two pans were boiling away on the stove.

"Yeah." Zac stared at his intended meal in bewilderment. "I'm starving, what are you cooking?"

"Steak, with a mixture of vegetables," she replied cheerfully.

"Where did you get the food?"

Melissa smiled knowingly and opened cupboards revealing shelves extensively stacked with packets and cans. Without a word she marched over to the refrigerator-freezer combination and swung open the doors like a circus ringmaster opening a curtain to disclose his prize attraction. They were both jam-packed.

"But how?" Zac asked.

"It was already here, Zac. Maxwell had left a note on the kitchen counter. I meant to tell you earlier, but well, we were busy making up. It said we don't need to buy groceries. It's all done for us."

"Wow."

"Yeah, I couldn't believe it. It went on to say if there is anything we want not here or anything here we don't like, write a list and it will be sorted."

Zac stepped forward for a closer inspection of the steak. Both the steaks looked expensive, thick-cut prime fillets with fine marbling through them. "I think I'm gonna get used to this," he lightheartedly remarked.

"How did it go today?"

"Really well, surprisingly. The guy is a legend, although it was long-winded, and the tests were boring. The chat we had about everything that's happened to me really opened my eyes. Maxwell knew the how and why with my feelings before I did. He helped me to realize a few things I didn't before."

"With Roy?" Melissa's voice was laden with reservation. "You told him everything?"

"Yeah, and he was really cool with it all. He used to be a practicing psychiatrist, so he said he had heard it all before. I feel so much better for talking to him, sharing myself. It really feels like something has been lifted from me. He recommends having regular sessions to work through all the bad things in my past."

"Well, if you feel comfortable doing that, I don't know whether I want to open up to him yet. Don't you think it's a little weird telling your boss and your landlord your innermost secrets? Don't you think it leaves you exposed?"

"Exposed?" Zac snorted. "What do you think this guy is gonna do?"

Melissa returned to chopping vegetables. Feeling as if Zac considered her hare-brained.

Zac waited for her reply. When it didn't come, he began to consider how he had let her down the previous night. "One thing that really came across in our session," he said, moving towards her, "is how much you mean to me and how much I love you." Walking up to Melissa with her back facing him, Zac circled his arms around her and pulled her in tight for an embrace. Initially she made her body stiff and awkward, resisting his advances. A second or two later she stopped the chopping knife cutting and relinquished her body into his protective grip.

"You know I love you, darling."

"Yes … I love you too," she responded.

CHAPTER 9

The next morning Roy returned home from his shift at the factory. His body was drained from the lack of sleep. He had seen his doctor several times about his insomnia. The doctor was not especially compassionate about his complaint. He was also uneasy about Roy being a recovering alcoholic. He had repeatedly refused Roy's requests to prescribe him sleeping tablets. It was just too much of a risk, he might become dependent on the sleeping tablets as a surrogate for the prior addiction. He suggested that Roy should have therapy to alleviate his fight against his former addiction and to help him to comprehend the resultant problems surrounding him, to deal with the fallout of his personal misfortune. Roy was far too proud for that. He was an old-fashioned man, not prepared to get in touch with his feelings.

Roy lay down on the bed fully clothed, staring at the ceiling, looking at the cracks and marks he knew so well. Like a prisoner locked in a cell for endless days, every aspect of the brick and metal work analyzed in detail to pass the time. Like a prisoner, Roy felt trapped, trapped in an unexplainable limbo.

"Take a seat, Melissa," Maxwell said. They were settled in the great room. Maxwell knew she would not be at ease in the office. He also wanted to maintain the boundary of Zac's work site being out of bounds.

Melissa timidly sat, gazing around the magnificent structure. Even now she found it hard to contemplate a room this eccentrically implausible actually existed. As she elegantly sat in the seat, her long fair hair slid over her face. A soft petit hand lifted, sliding it back behind her shoulders with an effortless velvety motion. It was an involuntary action Melissa habitually carried out, which would cause any man in the vicinity to take notice of her.

"I take it Zac told you of his day yesterday?" Maxwell asked, remaining focused on the job in hand, not being distracted by the vision in front of him.

"Yes, he was very enthusiastic about what happened. I have to say I was quite surprised. He is usually very reserved about personal feelings and his past."

"Except with yourself?" he asked.

"Even with me," Melissa countered. "Sure, he's told me all about what happened, but he's never really elaborated on it, only the basic facts. Very little about how he felt about it at the time, and nothing on how he feels now."

"Does that annoy you?"

"Not really. I think he's just a naturally private person. Like I said, I was surprised he opened up to you so easily."

"Well, it wasn't easy. Let's just say I'm well practiced at extracting information from people." He gave her a kind smile. "What about yourself? Are you happy to talk to me about yourself?"

"I can't say I'm overjoyed, but I don't have a problem with it. I'm selective about who I open myself up to. I guess you're okay, besides after what you did to Zac, I don't think blocking you out would do a lot of good." They exchanged a mutual grin. "Zac has explained how important it is for your computer program."

"Yes, that's correct. It's absolutely vital I get as much background data for the computer to learn from as possible."

Melissa moved forward in her chair. "One question," she posed.

"Yes?"

"Zac tells me you're an experienced psychiatrist, so why don't you just use the profiles from your past patients? You must have loads of notes you could use?" She retreated back to her original position.

"The simple answer has two reasons. Firstly, I haven't got their permission to use their data in such a way. It would be completely unethical of me to do so without it. Secondly, with my past patients I was only concentrating on getting to the root of their problem and then treating it. For the computer data I need a complete psychological profile. I'm sure Zac mentioned the endless tests in between these sessions."

"Yeah, I think endless was the word he used as well."

They both laughed.

"Well, these sessions..." Maxwell started as he composed himself, "are only parts of building the complete profile."

"One concern I do have is confidentiality."

"Of course, but I can honestly reassure you, anything you say to me stays completely between us two, with no exceptions. If you were to ask me a direct question about something Zac had said yesterday, I wouldn't be able to give you an answer." Melissa turned her gaze to the commanding view out of the immense window. A small frown appeared on her delicate face. "You're worried about Zac getting access to your profile while writing the program, aren't you?"

She shot her head back towards Maxwell. "How did you know?"

"I'm so good, sometimes I amaze myself," he said with a straight face, and then instantaneously burst into laughter. "Only joking," he added. Melissa laughed in return. "Seriously, it's a legitimate concern. Zac will have no access to any of that information, nor will he be present when I use it. His job is to create the structure of the program, its backbone if you will. He will write and produce routines and sub-routines for the computer to follow. I will be personally responsible for entering all of the personal information." Melissa looked slightly confused but was following him for the most part. "A simple way to put it is, Zac and any other of the remote programmers will form a flow chart to my specification but have nothing written in any of the question boxes. Afterwards I will insert the necessary information to make the flow chart work and make sense. It's the way it would be even if the information wasn't sensitive. He'd stick to what he's good at and myself alike."

"Okay, that makes sense."

"Right, shall we begin?" Maxwell rubbed his hands together before producing the Dictaphone. He held it up to Melissa. "Is this okay?"

"Sure." She would have preferred it not to be produced but did not have the same reservations as Zac.

"Okay, great." He set it down on the table between them. "Tell me about Zac, how you met, how you got to this point and what he means to you?"

Melissa went on to talk about their primary meeting in the nightclub. She said how great he had been throughout the course of the relationship. How he had been so dependable, always there for her. How she saw him as her rock. That he never really let her down in all the ways significant to her. She divulged knowing she was very demanding on Zac and his attention. Maxwell could perceive where this was going. He really did not need to guide her much. She was happy to talk about things personal to her and he only needed to occasionally nudge her into the correct direction.

Melissa was finding Maxwell fantastically easy to talk to. He had a noticeable charisma, putting her at ease. As she spoke, she frequently looked right at Maxwell, trying to study him, as he was her. He was in tremendous shape for his age and had a cool, sophisticated appearance. She couldn't help but hold a slight attraction to him.

"Why do you think you're so demanding on Zac?" he asked.

"Don't know, I guess it's just who I am."

"What's your relationship like with your father?"

"Not good," she admitted. "Well, pretty awful really."

Maxwell was not at all surprised. All of Zac's qualities she highlighted were features a daughter looks for in her father.

She continued to explain what had happened when he

departed from her and her mother's life. How she could not let him back in afterwards.

What did surprise Maxwell was how well adjusted and stable her emotions and feelings were. Of course, it had hurt her intolerably when Jim walked out, especially in such a spineless cowardly manner. Melissa tried to bottle it up, but her eyes welled with tears. She had deliberated with her mother about how she felt, confiding in her closest friend, letting out the anguish and sorrow.

Later on, after being with Zac, she had reflected back on what happened and permitted her mind to do something to liberate her from the usual mental idiosyncrasies of such an emotionally damaging situation. She forgave her father. Nevertheless, Melissa did not want anything more to do with him, but let any loathing or animosity pass. When Jim did get back in contact with her, she advised him of this candidly. He had not understood.

"If you forgive me, why won't you see me again?"

"My mother for one. My loyalty lies with her now," Melissa responded resolutely.

"I'm not asking you to take my side. I just want to see you again. It's your birthday, don't do this. I miss you."

"I miss you too, Dad," Melissa's bottom lip quivered slightly against the telephone receiver. *"But this is the decision I've made. You're gonna have to live with it, the same way I had to with yours."*

"You sound like you're still angry. I don't think you have forgiven me," Jim returned.

"Dad, please listen and try to understand. I have forgiven you. Not for your benefit, but for mine. I don't wish for or feel any malice towards you. I do miss you, but not enough to bring you back into my life." Melissa's voice

had a detached conclusiveness to it.

"But, Melissa," Jim's tone of voice became flustered at the other end of the phone. "This can't be it. I still need you. Please don't do this," he begged.

"Sorry, Dad. I have made my decision. You're forgiven. Goodbye."

"But, but–" The last words she heard from him before setting the receiver down.

"Did he try to contact you again?" Maxwell asked her.

"Nope. To be honest, I'm a little saddened he gave up so easily, although any further attempts would have been a waste of time. I was relieved he wasn't bothering me, but more especially for Sally, my mother. I was worried he might try using her to get to me."

Maxwell's mind whirled. He needed to establish a weakness in Melissa, a chink in the armor through which he could attack. Although this area principally appeared to be the apparent choice, her wonderfully balanced approach towards it all presented Maxwell with serious doubts as to its feasibility in his master plan. Even when he suggested all the qualities Melissa mentioned in Zac were all ones she would look for in a father, she didn't bite. Melissa thought about it and agreed. Get a shovel, Maxwell, we're going to have to dig a bit deeper, he thought.

"Tell me about the future, where do you want to be in ten years' time?" Maxwell rubbed his chin attentively as he waited for her response.

"To be happy?" she gave Maxwell a cheeky smile.

"Good answer, anything else?"

"Yeah, I'd like to think Zac and I would have a nice house in a good neighborhood, with the whole couple of kids and a dog thing going on. A decent American family."

"Sounds pretty Mr. and Mrs. Average?"

"Yep."

"But Zac has the potential to earn fantastic amounts of money. With all that potential wealth, you're happy to be average?"

"Okay it's easy to think like that, but the reality is huge wage checks mean huge amounts of hours. I want a husband and a father to my children, not a stranger."

"What about here, you know I'm gonna need Zac to participate heavily for a couple of years to make this work."

"I know that, but that's okay. He needs to get his career started and give us a strong foundation before we can have kids. I can just about handle him doing the long hours until then. All I need to do is find an interest to occupy myself while we're living here, if you don't mind me saying, in the middle of nowhere."

Perfect, Maxwell thought to himself. Absolutely perfect.

CHAPTER 10

Ryan sat expectantly in Maxwell's private living quarters. The view out of the window was still breathtaking. It was impossible to tire of. Not as sublime as the full panoramic view out of the great room, but unattainably fantastic, nevertheless. Ryan found himself split between his morals and his desire to act. He knew he had entwined himself into something dark and sinister. He was already in too deep to get out, so his mindset was beginning to shift. He was thinking more & more about what he had actually been hired to do.

He hadn't landed a single acting role since he arrived in Hollywood and that area of his psyche was ravenous. Yearning is a powerful force and slowly Ryan allowed himself to emotionally explore. It had been a long wait, but the time was near, partaking in what he had been born to do. Okay, there was no real audience for him to perform to. No admiration of the masses. No bright lights or picturesque women fighting over themselves to get in his line of sight, just an audience of one, Maxwell.

He reasoned with himself that this strange gig did have a few things going for it. Firstly the challenge; it would be tough to pull off this role. He already knew his objectives for the performance, what Maxwell wanted him to achieve. He now waited to be instructed about his character. The other stimulus for him being here right now was the money, lots of it. Enough cash for him to go back to Hollywood and support himself indefinitely. No waiting on tables for twelve-hour shifts, thus freeing him up to attend each and every audition he suited. In Ryan's mind there was never any doubt he would eventually make it. He just had the constraints of having to pay to live getting in his way.

He looked around the room. Some artwork hung from the pale finished walls. Not to his taste, all modern art, quite strange and contemporary. In fact, it was slightly intimidating. He could not decide whether or not they were valuable. He did love the leather couch he was sat in. He knew that was expensive, just sensing the quality.

The door suddenly swung open. Maxwell strolled confidently into the room. His appearance was upbeat, body language open and excited. His eyes, however, were groggy, red from lack of sleep. His body was surviving on exhilaration like a child up early on Christmas morning.

"Hi, Ryan, are you ready to excel?"

"Hi, Maxwell. I've never been more ready."

Maxwell smiled, offering Ryan one of two cups of steaming hot coffee in his hands. Ryan took it and reclined, his hands under his nose, letting the resonant dark aroma inundate his senses.

"Hmm." Ryan murmured appreciatively. Maxwell gave him a knowing nod, impressed by his awareness for the finer things in life.

"Right, well," Maxwell started, as he sat himself down getting settled. He pulled a dossier out from under his arm and opened it. He flicked through the pages undertaking one more browse, like a doctor about to reveal test results to a patient, just doing one final check to be definite. "Okay, Ryan, here's the low-down. I've already said you're a handyman around the place as we agreed."

Maxwell and Ryan had discussed what role would be mostly believable for Ryan after he first arrived. Ryan had indicated he had worked as a set builder in between waiting tables while trying to obtain roles in Hollywood. Maxwell's ears had pricked up at the mention of set building. Once Ryan had elaborated, they decided a handyman would be the perfect rationalization for his presence.

"Now I've written up who you are on these sheets." He

held them up for Ryan to see. "We'll go through it now, but you must study these continuously throughout all of this. If any alarm bells start to ring that you're not who you say you are, or your story changes in any way, your chances of your role being triumphant will be significantly reduced. As will your payment at the end. Understand?"

"Yeah, sure," Ryan obediently replied.

"It's important this becomes your truth. You must believe it yourself. When you're telling lies all over it's only a matter of time before you slip up and forget something you've previously stated. By sticking to these facts, treating them as your real self, it will help to reduce the risk of slipping up."

"Yes, I understand completely."

"Good." Maxwell selected the top sheet and started to read from it. "Right the basic facts. Your name is Alex. Your date of birth remains the same. Your parents were Barbara and William. You grew up in New Jersey. That okay so far?"

Ryan nodded. "Yep."

"All the schools you attended are listed here. Any friends, teachers or general stuff from your childhood keep the same as your real life. It makes things a lot simpler and Melissa or Zac won't know the difference. Remember it happened in New Jersey, though." Ryan nodded again. "Obviously it goes without saying, don't mention you're an actor. I think that's one detail we can leave out. All these other details you can learn in a minute. I suggest you spend the whole day today studying them. I will assess you tomorrow morning. Think of it as a mini test and if I'm happy you can get to work."

Ryan unexpectedly felt a burden of pressure coming down on him. He didn't like tests. Maxwell already knew this. He always had to be one step ahead of everybody around him, using his expertise to get the upper hand. Ryan had been easy to pick apart, not much in the way of depth to him, unproblematic to manipulate, perfect for his scheme. He knew the anxiety of a test would force Ryan to really knuckle down and genuinely establish his new persona in his own mind. He had deliberately used the word "test" to invoke the necessary triggers in Ryan's mind.

"After today I want you to read through all this twice in the morning and twice before you go to bed. Everyday. It will eliminate inconsistencies. Okay?"

"Sure."

"Right, now I've found you an easy way in." A smug smile of satisfaction spread across Maxwell's face, reveling in his own ego. "We're both handy swimmers, right?"

"Sure. I'm not at your level, but I can hold my own in the pool." Ryan loathed Maxwell's brilliance in the pool. It was another natural attribute Ryan had discovered he excelled at, only really getting into the sport after taking acting seriously, to maintain his perfect physique. Keeping it refined and toned was a vital parameter to any serious young actor's package. Ryan had been all track and field throughout his childhood but was average at best. Ryan didn't enjoy mediocracy so when swimming permitted him success his other athletic interests were cast aside.

Although Ryan was better than most, his lack of years of dedication to the pool revealed themselves against Maxwell's flawless technique. The classic age versus experience battle. Experience took the trophy.

"Well, you're probably going to like this," Maxwell continued. "Although you're my handyman, you're also my swimming coach."

"Swimming coach? You're better than me," Ryan exclaimed.

"Well, Alex – we'd better start using your character name – they don't have to know that, do they? Your story goes that you were an exceptional swimmer, competing at the highest level. You were a national hopeful until one day you slipped and smashed your shoulder on the side of the pool. Your career was over. Four operations later the shoulder has mostly recovered, but any chances of making it professionally were gone. The dream taken away from you still haunts your soul, but you were man enough to say that there were other things you could do. You would not give up on life. You started instructing, but it didn't pay all the bills, so you worked part time as a handyman. Which is how you got the job here, you were needed on both fronts.

"Sounds plausible," Ryan agreed.

"Now the reason for this is Melissa is going to be very bored. There is nothing for her to do here. I will be working Zac around the clock, impacting on both her boredom and loneliness alike. After you befriend Melissa, which will be easy, because you're going to have the model personality for her, you can then offer to coach her in the pool. I'm hoping it will seem the perfect and only real hobby she can take up here. It'll give you plenty of time alone with her, and the chance to win her admiration."

"Yeah. This is gonna work," Ryan nodded to himself.

"Make no mistake, Alex. She loves Zac, a lot. It's not going to be easy to succeed, but if we play it out right, there's no reason for it not to. Remember, we're holding all the aces."

CHAPTER 11

Melissa's mind detected an intrusion, something unwelcome. It took only seconds for the conscious part of her brain to fire up and gauge the situation. The infringement was a loud unremitting buzzing noise. It was the alarm clock, Zac's alarm clock. She sensed him lying motionless in a state of slumber beside her. A few more seconds passed, but still, he did not react. Melissa meanwhile was not enjoying the deafening electronic droning infiltrating her ears. She opened one eye to read the time on her own alarm clock, 6:30 am. It was hardly a desired time to be awoken. Lying face down she extended her elbow and gave Zac a gentle jab. Still nothing.

"Zac," she said in a loud annoyed tone. Still, he lay unaffected. Her elbow gave him another jab. Nothing gentle that time, perhaps a little stronger than she had intended.

"Ouch." It had worked. Zac's hand extended out of the bed, blindly feeling for the off button, but to no avail. Finally, he resorted to his good old proven technique of pressing his hand at full span down on top of the alarm, attempting to push as many buttons as possible simultaneously without reprieve. It worked. Silence fell across the darkened room. For a few seconds everything remained still, the atmosphere of the room basking in the newfound calm and tranquility. Soon after Zac sat upright with an almighty yawn.

"Sorry. Did I wake you?"

"Yes. It doesn't matter. Take a shower and I'll make your breakfast before you start work," she less offered than commanded. There was no way she could get back to sleep now. She figured she may as well spend some time with Zac before he disappeared down into the "off limits" office.

"If you're sure, darling."

"I'm sure."

Zac didn't stay long. He wolfed down his pancakes with maple syrup. Not even observing how light, fluffy and impeccably balanced they were. Between every mouthful Zac fired out computer gibberish, trying to explain to Melissa what he was endeavoring to do. She did not mind, though, glad he was excited about his job. As for the pancakes, if he did not complain, then they were good. The only thing she did want was for Zac to stay a bit longer after breakfast. She invited him to, but he said he had too much to do. With that and a kiss he was gone.

Melissa sat at the kitchen table for some time after he had departed. She sulkily slid the remains of her half-eaten pancake on and off her knife. She recognized her feelings were selfish, but the same question kept running round her head, what the hell am I going to do now? After leaving her promising career back home the sensation of having no purpose in her life rang true and loud. Once she knew the location of Maxwell's house, Melissa had looked for the nearest jewelry store of the chain with which she was employed. It had not delighted her to discover out here in the edges of civilization the nearest location was over sixty miles away. In fact, no major jewelry store chains were within anything like a sensible commutable distance. Any stores locally positioned were all independent, and run as a family business. She was certain she could find employment, but not in the most senior positions of the business. Melissa had worked so hard to get to where she was, why should she now make do with sales assistant? The realization hit home that she had forgone her own career to enable Zac to follow his. That was okay, but it did not eliminate the hole now left in her life.

Eventually she cleared and washed up the breakfast clutter and took a long refreshing shower. At first, she considered having a bath, but decided against it so early in the day. At least that would be one thing to do later.

After getting dressed and drying her hair she took her time over doing her make-up. When finished she glanced at the time. 9:45 am. Damn. For half an hour the gap was filled with television, channel surfing. She could not get into anything, the truth being she was no great fan of television at the best of times. She preferred to be active and had no idea how Zac could sit for hour after hour in front of a computer monitor, then come home and do the same in front of a television set.

Her next idea was to pull a chair up to the window and really take in the great view. After sitting there for a further ten minutes she decided the scenery and the lake were a fantastic image to sit and chill out to. What it didn't substitute was the gap of having no purpose to your day. Melissa turned her head back into the room and surveyed for some inspiration. None came.

Bang bang. A knock came from their front door. Melissa flinched, and then froze. Who was that? It couldn't be Zac, he would come straight in. It must be Maxwell, she reasoned. Bang bang. It knocked again. Melissa slid off the chair, letting her hair fall forward on to her face. As she ambled towards the door, Melissa seductively slipped it back again. Pausing at the mirror she checked herself, an unnecessary task, having had so much time to get ready, she knew her clothes and make-up were immaculate. As she approached the door, something made her jolt to a halt. The lock clicked. Someone had unlocked the door from the outside. In the split second before the door opened, Melissa's mind went into hyperdrive. What should she do? Retreat back into the living room? Hide? Lock herself in the bathroom? No. It was probably Maxwell checking whether she had left a list of wants and not wants for their groceries. She had taken a long time to answer the door. Maybe he assumed she was not in. Even so she did not like the idea of him just walking in. What if she had been asleep, or in the bath with the bathroom door open?

The door opened to reveal someone not expected. A man. It was a strange man, a stranger walking into their private part of the house. An almighty scream was lodged up in the back of her throat, inclined to fire at an instant's notice. Terror and adrenaline coursed through her body, while her mind stayed focused, weighing up the risk and what action could be taken, should the situation worsen.

Ryan looked up after opening the door. His face instantaneously filled with surprise. He jumped back.

"Jesus. Sorry, I didn't know you were in here," he blurted out. Melissa analyzed his face and body language. Her primary functioning brain quickly recognized the immediate threat was subsiding. Nevertheless, who the hell was he and why was this stranger entering her living quarters? Adrenaline was still being pumped into her body. She took the opportunity to grab the offensive.

"Who are you? What are you doing, coming in here?" she shouted defensively. Ryan almost swallowed his tongue in an effort to hastily reprieve himself.

"Sorry, I'm sorry. I'm the handyman, Alex. There's a kitchen cabinet door loose. I came to fix it. I'm sorry. Maxwell told me to do it before you arrived, but I hadn't got around to it. Sorry."

Melissa held her position. The reason did seem viable.

"I knocked, I thought you were out," he added.

She had noticed one of the cabinet doors did not shut correctly. The hinge slid back and forth on its mounting, meaning it required lifting slightly to shut. She looked down. In his right hand was a toolbox. A tool belt hung loosely from his taut waist. She relaxed.

"You scared the living daylights out of me." Her voice comprehensively lightened with relief. A welcoming smile broke on her attractive face.

"Yep, I think I did." Ryan stepped forward through the doorway and extended his hand. "Alex."

Melissa walked forward and shook it. "Melissa."

"Well, Melissa, now that I've completely terrified you, would you mind if I have a look at your cabinet?"

"Sure. Sorry." She gave him a sheepish grin. "Come in." Melissa motioned with her hand for him to enter. "Would you like a coffee?"

"Now that would be lovely, just the thing to settle my nerves." They both laughed.

Melissa led him into the kitchen. She picked up the kettle with one hand and pointed to the defective cabinet with the other. "It's that one I think." She took the kettle to the sink to fill.

"Thanks. I'd better check them all while I'm here."

"Good to know you're thorough."

"I think it's the least I can do." This is going to be easy, he thought to himself.

While the kettle was boiling, she took the time to inspect the new handyman. Not that she intended any more from him than tightening a few loose screws or repairing a leaky faucet, but it never hurts to look. She would have to admit, he was impressive. Not an ounce of fat on his whole body. His muscles not oversized, but perfectly defined. His hair was light and clean, white teeth and, surprisingly considering his line of work, professionally manicured fingernails. Maybe he has too much time on his hands as well, she reasoned to herself.

"Sugar?" she asked.

Ryan looked up from the cabinet. He considered the old "No, I'm sweet enough already" line, but decided against it. Maxwell had told him to be charming, but not slimy and unoriginal. One-liners would not cut the mustard with this one. "No thanks," he responded looking at the cupboard hinge he had loosened a few days earlier. "So, what's the story with you two?"

"Who? Me and Zac?"

"I didn't know your boyfriend's name, but yeah."

"Zac is here to help Maxwell with his computer program. I'm here cos, well he is."

"Oh. Here for long?"

"Yeah, a few years I think."

"Wow. Hope you brought a big crossword book." They exchanged an ironic smile. "I have to warn you it can get pretty boring out here. I'll be glad to have some more company."

The kettle boiled. Melissa proceeded to make the coffee.

Ryan shut the door. Opened it, and then shut it again. "Done," he declared, before checking the rest.

Realizing he was going to be finished Melissa took the two drinks over to the kitchen table and took a seat. After the last cabinet had been assessed Alex removed his tool belt and set it down next to his toolbox. Melissa pulled a chair out.

"Have a seat," she offered with a warm smile.

"Thanks." He engaged eye contact with her and held his smile back for a little too long. Melissa could feel her cheeks beginning to redden, much to her annoyance.

"I have to admit I'm really bored already. Maxwell said you live here too."

"Certainly do."

"You must have a lot of free time on your hands as well, I'm sure there can't be that much to fix around here."

"You're right on both counts. I'm not just the handyman, though. Maxwell has a bit of a compulsion for swimming. I'm sure he's mentioned it once or twice."

"Only several times, but I haven't been here long, I'm sure it will be mentioned again," she joked.

"Well, I used to be a pro swimmer. I was going to swim for America."

"Wow. That's fantastic."

"Yeah it was, until I busted up my shoulder really bad."

"Oh no," Melissa put her hand to her mouth.

"Several operations later, it's back pretty good. Just not good enough to compete at that level though."

Melissa listened intently with a concerned and sorrowful frown.

"Don't worry, it's testing, but I'm coming to terms with it. I started coaching, which I really enjoy, but it doesn't pay very well. So I began doing the handyman stuff on the side. Guess I was perfect for Maxwell, two employees for the price of one." He stopped to take a sip of coffee. "Hmm, nice."

"Thanks," Melissa beamed.

"Not that I'm complaining. Maxwell is a generous wage

payer and a good swimmer. Not too much for me to do but finely hone his technique."

"But you get quite bored up here?"

"Very much so. What about you, do you swim?"

Melissa's mind immediately shot back to her school swimming lessons, where she was much more self-conscious and under-confident. It had been hard enough to leave the changing rooms with just a swimming costume on, being ogled by the boys in her class, let alone tolerate the ear-piercing screaming swimming instructor who the class benevolently nicknamed "Fat Witch" on account of her verging on obese figure and wickedly evil tongue. Many had often speculated how many decades had passed since she last took a dip herself, and when she did, how much the water level rose. Her favorite tool, the whistle, was used to ear damaging effect. The screech in her voice was not far behind.

Melissa remembered to herself how little understanding or empathy Fat Witch had shown to a bashfully shy and delicate student who needed encouragement, not discipline. This woman had locked the carrot in the changing room and had lost the key, endeavoring to use the stick twice as hard to compensate. Unsurprisingly Melissa had grown a strong aversion towards swimming and instructors alike.

"Not very well. I wouldn't drown. I can swim, but I wouldn't break any records either," she replied.

"Well, to help pass the time, I would be more than happy to give you some coaching. Free of charge, of course." Ryan's voice was a little needier than he had wanted, but he had got the necessary question out, without it sounding forced.

"Oh. Thank you, but I'm really not into swimming." Melissa was not at all keen on this idea. Damn it, Ryan thought to himself. "I wouldn't want to waste your time," she furthered.

"Honestly it wouldn't. Come on, it'd be a laugh and something to pass the time. Just give it a try." Ryan appreciated he could push it no further. If she declined, he would risk ruining any chance of a close friendship by pursuing the topic.

Melissa paused. She really didn't want to do it but had taken an instant liking to Alex. If she declined, he might take it as a negative signal. She needed as many friends as was feasible in this lonely place. Better to be diplomatic for now. "Okay, I'll give it a go, but I haven't got a swimming costume, so it will have to wait until I get one." That should buy some time, she contemplated.

Ryan felt a wave of relief wash over him. "That's great. It'll be fun. Honest."

CHAPTER 12

Zac's fingers assaulted the keyboard with speed and vigor. He disliked the phrase "in the zone" but he did enjoy sporadic interludes of genius. His brain would work so rapidly and fluently his typing labored to keep up. The majority of his time was spent either carefully considering each line and its implications before typing it in, or staring vacantly at the computer screen, hoping for inspiration. So when Zac attained such a productive point, the last thing he wanted to do was stop. He might be able to write half a day's work in the space of an hour.

Zac took a second to look at his watch: 8:30pm, this was not good. He realized that Melissa would have been expecting him back hours ago. He hadn't made it back up for lunch, there was just too much he had to do. He had made himself a sandwich in Maxwell's kitchen, and then taken two packets of crisps and a can of Coke back to his workstation. In total it expended less than ten minutes in wasted time. If he had gone upstairs for lunch it would have been half an hour at the very least.

Now with time progressing he had peaked. An hour or two earlier he was subdued, getting tired and thinking of calling it a day. Then it all changed. He got his second wind. It was now all hands on deck. He felt fresh and productive. Melissa would just have to understand.

Melissa had been keeping Zac's dinner warm for an hour now. She checked it again in the oven. It was getting really dry. She elected to switch it off before the chicken in a red wine and onion sauce with mashed yams, potatoes and spring beans was completely ruined. After placing the dinner in the microwave ready for him to reheat, she started to write him a note.

◆ ◆ ◆

Ryan sat in his living quarters, his bare feet up on the coffee table crossed over each other. In his lap a bowl of cornflakes, which he slowly worked his way through. Directly in front of him the television set, showing a rerun of *The Simpsons*, blared out. Although Ryan had watched the particular episode many times before he never tired of seeing them again. Banked around the television were additional monitors. They showed CCTV footage from around the house. Ryan could see Zac working hard away at his computer. He was not going anywhere for a good while yet.

Melissa, on the other hand, was getting impatient. He had kept an eye on her movements for some time now. She paced their apartment like a caged animal. Ryan's ego was fading out the reality of what he was involved in and where it might ultimately lead. The kitchen "act" was a real buzz. As he left, he was filled with a long-forgotten sensation; The feeling when you know you just nailed a scene. He had missed it and was now starting to enjoy himself, pushing the considerations of motive and final outcomes to the back of his mind. He took sincere fulfillment from Melissa's evident boredom. The more time she spent in this state, the easier his job would become. He almost couldn't wait to meet with Zac face to face and yearned to shake his hand. Not as an acknowledgement or greeting as Zac would think, but to secretly thank him in an underhand approach. Thank him for neglecting his girlfriend, making his job so much easier. Ryan's mind prolonged the fantasy. He conjured up an image of himself collecting his first Oscar and thanking Zac for starting his career in his acceptance speech.

Ryan was snapped back to reality by Melissa's next move. Unnoticed by him, she had left her apartment. He had to refocus rapidly, not sure of where she was going, but understanding there was a fair chance she was searching for him. Most probably she would check the pool. He had no time to waste. Setting down his cornflakes, he grabbed a towel and made for a flight of restricted and remote stairs at the back of the house. They were constructed for use in an emergency like a fire. The stairwell gave Ryan a timing advantage. He could move to where he needed to be without Melissa suspecting anything was amiss, such as simply being at the pool before her on the anticipation of her attendance. It was the pool he headed for.

Melissa exited the elevator at Maxwell's living space and the office level. She stepped into the great room. Empty. Next, she tried the kitchen, but still nobody. Melissa walked up to the office door, her hand poised to knock. Zac had to be in there. So might Maxwell. She speculated he would not take kindly to Zac being interrupted. He had told her the office was inaccessible, but she only wanted to ask Zac how much longer he would be. Surely, he could not be angry for her undemanding enquiry.

She didn't knock. Melissa walked back to the elevator. As she entered, she afforded herself one more look at the office door, virtually willing Zac to telepathically perceive her presence.

"Pool," she finally commanded. The doors slid shut.

As the door opened, she heard the sound of splashing. Someone was swimming. She hoped desperately it was Alex, alone. Stepping forward away from the elevator she promptly secured a view of the swimmer. It was Alex. He cut through the water in a graceful, efficient stroke. His alacrity through the greenish blue liquid appeared effortless, leaving virtually no splash, slicing through with body and water as one. Melissa could not help but be impressed. Alex seemed oblivious to her presence and she felt naughty, partly for being an undisclosed voyeur, but also deeply immoral for her unbridled sensation of lust, watching his toned and athletic body as he swam.

She quietly walked over to a nearby lounger and sat just marveling at him traveling up and down the pool. Melissa was not aware Ryan knew perfectly well she was close at hand. His confidence astronomical, he swam outstandingly, showboating to his audience. He was aware she would not find showing off desirable, as Maxwell had told him so. But as she thought she was undetected he could flaunt without risking antagonizing her.

After a few minutes, once he was sure she had received a beneficial eyeful, he faked noticing her and swam over towards her lounger.

"Hello again," he said with a mischievous smile.

"Hi." She gazed at him for a few seconds. "I'm not disturbing you, am I?"

"Not at all. I'm glad to see you."

"Thanks." She felt a little embarrassed at the compliment. Her cheeks flushed and she stared down at her feet.

"Where's Zac?" he deceitfully asked.

"Dunno." Her eyes raised to converge with his. "Guess he's still working, but I haven't heard a thing from him. I'm not allowed in the office to find out."

"Well, that makes two of us. I'm only allowed in there when something needs fixing."

"The outcasts," she teased.

"Yeah. Still, we can be friends while they're both busy locking themselves away, getting square eyes."

She laughed, brushing her hair back over her shoulder. Ryan remembered the tendency he had noticed last time they spoke, in the kitchen. She was exquisite. It made his job significantly easier. He would have been diligently making a play for her anyway, regardless of his unique employment circumstances.

"I'd like us to be friends," she matched.

"Great." With that he dipped his head under the water, and then ejected himself up, out and over the side of the pool. All his muscles protruded and the sinews stretched taut in the movement, emphasized by the water cascading down over them, like a miniature waterfall, and just as eye catching.

He grabbed his towel and sat on the lounger next to her. For a fleeting moment they only gazed at each other. Melissa identified a potent chemistry between them. She could not quite put her finger on why it was so potent and intense. She did know it was going to be perilous spending so much time with him. In her normal world, if she had ever encountered someone like this while with Zac her reaction would have been to not encourage the connection. Playing with fire only has one long-term outcome. Not that she had ever met anyone like Alex before. Here, though, in the incarceration of isolation, not only was she instigating the friendship, she was also enjoying the intimacy and thrill of the sexual tension between them.

"Someday soon we can take one of Maxwell's cars and drive into town. So we can get you a swimming costume."

"Okay," Melissa's voice was heightened with reservation.

"You don't sound keen."

"It's not that. Just something from my past."

"What?"

Melissa went on to divulge all about Fat Witch and the reason for her longstanding hatred of all things connected with swimming. When she finished, she was surprised by Alex extending out his hand and grasping hers.

"Please don't think it will be anything like that," he said. "I want to do it for fun. I certainly won't be shouting at you. Or blowing any whistles, for that matter."

Melissa hardly heard him, she was preoccupied by the sexual buzz Alex had created in her, merely by holding her hand.

"Okay. I'm sure it will be fine," she uttered breathlessly, before awkwardly retracting her hand.

"Great. We could make a day of it. I'll show you round the shops. We could go for lunch?"

"Yeah, that sounds nice," she agreed, trying to swallow the lump in her throat.

◆ ◆ ◆

Over an hour and a half later Melissa opened the door of their living quarters. Zac was back. Melissa could not help wishing she had returned before him. Zac sat at the kitchen table eating his microwaved meal. He must have returned recently.

"Hi, Zac," she managed as nonchalantly as possible.

"Hi. Where have you been?" he asked with a mouthful of food.

"I wrote you a note."

"Yes, I read it. It only said you were about in the house and wouldn't be long."

"I was down at the pool," she revealed as she parked herself on the kitchen worktop behind Zac. She anticipated a multitude of questions. Although nothing improper had occurred, her conscience was guilt-ridden. The potent sensation of a sexual implication ran through her mind. She elected not to sit right in front of him. Trying to hold eye contact throughout any of his questions was an intolerable task.

"At the pool? But you don't even like swimming!" Zac exclaimed.

"Well hopefully that's going to change. I'm going to get some swimming coaching," she exposed in a positive tone.

"From Maxwell?"

"No." Melissa paused slightly before broadening her answer. She did not mean the delay, but it was enough to stop Zac from eating and turn his head round to look at her. "Turns out the handyman, Alex, is also a swimming ace. He coaches Maxwell already and offered to coach me for free," she carried on in her cheerful manner, but could not help it sounding slightly fabricated.

"How old is he?"

"About our age," she answered honestly.

"Is he good looking?"

"What's that got to do with anything?" she took the defensive sharply.

"Just asking."

"He's okay, I suppose. I didn't really notice," she answered somewhat less honestly.

"So why does he want to give free coaching? What's in it for him?"

"A friend. I know I need one, if today is anything to go by."

"And is that all he wants?"

"If it isn't then I will put him in his place. I've got you, I don't want anybody else. All I need is a friend, so please don't make this difficult."

Zac's options for maneuver were waning. He was convinced Alex would want more from Melissa than just a friendship. In spite of this he had to trust her. The more he interfered and tried to thwart their friendship the more it would bring them together.

"Okay, darling. I know I can trust you. It's just other people I worry about."

CHAPTER 13

A week passed by in a blink; both Zac and Melissa were settling into their new routines. For Zac it involved working every hour he could possibly stay awake. His head spun with the awareness of the mountain of work ahead, it was worse than his imagination had permitted. Faced with this seemingly impossible volume Zac threw himself into it completely and utterly. It was his way, his method of dealing with pressure: work harder. Of course, guilt floated throughout his psyche for so comprehensively neglecting Melissa, but he could see no other path. He consoled himself with the likelihood she would understand. That she recognised this sacrifice was for them both, for their future together. Setting them up with a financial security that would last their whole life. Yet at the same time a danger existed, the threat of Alex played cruelly on his mind.

He empathized with her very obvious boredom. Yet she was lonely and spending greater amounts of time with Alex. When he left her early one morning she had told, not asked, but told him that Alex and she were going out the next day to buy her a swimming costume. As he switched off his computer for the night, Zac determined it was essential for him to see Alex for himself. They had both resided in the same house for over a week, he was Melissa's newfound best friend, yet due to Zac's obsession with his master, the computer screen, he had been unable to assess this very real risk to their relationship with his own eyes. He would tomorrow, for sure.

The following day Zac sat at his workstation working away. Attempting to remain absorbed and not think outside his computer world. Maxwell was behind him doing the same, seemingly without the same concerns. Zac was undoubtedly unfocused today.

Earlier he had purposely set out to encounter Alex somewhere round the house. He had found him in Maxwell's kitchen. Zac made himself a cup of coffee while he spoke to Alex, immediately feeling sick when he realized how attractive the guy was. Melissa had professed not to notice. Rubbish, it was impossible not to. He would have felt more reassured if she had just admitted Alex was stunning. The fact that she had tried to dupe Zac, illustrated she was attempting to conceal her feelings. Not an encouraging sign.

"So, I hear you're going to be coaching Melissa in the pool." Zac tried his best not to sound threatened.

"Yeah, certainly am."

"And you're taking her into town today to get a swimming costume?"

"Yep. It'll be nice to get out of here for a while."

Zac smiled and silently nodded. He desperately wanted to say, "Keep your greasy hands off my girl or I'll kill you," but knew it would not change anything. If Melissa found out he was reading the riot act to her new friend, he really would be for the high jump. Underneath a dark aggression simmered. Zac had lived through a period of noticeable aggression during his years of neglect and grief while his father had nursed the bottle. He had gotten into a lot of trouble at his school and they only knew the half of it. His classmates were so scared of him, most of his behavior went unreported. The playground code of silence. That was a different Zac, not the person he was now. Even so that Zac existed and he was very aware of that fact.

"Well, drive carefully." What else could he say? He grabbed his coffee and mentally kicked himself as he walked out.

Later on, at his computer, every other thought running through his mind was what Alex and Melissa were doing. He had to snap out of this. It was affecting his work severely. The problem was obviously here for the long term, so he knew it was fundamental to deal with his state of mind.

"I'm going to stretch my legs for half an hour Max."

"Okay, Zac. See you later."

With that he was gone. After taking the elevator down to the car park he noticed the X5 was gone. Shit. Not only does he get to take my girlfriend out for the day, but he also gets a fantastic car to do it in, Zac cussed in his mind. Head down, he dejectedly stepped outside. He inhaled deeply into his lungs letting the clean fresh air clear his mind. After a few seconds he let it all sail out, his problems, tensions and everything else.

The air was cold and revitalizing as Zac slowly made his way down the drive. He intended to find a road to the lake. It soon became apparent this would not be as easy as first anticipated. The driveway was a good deal longer than he had remembered in the car arriving. Plus, it ran steeply downwards off the hillside. It was going to be remorseless work walking back up. He carried on regardless. Upon finally reaching the road his expectation of an easy route on to the lake was quickly dashed. All he could see in front of him, left and right was steep hillside. No sign of a nearby road cutting through. After a meticulous inspection he noticed a rough old track, steep and overgrown. It climbed up over the hillside. Zac turned back toward the house. The last thing he wanted was to arrive back in the office hot, sweaty and dirty. After taking two steps he turned back towards the track, opting to resume after coming this far.

He crossed the road and clambered up the hillside, sometimes having to use his hands for extra traction and leverage. The climb appeared to go on forever, but eventually his determination paid off. He reached the summit and could not be disenchanted with his reward. The lake was a depiction of splendor. As a bonus the other side of the hill was a significantly kinder decline. The track leading down was also in a far healthier condition. He carefully stepped down the hillside to the lake's edge. An old wooden bench sat on the shore. Zac took a seat and with a prolonged inhale though his nose, took in the vision and all its allure, the sunlight shimmering on the surface. Zac's initial enticement back at the house now captured him in a far more passionate fashion. In close proximity the way the light glimmered and sparkled on the surface teased the viewer like a dance. Virtually hypnotizing him into an involuntary condition.

What really captured Zac in this oasis was the plentiful wildlife. Over such a tranquil spot it seemed ironic death and violence was commonplace, particularly in the graceful flight the birds took over the water, gliding and swooping with such effortless control, and then suddenly with a quick sharp change of direction, diving into the drink, emerging seconds later with an innocent fish impaled on their beaks. Zac had a childhood passion for animals and wildlife in general, but all passion for anything had vanished the day of the accident. Any event, hobby or pastime with connecting memories to his mother were gone. In her death it all evaporated with her.

Now though, whilst sat all alone in such a therapeutic location he allowed himself to benefit from the spectacle of undisturbed wildlife. He took a second to look at his watch. Twenty minutes had passed since leaving the office, although he had the impression of being a world away. Zac knew he had to return, however he opted to seize another quarter of an hour in his paradise.

Just then something caught his attention, a rumbling noise. As it intensified, he identified it as a vehicle driving on a dirt track, off to his left. The motor vehicle was getting closer. He sincerely hoped it was not Alex bringing Melissa here to enjoy the view. If it was him, he could only have one purpose on his mind. Zac considered hiding, so if it were them, he could observe them alone together. Prior to considering how paranoid he had become, Zac twigged to one obvious problem with the hastily conceived plan – there was nowhere to hide.

Without options he sat tight to await the mystery vehicle's arrival. To his surprise a battered old jeep rounded the corner.

The wheels hopping and dancing all around as the worn suspension tried to cope with the potholes and loose gravel. A shower of dust and debris kicked up from the tires, hung suspended in the air, like a rolling bank of fog. Still traveling at speed, the jeep was heading straight for Zac. He sat attentively watching, beginning to wonder if it was going to stop. Then all in one very belated dramatic maneuver it broke into a skid and the backend slid round to face the water. Momentum carried the dust to Zac. He instinctively closed his eyes and protected his face with his hands.

After sensing the tingling of millions of mini missiles had depleted, he opened his eyes to witness a young woman jumping out from the jeep, seemingly oblivious to his presence. She was tall and casually dressed. A baseball cap and sunglasses obscured his view, but he could perceive she was striking. A ponytail of long blond hair jutted out from the back of her baseball cap. Her clothes were certainly not suitable for the cold winter weather. Her T-shirt and shorts were baggy, but it was still possible to judge her petite frame and slim figure. She walked around to the back of the jeep and lowered the tailgate. Immediately a golden retriever leapt out from the back and dived with a colossal splash into the water. Any enduring fragment of the former tranquil ambiance was now eradicated.

Zac did not mind. "Hi," he offered.

She swung round in surprise, startled by the voice. Zac realized she genuinely had not noticed his presence and felt remorseful for alarming her.

"Hi," she replied after swiftly assessing him. "I didn't see you there." She placed her hand on her chest as if to calm her beating heart. Zac endeavored not to notice, but the action tightened her T-shirt revealing the outline of her shapely chest.

"No. I noticed," he said with a grin.

"I'm sorry I must have covered you with grit."

"Nah, it missed me," he lied. After a quick glance at her seemingly amphibian dog she broke into a warm summer of a smile and gestured with her hand toward to the bench. "Mind if

I join you?"

"Not at all." Zac slid along the bench like a typewriter cradle, giving her a more comfortable amount of room. She sat. For half a minute they both looked intently in unison out across the water. The dog meanwhile had now calmed down from its early exhilaration of disembarking the vehicle at the lake. He finally observed Zac's presence and swam as the crow flies toward him, eager to scrutinize and investigate, as dogs do. Upon reaching the water's edge it clambered out, and proceeded to give itself a comprehensive and gratifying shake. Water flew off in every direction, the beads catching the sunlight, shimmering like a shower of tiny jewels and diamonds. It was a heart-warming moment, which was evident in Zac's expression. Once the surrounding area had been soaked the dog approached him, tail wagging. Zac gave the sopping wet dog a hearty stroke.

"Buster, Buster, leave him alone," the woman commanded. "I'm sorry." Already Buster had managed to rise on his back legs, one wet paw on Zac's lap, the other on his arm and was licking away at his face. Zac found it not too dissimilar to when he was young, and his mother would lick a paper towel and use it to wipe marks off his face. Not pleasant, but strangely not offensive. Zac let out a chuckle as he ineffectually attempted to protect himself from the over exuberant hello. Once fulfilled Buster jumped down and returned to his watery playground.

"I'm not used to seeing anybody else here. I'm Lisa by the way."

"Zac." They shook hands. "To be honest it's my first time here."

"Oh. Well normally you'd get to enjoy the peace and quiet, uninterrupted." Lisa looked around "Where's your car?" she asked in a confused tone.

"I walked here."

"Walked?" she exclaimed. "This is the middle of nowhere. Where did you walk from?"

"Oh, not far, just from the house on the other side of that hill," he said, pointing behind him. Lisa stared at the hill. Her face retained the confused expression.

"That's my uncle's house?" she said, her voice filled with perplexity.

"Who? Maxwell?"

"Yeah, you know him?"

"I work for him."

"Oh." Lisa thought for a moment. "Ah, his computer program, I'm guessing?"

"Spot on." Zac hunched his back up and then squinted his eyes. "My name's Zac and I'm a computer programmer," he said in a mock nerdy voice.

"Stop it." Lisa laughed out loud. She gave him a slap on his arm. "I'm Maxwell's niece."

"Well, I'm pleased to meet you, Lisa," They shook hands once again.

"I'm sorry to say I'm not quite so pleased to meet you."

Zac recoiled slightly, reacting with momentary indignation at the remark. "Oh. Why?"

"I bet you're staying in the guest living quarters?"

Zac, still miffed, gave a nod to confirm.

"Well, that's where I normally stay." As she spoke a large smile suddenly erupted onto her face.

Zac relaxed, grasping she was teasing him. "Sorry about that."

"Yeah. I bet you are." Humor was again apparent in her voice. Zac studied her for a second.

"Where will you stay now? I'm guessing you're staying?"

"For a few days, and don't worry. I'll just have to make do with the spare room in Maxwell's living quarters."

"Not the one Alex is living in?" Zac squirmed unnervingly.

"Nah. He has a couple of spare rooms. Don't feel too guilty, I'm sure I'll get used to a box room," she mocked.

"Oh, I'd like to feel guilty, but I like the view from our place too much."

Holding a combined smile, they both looked out to the lake. Lisa's dog continued to swim aimlessly around, a blond head sailing through the calm lagoon, a small wake left behind.

"Our?" Lisa finally remarked.

"Sorry?" Zac failed to understand the question.

"You said our place. You have a wife?"

"Girlfriend," Zac corrected.

"Oh. Well, I'll look forward to meeting her."

Zac thought he detected disillusionment in her voice. Truth was, she was purposely being moderately obvious. Zac decided to take it as a compliment.

"What's your opinion of Alex?"

"He's okay," she answered. "A bit too serious at times. Why do you ask?"

"He's taken Melissa, my girlfriend, into town."

"Ah, I see," she said with a shrewd expression on her face. Lisa turned back to the water. Buster had located a substantially sized branch floating in the water. Far too sizeable for the dog to happily hold in its mouth. Yet he persisted, laboring to compel the cumbersome object to comply against the incessantly changing direction of his swim. The dog emphatically left a more impressive wake now.

"Well, it was really nice to meet you, but I have to get back to work. I've already been much longer than I said I'd be."

"Maxwell still the slave-driver?"

"Yeah, something like that." Zac stood up and dusted himself down.

"I can give you a lift back if you want?"

"Oh, thank you, but I don't want to be any trouble." He looked out at Buster, toiling to keep pace with such a large branch in his mouth. "Besides I don't think he would be too delighted at play time being cut short."

Lisa laughed with gusto. It was a stout laugh for such a petite girl, yet at the same time endearing with a soft female undertone. "It's no problem. I was only giving him a quick dip. There's plenty of time over the next few days to clear the lake of driftwood." She stood and walked to the water's edge. She called out to Buster several times. The dog pretended not hear the calls, hoping she would give up and let him continue. Soon after the persistent shout intensified, becoming more audible and commanding. Buster knew his time was up.

The journey to shore became more problematic than it might have been. Buster, already tiring, had to negotiate through reeds and bracken with his decaying wooden prize. There was never any question of discarding it, however. Buster would sooner risk drowning than let that happen. Eventually he made it to shore. Lisa helped him out of the water, by yanking his collar up and out. Quickly she made her retreat before he shook himself. The first attempt proved futile. Buster reluctantly dropped his trophy and did the job properly. When finished he attempted to reclaim it, but with it being much heavier and unwieldy out of the water he found it impossible to get a purchase.

"Buster, get in," Lisa said firmly, motioning to the jeep. After giving the branch a long sorrowful look, like a dieter walking past an "all you can eat" buffet, Buster did as he was told.

Zac was not prepared for the ferociousness of Lisa's driving. She gunned it down the old beaten trail as if she was on a racetrack. Zac prioritized fastening his seatbelt. A lesson well learned. Nervously he held on, listening to the rumbling of the tires fighting the rough ground for traction.

The track ran in a long sweeping curve, always tightening. Zac could feel the jeep slipping towards the embankment. Just before it seemed the jeep would topple off the road it straightened out. No prospect of Zac relaxing though, the straight road only encouraged Lisa to accelerate harder. In the distance Zac observed the end of the track, joining onto the main road. He silently prayed to himself, God, or anybody else listening, for her to stop drag racing and just start braking.

Reaching the point where Zac was about to remonstrate, Lisa anchored up. The vehicle squirmed left and right, on the very periphery of control, rubber failing to bite on the broken surface. Zac shot Lisa a sideways fleeting look. She sat at the controls with a slight smile on her face. No sign of anxiety or trepidation. She was prettier than Zac's first judgment. Her extreme confidence, although petrifying, was also extremely charismatic and alluring. Zac's attention snapped back to the rapidly discontinuing road. Just when it seemed to be too late the jeep came to a halt. A microsecond check left and right confirmed all clear. They continued on to Maxwell's house bordering on warp speed.

"Hi, Uncle!" Lisa burst out loudly as Zac and she entered the office.

"Lisa!" Maxwell exclaimed with a smile so large the corners of his eyes creased up. The two gave each other a long heartfelt hug. Zac felt slightly awkward, uncomfortably stood beside them, looking completely out of place. After what Zac considered a slightly overbearing greeting, Lisa spoke first.

"I'm sorry, but I picked up a stray on the way here." Her eyes fell on Zac in an artificial incriminating way. Zac gave a little self-conscious smile and hurriedly returned to his desk. When the greetings were all over, Maxwell switched off his computer and the two of them left, leaving Zac to work alone.

"How did it go with Zac?" Maxwell asked after they had retired to his private study. He handed Lisa a can of lemonade.

"Good, I think," she answered, cracking the can open. "He seemed to like me. I'm guessing you already know he's very concerned about Ryan."

"Alex," Maxwell corrected. Lisa gave him a bewildered look. "Always refer to him as Alex."

"Sorry. I didn't realize it mattered when it was just us two." Lisa felt harshly treated. Her tone was anything but apologetic.

"It's easier for all of us. Plus, it seriously reduces the risk of a slip-up in front of Zac or Melissa," As aggrieved as Lisa felt she knew he had a point. She took a long swig from her can. Its icy bitterness hurt her sensitive teeth but invigorated her senses.

"So, what's next?" she asked.

"Have you been studying your sheet religiously like I told you to?"

The aggravation restored to her sweet little face. "Yes. I have," she heatedly stated. "I know it all off by heart."

"Good. Keep studying it."

"There's no need. Like I said, I know it all off by heart." She gave Maxwell a hostile stare. He held it raising an eyebrow in a questioning manner. It took a while, but Lisa caved in. She looked away, then down on the ground. "If you think it's necessary."

"I do. I do," he repeated for additional emphasis.

CHAPTER 14

The following morning Zac awoke with an uncomfortable knot of dread in his stomach. He had been arguing with Melissa again. He looked over at her. She lay on her side with her back toward him. Her skin was so white she almost disappeared into the bed sheet. Her shoulders spotted with freckles like speckled bird's eggs. She only ever slept in that position when they had gone to bed on a row.

Unsurprisingly the argument stemmed from Melissa's jaunt with Alex. Melissa had been subjected to being on trial upon returning. It was not quite, "How was your day?" More like an interrogation with almost no question having a correct answer. In the end Melissa realized no matter what she said, Zac was just getting more and more wound up. She opted for silence. That did not work any better as Zac's paranoia was in overdrive.

He got up and took a shower. His mind rolled like a barrel down a hill, recognizing the severity of the problem. He understood Melissa needed company. Conversely, he could not permit this friendship to develop. Certainly, it would only be a matter of time before Alex made a move. Zac assessed his options. If he apologized to her before leaving this morning, the danger of Melissa responding to any advance would be slim to nonexistent. On the other hand, by apologizing now he would be accepting and consenting to their friendship, an objectionable outcome at the least. Zac let the torrent of water pour onto his head, keeping his face down, so the water ran off, permitting him to breathe.

If Zac left without a request for forgiveness, he would have stood his ground. It might mean that once Melissa had calmed down, she would cancel the swimming lessons and just see

Alex in passing. That was unlikely. More probably she would go ahead anyway. If Alex did make a move the likelihood of it being reciprocated would be amplified. Riled by Zac she might respond just to spite him.

Zac made a half-hearted attempt to wash. His mind was too extensively preoccupied to complete the job thoroughly. He reasoned that it was doubtful Alex would make his move so soon, he was almost certainly intelligent enough to grasp the importance of building a strong camaraderie first. Establishing a strong united friendship was undoubtedly his tactic, Zac was certain of that. If he did make his move as early as today, surely Melissa would not consent. He had to trust her that much. The judgment was made. After switching off the shower, drying and dressing, he made himself two slices of toast. Then he left for work without a word to Melissa, still lying motionless in the bed.

She had been awake the whole time, pretending to be asleep. She had lain in suspense of Zac kissing her goodbye. At first, she felt stunned and distraught that he had not backed down yet. It shortly turned to anger. What the hell had she done wrong anyway?

Ryan sat at the table. His drained bleary eyes struggled to remain focused. The replenishing scent of fresh coffee invaded his nose, keeping him functioning. It was fair to say Ryan was not a morning person. He recognized he drank too much coffee, a substantial vice in his life, gone too far. He was virtually unable to function without the socially acceptable drug.

His time in Hollywood had furthered the quandary. While working as a set builder the entire workforce consumed coffee as if it were more essential than air or water. During his time waiting tables unlimited coffee was obtainable free of charge and Ryan took full advantage. Being free, he drank it to such an extent he bounced off the walls all the way home. This chain of events led to him being incapable of uninterrupted sleep. Of course, then drained in the morning, it compelled him to drink more of the rich dark drug to operate. Now caught in the vicious circle he certainly needed a fix before putting up with Maxwell. He groaned inwardly as the study door opened. Both Maxwell and Lisa entered.

"Good morning, Alex," Maxwell said.

"Morning." Ryan did not address Lisa. He undertook a prolonged slurp of his wakeup fuel. He could almost sense the stimulant's intoxicating energy coursing through his veins.

"Have you read your character sheets twice this morning?"

"I have," Ryan lied.

Maxwell leveled a harsh unbelieving stare at him. "Just make sure you do before you meet Melissa." He gave Ryan a "do not kid a kidder" look. Ryan shamefacedly dropped his eyes down to his coffee and gave a nod. He noticed that Maxwell did not ask Lisa the same question. Goodie two shoes, deliberated Ryan.

"Right." Lisa sat down as Maxwell addressed them both. "We are at a delicate stage today. While Lisa is here for a few days to build her friendship with Zac, we must keep her away from Melissa. Naturally Zac is extremely concerned at your friendship."

Ryan nodded impassively. Naturally, he thought.

"He is putting masses of pressure on Melissa to discontinue your relationship," Maxwell continued. "So far, so good. Her need for a companion outweighs any emotional manipulation he can throw at her. That is, of course, while she thinks there is no threat of Zac participating in a similar relationship. Now, from his psychoanalysis I know Zac will not offer up any information about his soon to be growing relationship with Lisa. So, if you two don't meet yet, we won't have a problem. If you do meet, she will almost certainly feel threatened and offer up the end of her friendship with Alex in exchange for Zac to do likewise." Maxwell gave his chin an extensive concerned rub as he considered this. "Let's make no mistake, guys, if that happens it could be curtains for this whole venture." He slumped back in his seat. Point made.

Zac clacked his computer keys. Yesterday's work was of such a poor quality he virtually had to discard the whole lot. He appreciated his mind had been preoccupied, over on some yonder hill, and his programming had reflected the fact. Small strands of his usual consistent programming infiltrated the mass of feeble, amateur efforts, abundant in holes and glitches. He could not permit the poison of his own thoughts and insecurities to attack his work. Not now. Not after arriving at an early pinnacle of his short career, a foremost landmark in his life.

He buckled down and intensely stared at the screen like some cowboy in a black and white western. Inspiration came. Zac seized it, like a hungry lion in a barren safari. For several minutes the conventional Zac returned. Not a thought for the world outside his computer.

Zac failed to maintain it. Negative sensations, not even sufficient to be considered thoughts began oozing inside. Before he could stop it, they were streaming. A very potent contaminate indeed. Eventually Zac surrendered. He stopped working and tried to run the thoughts through his mind. As if once processed they would expire, like a computer. However, computers work completely differently from the human mind. They only follow commands, have no intelligence or conscious thoughts. Without commands a computer is merely plastic, metal and silicon.

Zac endeavored to rationalize the facts in a logical manner. His partner was to all intents and purposes, extremely beautiful, eye-catchingly beautiful. Pick her out of the crowd beautiful. Persistently throughout their relationship, Zac had put up with unwanted attention. He never found it settled comfortably with him but accepted it as a worthwhile price to pay. As he perceived the escalating situation, the significant difference this time was not so much unwanted attention, but a direct threat.

In normal circumstances, for instance if Melissa and her friends took a night out, Melissa would get chatted up numerous times. In truth she enjoyed the attention and compliments. To feel wanted is to feel good, but yet she was always careful not to lead anybody on. The key difference was she did not require their friendship, her real friends were right there. She did not crave sexual attention. Zac was her man. Now though, the scales had tipped, the balance was lost. Zac speculated how she could find her equilibrium now, with no friends and currently only a part-time lover at best. Exasperatingly Alex seemed to be the missing part of her new jigsaw. As much as Zac wanted to trust Melissa with blind faith, turning a blind eye would only make Alex's objectives much more straightforward.

He stared back at the computer screen. Zac posed himself a question, what am I going to do to tip the scales in my favor? He hit a few keys on the computer, slumped back and viewed the screen. It read "Fight Back."

CHAPTER 15

Melissa examined herself once more in the mirror. She was about to meet Alex down at the pool for her first lesson. Her self-ogling was not out of vanity, but insecurity. Melissa continuously failed to see what was staring her in the face. Her freckles, although much diminished since childhood, were still a prominent feature. She had always detested them, right back to childhood, feeling they gave her a tomboy appearance. Coupled with the boyish short haircut her mother insisted she have, it often led to others confusing her sex, the fundamental reason for her obviously feminine locks today. When in her early teens Melissa told her mother, she was growing her hair, Sally did not object. Her freckles she could not do much about, but every other fragment of her was an undertaking to look as womanly as possible. She was in fact all woman, she being the only person unable to see it. Reflection checked, she snatched her towel and headed for the pool.

As the elevator doors slid open Melissa was pleased to be greeted by the familiar sound of water splattering and splashing. Alex was already in the pool.

"Hi," she announced as she turned the corner, almost instantly freezing to a halt. It was Maxwell in the pool. He had seemed not to notice her as his head was submerged, his body cutting through the water with seemingly unfeasible velocity.

"Hi, Melissa," the correct voice returned. Alex was sat in the corner, toweling himself off. She smiled sweetly at him and strolled over, staging her best attempt to walk towards him confidently, albeit the insecurity of wearing just a swimming costume and towel left her inelegant and rigid. "Perfect timing. Maxwell is just finishing up."

"You're sure he won't mind me taking up your time?"

"No problem." A voice unexpectedly announced from behind. It was Maxwell clinging to the edge of the pool like a chimp on a branch. "No point in him wasting his teaching talent on an old timer like me."

"Thanks," she smiled.

Maxwell left soon afterwards. Once in the water Melissa's long-forgotten scars from Fat Witch reignited, causing her to feel more self-conscious than when she had stood at the poolside half naked.

"Okay, just swim a few lengths. I want to see what you already know."

Melissa gave a childlike nod and began. She immediately realized the mediocre technique from her youth had not exactly improved with years of no practice. Mindful an attractive male was also studying her meager effort was an embarrassment beyond. All she only think was Alex was used to coaching an expert. He must be cringing right now.

She completed two lengths, and then grasped the pool side. Her cheeks flushed, half from the exertion, half from the embarrassment. She looked at Alex far from expectantly, almost anticipating him to be doubled over with laughter.

"Not bad, Melissa," he called out.

"You're patronizing me," she returned.

"Not at all. Your basic technique is good. Okay, it's obviously rusty, but in free style you're far from a beginner."

After the lesson was wrapped up Alex tossed her a diet Coke. She sat on the lounger dripping chlorine-treated water on the floor. She wrapped herself in her towel then opened the can.

"Thanks," she offered, holding it up to him, before taking a long, much required drink.

"Now what did you think about the lesson?" He held a long smile. "Am I as bad as Fat Witch?"

"No, I really enjoyed it. I can't believe the difference after just one lesson. It's nothing like before."

"Aha, another satisfied customer. It's always a pleasure."

He mimed tipping an imaginary hat at her.

Melissa took another swig of her soft drink and lay back on the lounger, primarily looking at the ceiling. Not much to see. Eventually turning her head round to look at Alex. He was already gazing back at her. They both retained the familiar smile, but this time neither looked away.

Inside Melissa's head alarm bells were ringing loud and clear. She comprehended the tightrope she was walking, but desire is a compelling force. She willed herself not to persist with this undeclared mutual lust. After some time, Alex eventually broke eye contact moving them down her body. For the first time in her life Melissa encountered the sensation of a man undressing her with his eyes. Not that she was wearing much to remove. The impression was electric. Being so close to naked was such a thrill. Melissa suddenly became aware of her heart pounding in her chest, and the deepness in her breathing. She surmised her cheeks were ready to camouflage against fire trucks.

Maxwell had now joined Zac in the office. Zac barely noticed Maxwell's arrival. Striving to work effectively coupled with fretting about his girlfriend's faithfulness had thoroughly engaged his mind.

Maxwell sat away from Zac. He appeared deep in thought. Zac glanced over at him. Maxwell had not typed a thing for some time, he was just completely transfixed on his monitor. Zac could not make out the point of interest, the screen was turned away from his line of sight.

Maxwell stared intently into the screen. He could hardly believe how well the plan was working. Everything was slipping into place beautifully. Holding all the aces and having a few up his sleeve, just in case. Of course, this was the easiest part. Maxwell had regained his lost confidence that everything would work out for him. It now burned brightly on. Any doubts of recent failures in his life were instantly extinguished. Blind faith was sometimes a man's best friend, but other times his worst enemy, the rise and fall effect.

The image on the screen he viewed was a swimming pool. Two figures locked together by their own intensity. Maxwell could not help but rub his chin in expectation. Was this about to be the climax of the first part of a scheme so devious and outlandish it had made the hairs on the back of his neck stand on end? This was certainly much sooner than Maxwell had anticipated, but with the obvious chance presented, he willed Ryan to act.

Melissa's heart already seemed to be at maximum rate. That was before Alex rose from his lounger. Then she half-expected it to break out of her chest. Alex slowly, but purposefully, walked towards her. Upon reaching Melissa's lounger he lowered himself to a squat position beside her. They were back to unbroken eye contact. Melissa felt paralyzed. She did not think she could move away even if she wanted to. Not that she did, instead she threw a mental blanket over her alarm bell.

Alex lifted her hand to his lips, still maintaining eye contact. He awarded it a gentle drawn-out kiss. When he finally released her hand, she brushed it against his cheek, unpredictably smooth and velvety for a man. After only half a minute or so, although to Melissa it was a lifetime, Alex tilted in and kissed her lusciously on the lips, caressing the fleshy islands with proficient effect. Ryan knew he was an accomplished kisser, had been told so many times in the past. He had certainly practiced emphatically. Melissa unquestionably thought so. All the electricity of their flirting now channeled its way through her body. Senses erupted as if she were a smoking volcano blowing its top, her head giddy and faint, any contemplation of right or wrong now entirely suppressed, buried deep in the ground. At this moment they were the only two. The rest of the world did not exist. Before Melissa could collect herself, Alex slid down, attentively kissing her neck. She let go a moan of gratification. Her body so charged with electric, she almost deemed herself unsafe so close to the pool.

Maxwell watched with bated breath. He willed the scenario to continue, the back of his mind knowing this had occurred much more prematurely than he had imagined, her loneliness and desperation not yet reaching anywhere near adequate levels to render this a sure thing. Yet Ryan gave the impression of playing his part impeccably. Maxwell regained renewed faith in him. He hardly dare breathe himself. Now it was Maxwell's turn to feel like the voyeur. The act proceeded to advance. Ryan slowly removing Melissa's swimming costume, peeling it back with his hands. His lips kissing every part of newly exposed flesh. Then abruptly Melissa's hand extended out and constrained Ryan. Maxwell winced. So close. He could see her say something to Ryan but had no idea what through the muted screen. Directly, without remonstration, Ryan rose from her and walked away.

Maxwell's blood boiled. How could Ryan give up so easily, at such a critical point? To stop now might signify no further opportunities. Maxwell continued his surveillance, bemused. Ryan moved over to his bag and rummaged through it. Much to Maxwell's relief Ryan produced something completely transforming the situation. Melissa had asked him for something, confirming her intention to continue. It was a condom.

Subsequently Maxwell watched a pair of youngsters in the throes of passion. He waited and waited. Hoping Ryan would do the same. Then when the time was right, he commenced phase two.

CHAPTER 16

In the throes of heightened passion Melissa detected a noise that made her blood run cold. On top of her Alex seemed oblivious to the sound. She put her hands determinedly on his chest in an attempt to stop him, but her endeavor was far too belated.

Ping! The noise signified the elevator arriving at the pool level. In the split second before the doors opened, Melissa desperately tried to move away. Although without Alex's cooperation she was going nowhere. Turning her head towards the obstructed view of the elevator entrance she willed it not to be Zac.

Her firm pushing then amalgamated into the thumping of Alex's torso. Still, he failed to desist. Melissa's heart sank. Zac impassively walked into view. Watching him round the corner, she had a sensation of slow motion. Now facing the spectacle, Zac looked up only to be utterly crushed by what he witnessed. He could not process the entire image thus far, being only able to focus on Melissa looking back at him with horrified eyes.

Unable to convey or recognize any direct feelings Zac only experienced a deep emptiness. His soul was being destroyed. Finally, Alex responded to Zac's presence. Still on top of Melissa, he turned his head to view Zac. The apparition of a man reminded Ryan of a little boy, lost and forlorn. Zac remained frozen on the spot. Ten seconds had passed, nobody had said anything. Without sensation Zac lingered on the edge of reality. His mind walked spellbound through a giant field of corn, absolutely disoriented, unable to locate the gate.

Then something changed.

Alex, still on top of Melissa, gave Zac a smile. An "I won" smile. The transformation in Zac was extreme. A detonation occurred deep within his mind. It fashioned an explosion of unsurpassed energy. A twenty-megaton thermonuclear blast ripped through him.

Without forewarning Zac sprinted toward and hurdled into Alex, tearing him off Melissa. Alex panicked slightly as hands and nails seized at his face. The typical Hollywood type – anything but the face. It was too late for that now. Zac dragged him to his feet and let go a shotgun of a punch, his whole body following through, enhancing the blow. It landed cleanly on Alex's nose. A sickening crunch echoed through the air as bone collapsed and splintered.

Ryan had not been expecting this reaction. Maxwell had insisted from looking at Zac's profile he would just run and cry. He informed him the only risk of aggression would be much later if Ryan remained at the property. This would not be problematic as Ryan would be paid and sent back to Hollywood without delay. In reality Maxwell knew Zac would explode immediately in this manner, but he had decided against enlightening Ryan.

Zac's assault against Alex was far from concluded. Now on his knees with blood streaming from his repeatedly hit nose and splattering onto the tiled floor. Melissa incessantly shrieked in pure terror. She wrapped herself in her towel, petrified of the animal her boyfriend had become.

Worse was to follow. After Zac concluded raining down a series of blows on Alex's bloody and battered face, he dragged him half-conscious into the pool. Both figures fell into the water. Elegant sinews of blood drifted through the liquid. Weakly, Alex tried to stave off further attack. His effort drastically insufficient, as Zac began to hold Alex's head below the water, his victim's arms flailing ineffectively against Zac's face. Zac shot a solitary glare at the screaming woman he felt he no longer knew. She saw only hate in his eyes.

Zac returned his attention to the submerged figure within the water, his hands more vehemently pushing and pulling Alex as he frantically tried to free himself. His weakness from the beating proved too great. He was completely at Zac's mercy, not a quality Zac was likely to exercise in the near future. Alex's body tightened and tensed. His strength returned momentarily, but it was not enough to free him, and rapidly afterwards his body changed to a limp and lifeless state. Zac abruptly recoiled as if taken by surprise. In the flick of a switch reality steamrollered him. He stared again at his hysterical girlfriend. This time panic and terror filled his eyes. A million thoughts ran through his mind like a stampede, with not one comprehensible.

From nowhere a figure appeared. Without hesitation the person dived into the pool and in record time reached the floating stricken body. When it reached Alex, Zac identified the savior as his employer. Maxwell took Alex to the side and lifted him out, almost jumping clean out of the water after him. Firstly he cleared his airway, fortuitously most of the excess blood had sluiced off in the water. Maxwell frantically began resuscitation. Zac watched in a blurred haze, still unable to collect a solitary thought. Melissa persisted in her relentless screaming, although it had grown hoarser and more strained.

Maxwell's speed and expertise paid off. A short time after commencing the lifesaving act Alex spluttered, coughing out bloody water from his lungs. His body convulsed in pain from the assault. Eventually he managed to draw in a clean breath. Maxwell had just saved his life.

CHAPTER 17

Hours later Zac sat alone in the great room, the extraordinary view the last thing on his mind. How had everything gone so wrong?

His face in his hands, he wept, shedding tears. Years of anguish from horrendous events never released. Today, supplementary mounds of shit had been thrown on the already substantial pile. He could hardly comprehend how close he had come to taking another human life. Like father, like son. The one person he needed to unburden his heart to was Melissa. However, this was the same person who had instigated the scenario. She had gravely betrayed him.

Zac wanted to believe the relationship was salvageable, but in truth he recognized for him there could be no way back. Hurt and let down so many times, a hard veneer had formed over him. Melissa had been privileged to break through the veneer, to have gained his trust. She had secured access to something precious and guarded within Zac. What had she gone and done with it? Like a Trojan horse she had used a ruse to gain entry, only to create havoc once inside the protected walls. He despised her for that. He loathed how much he loved her; how much he was now going to suffer. He experienced repulsion at yet again being on the receiving end of such a wounding act, for doing nothing wrong, yet suffering at least as much as anybody else involved. Where had this curse afflicting him materialized from? The more he fought to stay on top, the more it dragged him down.

The large doors suddenly rolled silently open. Maxwell entered. His face looked heavy and grim. He stood at the doors for a period, as if full of trepidation. Zac did not look at him.

Eventually Maxwell stepped fully into the room and shut the doors behind him. As he approached, Zac hung his head even lower in shame. He sensed Maxwell's hand rub the back of it. The touch felt pleasant, comforting, fatherly. Maxwell took a seat opposite Zac. They sat in communal silence for what seemed an appropriate time.

"Well, Zac, what a mess." Maxwell spoke softly. Zac could detect disappointment in his voice.

"Is he okay?"

"Yes." Maxwell leaned forward. Again, he used a reassuring hand, this time on his knee. "You are very lucky. He will be fine."

Zac gave a sorrowful nod.

"I have spoken to him at length. He has agreed not to press charges."

"Press charges?" Zac exclaimed.

"Yes, well technically it was an attempted homicide."

"But he's not going to?"

"No."

"You're sure?"

"Yes."

Zac slumped back, deep into his seat. He gave his already red and puffy eyes a fleeting rub. "I guess you want us both to leave right away?"

"Well in one way it would be appropriate. But no. I want you to stay."

"Really?" Zac had not even entertained the possibility of staying and keeping his job. "What about Alex?" His voice carried an unpleasant snide undertone, more evident than intended.

"He will be leaving in a few hours, never to return."

"Oh. I guess he wouldn't want to stay after what I just did to him?"

Maxwell pondered Zac's last comment for a second. He did not respond. Zac was relieved, he did not want to hear the answer.

"Melissa is upstairs in your living quarters. I suggest you go and talk to her, as long as you think you can remain calm. Do not forget how lucky you are not to be spending the next thirty years in a prison cell."

Zac furnished him with a sheepish nod. "I know. I promise. No more violence." A single tear ran down Zac's cheek. Maxwell caught his eyes with his own. They were full of tears, reminiscent of water wells. "What am I going to say to her?"

"Not an easy one, Zac. Has she ever done anything like this before?"

"Never," he stated adamantly. Then the tone of his voice altered dramatically, "That I'm aware of."

"All I can suggest is at this stage it's best not to do anything too rash. You're still very much in shock. Give it a few days for your thoughts and feelings to balance and evaluate."

Zac raised his glance to connect with Maxwell's. The rawness affected Maxwell's self-reproach. Looking into Zac's eyes he questioned whether he was taking it all too far. Was he this desperate? Would successfully executing this malicious scheme actually return Maxwell's life to where he needed it to be? Some aspects, yes. But what price would his conscience pay? What debt would his soul bear? Then he detected behind the saturated eyes, something revealing itself in Zac, exactly the revelation he was hoping to observe, a hard and unyielding attitude. The fleeting doubt evaporated.

"It's over, Maxwell. Nothing will change that."

"Just give it a few days," he genuinely advised. Inside he knew enough about Zac to appreciate he would not change his mind. Zac gave him a look that said a thousand words.

"I'll need to sort out a flight home for her." Zac substantiated his intention with no emotion in his voice, a detached formal tone the replacement.

"Don't worry. I'll book one for tomorrow morning, whether Melissa takes it or not is up to you. Either way, it's not a problem." Maxwell knew there was no point in contesting his decision.

"Thanks, Maxwell." Zac rose from his seat and walked to the doors. Just before sliding them closed he halted briefly. "Maxwell?"

"Yes?"

"I'm truly sorry for..." Zac reflected for a moment, "... everything."

"I know."

He closed the doors.

Ryan lay on the couch in Maxwell's private study, his head throbbing and his vision abnormally blurry. It was the concussion limiting his thoughts and functions. Lisa sat beside him, cleansing his wounds with a damp swab.

"That bastard," he feebly whispered, his chest and lungs aching.

"Who? Zac?" Lisa asked.

"No, Maxwell. He assured me Zac would not be violent."

"Well, it's not easy to predict how someone is going to behave in such a situation."

Ryan weakly lifted a hand to his head. Everything he fingered felt damaged.

"Don't touch," Lisa commanded.

"My god. What has he done to my face? How am I ever gonna work in Hollywood now, looking like this?"

"It's not as bad as it feels. You'll heal up fine, a couple of weeks you'll be as good as new."

Ryan detected deceitfulness in her over-cheerful reassurance. "Maxwell told me Zac would just run away. He said everything from the psychoanalysis pointed to a non-confrontational reaction."

"Like I said, Ryan, at such an extreme time nobody can fully predict what will occur."

"Bullshit. He knew. He knew Zac would react violently. It's just he already had me and everything else in place. He wasn't gonna let a little fact like me almost getting killed stand in his way."

"Christ, Ryan, stop being so melodramatic. You'll be fine. You've done your bit, and you're about to collect a very tidy sum. What's the problem?"

"The problem is I've had a moment of clarity. All this, it's just so fucked up. I can't believe I agreed to it. You should get out now before it's too late." Ryan managed to sit up slightly. Although his head pounded and he felt so dizzy he could vomit, thoughts now coursed through him fast and clear. He looked at Lisa, her face transfixed with an irate scowl.

"It's all very well for you to see the light after you've earned your money," she sneered. "I'm yet to do my bit and I really, really need this. Don't fuck it up for me. I'm warning you, don't do anything. Don't say anything to anybody. Do you understand?"

Ryan observed a fire in her eyes. Her body language so belligerent he found himself too stunned for words, only able to manage a pitiful nod. She threw the blood-soaked swab at him and stormed out of the room.

CHAPTER 18

Zac entered his living quarters. Melissa lay on the couch, curled up into a protective ball comparable to a hedgehog without spikes. Zac could hear her sobbing, almost uncontrollably. Despite everything, part of him felt remorse for her distress. Before today whenever Melissa broke into tears, it had split Zac's heart in two. He would do anything to stop her crying, no matter what the reason, like an override trigger built within him. Now that very instinct kicked in. He wanted to hold her close and tell her everything would be fine. He craved to stop her tears and witness her most radiant smile, which only blossomed following upset. This time, however, the override itself was overridden by an untouchable reaction.

"Why, Melissa?"

Still, she continued to cry, not reacting to his question.

He approached and stood over her. "Why?!" he blasted.

Melissa braved a glimpse at him. Zac's stance was aggressive and heated, his face emitting disbelief. "I'm so sorry," she whimpered whilst remaining curled in a ball. Two reddened eyes peeked out from behind her arm.

"I didn't ask for an apology. I want to know why." Zac stepped in closer, his body entirely dominating her personal space.

"I don't know."

"Not good enough. Answer me, you fucking bitch."

"Please, Zac," her voice implored. "I made a mistake. I didn't do it to hurt you, there is no reason why." She began to choke on her tears.

"I'm not buying that. Why? Were you lonely?"

"Yeah maybe. I don't know."

"It's barely been a week," Zac shrieked. "Look at me!" He yanked her arm out and forced her to sit up. "Is that what our relationship means to you? Neglected for a few days so you cheat? Jump into bed with the first guy who comes along? How stupid am I? I thought we had something, something special. How fucking stupid am I?"

"Please, Zac. It wasn't anything against you. It really wasn't. I just didn't think. Please, I'm sorry."

"I've already told you, do not apologize to me. I don't want to hear it. Do you understand?" Zac's tone became increasingly irritate.

"Yes."

"Now tell me the truth, why did you do what you did?" The words felt polluted coming out of his mouth. He experienced the urge to spit after saying them as if to clear any dirty remnants left behind.

"He was just so nice to me," Melissa began. She wiped her eyes and cleared her throat. Zac sat down beside her, staring forward into space. "Coming here, leaving my mother. It was a big deal for me. To be honest, I quickly realized I was going to be very bored and lonely here. You were going to be working long hours. I would be left on my own all day, every day. There's nothing to do here for me. Although we haven't been here long, I looked ahead to nothing and to be honest it scared me." She paused and blew her nose. Zac said nothing, his face vacant. "Then, when I met Alex, he was friendly and charming. I guess I felt rejuvenated by his affection." Zac released a sneer under his breath. "Please Zac, you asked me to explain honestly." Melissa protested. He gave an impassive nod for her to continue. "I just sort of latched on to him. I know this sounds like I'm trying to excuse myself, but I'm not. I realize now, everything he did was an attempt to seduce me. I just didn't see it, blinded by the need for a friend. Now looking back, I really can't believe how stupid I've been."

They sat in silence for some time. Eventually Melissa attempted to hold Zac's hand with hers. He instantly snapped it away.

"Don't you understand? That's it. We're over," he growled.

"No don't say that. We can work it out. Please. You'll feel differently soon. I'll do whatever it takes. Please give me another chance."

"No." Resolve radiated from his voice.

"Please don't make a decision now. Give it a few days," she begged with tremendous desperation in her gesture and disbelief in her eyes.

"I'm sorry, Melissa. I've made my decision. I'm not changing my mind. Maxwell is booking you a flight back for tomorrow morning.

Melissa let out a slight whimper. She tried to grab onto Zac, as if she were a little child clinging to her father out of fear. He resisted the attempt and pushed her back. Melissa went back to her rolled-in-a-ball posture and wept frenziedly. Zac was aggrieved for her distress, wanting to console her, his anger diminishing, although equally not wishing to send her mixed signals. Giving Melissa false hope would not help matters for either of them.

They sat together for an immeasurable stretch without a word being spoken. Only the soft sound of Melissa continually sobbing was audible. Zac persisted in staring ahead into space, not looking at the woman he loved. It was just too painful to gaze upon what he was about to lose. He tried to question if he himself had been partially to blame. He did not believe so, he frankly could not see how. An opulent tapestry of feelings and emotions swirled around, lapping against him. Something did not add up. Quite what, he was unable to fathom, yet he sensed more at work, beyond what he was able to envisage. He wondered about Maxwell. Why had he sent him down to the pool, only to come down himself straight after? Not that he was unappreciative that he had. As much as he disliked Alex, killing him seemed rather extreme and he certainly did not relish the prospect of spending half his life in prison for committing such an act. The image of them both together incessantly flashed through his mind, giving rise to a nauseous sensation in his stomach. Eventually he snapped out of his haze.

"You had better start packing your things ready for tomorrow."

"No, Zac. I don't want to be without you," she cried, uncurling out of her ball, more coherent and controlled. Now ready to talk sensibly and try one last time to change his mind.

"Either you pack your stuff, or I will."

"Please, Zac. We need time to discuss things. We can't end it just like that."

"You should have thought of that before. Pack your things. Now."

CHAPTER 19

Maxwell drove Melissa to the airport. She was devastated. Zac had not even said goodbye. She went to bed after packing, not sleeping a wink, her mind and stomach somersaulting. Dark shadows in the room seemed to creep up on her, plaguing her mind. Zac had stayed on the couch and left early next morning, she presumed to work in the office. Disbelief consumed her. Even after what had happened how could he let her leave without so much as a goodbye?

Maxwell remained very quiet throughout the whole journey. Melissa had expected him to give her knowledgeable advice about the situation. Not to judge her but help. He was a psychiatrist, supposed to be objective and impartial. She figured out for herself he was not at all delighted with the disruption in his house. After all, it had cost him one employee and mentally scarred another. She concluded she should not blame him for having animosity toward her, after the disarray she had caused. What a price to pay.

Upon arriving at the airport Maxwell exited the car without a word, taking the cases out of the trunk and placing them on a nearby porter's trolley.

"I'm sorry, Maxwell," she offered as way of goodbye.

"Me too, Melissa." He stopped for a second and looked her in the eye. "More than you will ever know." His appearance noticeably anguished. Without another word he got back into the car and drove off.

Roy sat upon his windowsill, sipping an iced tea. The morning sun was scattered across the urban concrete view, slicing through it like an alien tractor beam, broken up by various tall buildings in the neighborhood. For all his problems and hang-ups, Roy found such moments gave him a tranquil satisfaction, a manner of inner peace he considered permanently lost. A long time ago in his former life he had often benefited from the sensation. Now, when such a moment was so scarce, like a rare flower bursting out of a remote hillside, it engulfed him. He grabbed it with both hands, not wanting to let go. Reality was, it disappeared as suddenly as it arrived. Roy never could tell when this spiritual balance would return.

His pained face relaxed, even the premature aging and bloodshot eyes from lack of sleep receded. Best of all, for the duration of the solace he experienced no guilt, merely empty corridors in his mind, tranquil, serene, telephone ring.

Roy's brain snapped back to reality. He stared a thousand knives at the phone. The moment was spent, ripped from his grasp by some anonymous person who chose that precise moment to contact him, much like the alarm clock taking you from the pinnacle moment of a fantastic dream. It was the ultimate cruelty of timing. Roy speculated it would only be someone selling insurance or such like. It would be typically fitting.

"Hello," Roy semi-barked, picking up the receiver.

"Pa?" Instantly Roy's mood changed. It was a call from his son. The son he loved as much as any father. The boy he had encouraged, nurtured and invested in. Only to hurt, let down and destroy. Although still distant, Zac had allowed him back into his life. The guards were still very much up, but Roy had to start rebuilding somewhere; re-laying those damaged foundations, hoping to rebuild a strong relationship.

"Hi, son, great to hear from you," he spurted eagerly. "How's the new job going?"

"The job's good, Pa. Hard, but well, you know."

Roy immediately recognized the uptight tone in his voice. "What's wrong?"

"It's Melissa."

"Why, what's happened?" Roy panicked.

"We've split."

"Oh." Roy had failed to see that coming. "Really? I thought you two were going good?"

"So did I."

"What happened?" No reply, just breathing. Roy presumed Zac was crying. Fair enough. "You can talk to me y'know," he offered faithfully.

"She cheated on me."

Roy felt his heart plummet like a runaway elevator. "Oh, son, I'm so sorry."

"Thanks."

Roy waited. He guessed, no, hoped, Zac would confide in him, but he did not elaborate. "I've got to say I'm really shocked. I honestly didn't think she was the type to do something like that. I don't know what to say, I thought it was going well between you two." Roy had to sit down, his legs suddenly feeling truly heavy like lead.

"So did I," Zac returned, lemons appearing sweet, compared to the bitterness in his voice.

"So where is she now?"

"On a plane home. She wanted to try again, but I couldn't. Not after that. I'd never trust her again. I just know it wouldn't work even if I forgave her. I just wouldn't trust her. Ever."

"I understand, Zac. What about the other guy?" Roy said the last word like it left a repulsive taste in his mouth.

"Well, I ..." Zac wanted to reach out to his father, tell him exactly how frighteningly close he had come to taking the man's life, but was unable to. "He worked at the house as well. He was sacked. He's gone as well."

"Right, well at least that's something."

"I guess."

"Do you want me to fly out to you?"

"Thanks, Pa, but I'm okay."

"It's no problem, it would be good to come and see you anyway. I want to help you." Roy's voice was consumed with need, the need to be a father again, attempting to rectify and compensate for his abundance of shortcomings. Another long pause passed.

"No honestly. I appreciate the offer, but really there's no need."

"Sure, son." Roy tried not to sound too disappointed. This was not the time to emotionally blackmail his son. "If you change your mind?" His voice trailed off.

"Thanks."

They spoke for another ten minutes, predominantly about Zac's job, rather than the break-up of his relationship. Roy guessed it helped Zac just to talk to his father at such a painful time. That meant a lot to him, hope still remained to rebuild many bridges. With it came newfound inspiration not to fall off the wagon again and to stay clean. Roy understood how thin the ice was under their relationship. What lurked underneath did not bear thinking about.

CHAPTER 20

Zac spent the majority of the remaining day working in the office. He astonished himself with his reinvigorated focus. He had expected to be further distracted as a consequence of the traumatic events that had occurred. Now, with bolstered determination and drive he threw himself into the one remaining thing he could still accomplish in his life. It was his now solitary offering to this world. Zac was presently mentally battered and bruised, but like a proud warrior he fought on. With no surrender, he would not lie down and die. Would not crumble, not like Roy.

As Zac typed away, he completely lost track of time, the stylish modern blinds within the office blocking out all signs of life, daylight or dark. The room was a total void, calculatedly designed to offer the occupants no sense of time outside its walls. No disruptions, no clock, even removed from the desk top screens, nothing to pull them away from their work.

Zac was subjected to one lone disturbance, Maxwell coming in and out a few times collecting paperwork or such like. Zac had no idea what the time was. At an educated guess, it was late afternoon or early evening. Relentlessly he ploughed on in front of his computer like a nerd possessed.

Whilst concentrating on an intensely tricky conundrum, he heard the office door open. So tuned into his work he failed to look up, determined not to lose his train of thought, Zac assumed it was Maxwell, but as the person approached from behind, he recognized it to be another. Agreeable perfume pleasured his nostrils. Not really Maxwell's thing. He broke from his unadulterated focus and spun around.

Firstly, he was relieved to see it was not Melissa, but in

equal measure delighted to find Lisa daintily stood in front of him, offering a plate of food. After recent events, he had completely overlooked her presence in the house.

"Hi," she addressed him with a radiant smile of pure whiteness. She could have been in a toothpaste advertisement. "I thought you could do with this." She offered the plate forward. Two stacked sandwiches overflowing with a selection of cold cut meats, cheese, salad and sauces.

"Wow, now that's what I call a sandwich," beamed Zac.

Lisa laughed, observing the eye-bulging delight in Zac's face. "Well, you should be hungry by now. You haven't eaten all day."

"What time is it now?"

"Just gone ten," Lisa answered without hesitation.

Zac's face tautened with surprise. "Really? I thought it was only early evening."

Lisa awarded him a smirk and shrugged her shoulders. "Now that's a sign you're in need of a break if I ever heard one." Lisa gestured to the door with her soft blue eyes. "Come on, keep me company for half an hour," she gently pleaded.

Zac let out a long sigh. "Yeah, okay then," he conceded, rising from his seat and out of the workstation. "Let's go to the great room." Zac took his prize sandwich and trailed Lisa out.

Half an hour became all night. Light, general chatter developed into absorbed and intense conversation. Lisa patiently listened as Zac poured his heart out to her. Only now was he beginning to deliberate on the full and uncompromising consequences the previous day's events had bestowed on him. Zac was now not only wounded, but also scared. It felt heartening and reassuring to confide in Lisa.

Through the night Lisa counseled Zac, making him realize that light did exist at the end of all the darkness of the tunnel in which he was currently residing, and it was light worth fighting to attain.

By now the delicate pioneering hints of morning became perceptible outside the wall of glass. Without additional discussion Zac pulled Lisa into him on the couch, to settle in and observe the sunrise through the most mind-blowing screen imaginable. Lisa snuggled her head into his chest. Zac warmed with a glowing sensation of comfort and security. He needed the affection; he required the attention. The two bodies grasped each other, touching, not in a sexual way, but in an innate loving manner. This was not to say Zac was not attracted to Lisa, also detecting mutual signals from her. For now, though, it was not appropriate to even consider such advances in the infancy of their newfound friendship.

Besides which, the opening prongs of sunlight began to shoot out from beyond the remote hillside sitting behind the gloom-filled darkness of the lake. In that instant all their conscious responsiveness pursued the indulgent beams, like searchlights reaching through the air, leisurely dropping down to earth as the sun climbed higher behind its mountainous partition. Eventually the sun peeked out from behind its shroud of rock. Mother Nature turned on her laser display, shooting beams indiscriminately across the watery surface, splitting out into a spectrum of colors. The view, already unfeasibly beautiful, was transformed into something profoundly beyond comprehension, the oasis within paradise.

Zac, much like his father, took the opportunity to disconnect himself from all the turmoil and anguish, subsequently floating across the ocean of his vacant mind, accepting the splendor before him. Somewhere entrenched within his soul he comprehended the reward for all the pain of life. The recompense of living, for all the hardship and grief, one solitary moment could prevail over it all. A single tear ran down Zac's cheek. For no reason, conscious or otherwise, just the raging torment of self, simmering deep underneath the freshly relaxed body and mind.

Light became further forced from the sun. Drifting away were the soft colors of the embryonic rays, developing into explicit unsympathetic beams. Zac had to squint to maintain the observation of this self-transpiring magnum opus. He looked

119

down at Lisa, but her awareness was elsewhere. Leant against his chest, sleep had crept up and snatched her away from Zac, despite even the sun's finest undertaking to astound.

Zac unhurriedly lifted his hand and ran it through her soft hair. An unexpected numbness of dread abruptly coursed through his body. Zac appreciated that unfeigned grief and anguish was on its way. Of that he was certain. It was the delayed agony and woe held back by the shock. When the sympathy and comfort of those around you has dried up and you are back to normal life, only then can you entirely acknowledge the true devastation of an atrocious event. Zac, though, was presently still at the station, waiting for that specific train to arrive. He implored Lisa to be enough and give enough to delay that train for a good while yet.

"Thank you," he articulated mutely under his breath, transfixed by his short-term savior. Tranquility had been restored within his body and without another thought he joined his new companion on her journey through slumberland.

CHAPTER 21

In a former life, Roy was perceived, not as a "super cop" or anything so intimidating, more as a gifted community officer, a body of reassurance and consistency, bringing safety to the streets. He offered guidance and direction for petty and rebellious juveniles, whilst giving simultaneous protection against the more perilous members of society. Predominantly Roy had an instinct for reading between the lines, identifying when something did not add up, almost a sixth sense where the slightest discrepancy triggered alarm bells in his head. After phoning Melissa, Roy knew masses did not add up.

It was a dicey approach, to telephone the girl who had just betrayed his son. Zac would have hit the roof, but Roy had to obtain her side of the story. After all, who the hell was he to judge? On a chart of betrayals against Zac, Roy was still safely top of the leaderboard. Roy dialed the number for Melissa's mother, on the assumption she had retreated back there. Roy's mouth dehydrated like a desert when he heard the ringing tone. His need for a strong drink to calm his agitated nerves became fiercer than for any period in his recent memory. Roy settled for a swig of water to saturate his parched mouth. Water failed to do much, but *que sera sera*.

"Hello?" A voice of more maturity than Melissa's answered.

"Hi. Is Melissa there?" he asked in the most innocent manner possible.

"Er…" Pause. "Who is this?"

"Roy, Zac's father."

"Oh." Sally's voice was overflowing with uncertainty. What does he want? she thought to herself. Surely, he did not mean to attack Melissa for cheating on his son? She did not in truth know Roy at all. Maybe he could be that interfering? What a cheek. There was no way that was going to happen, Sally told herself. "She's not really taking calls at the moment." Sally was satisfied with the level of authority she exerted in her voice.

"If you could just ask her if she'd speak to me. I'm not going to have a go at her or anything like that, I promise."

"Like I said, she's not taking calls today."

"Is this Melissa's mom?"

"Yes," she waited a moment. "Sally," she added.

"Okay good. Look, Sally, I completely understand you're protecting your daughter, but the reason I want to speak to her is because I'm really concerned for my son. Something about Maxwell and that house is bothering me." He took a breath. "Now obviously I'm not pleased about what Melissa is alleged to have done. However, that isn't any of my business. It's completely between the two of them. I just want to ask her about Maxwell. I want to reassure myself Zac is okay." Roy waited for a response. None came. "As a parent I'm sure you can understand that."

"Erm..."

Come on, Sally, Roy thought to himself.

"I'll ask her. No promises though." Sally didn't sound pleased to be backed into a corner with parent-to-parent emotional blackmail.

"Thank you." Roy waited for what seemed a lifetime. He sipped his water a few times, then a few times more. Eventually he heard someone picking up the receiver. He prayed it was Melissa.

"Hello?" A weak quivering voice answered. Roy scarcely recognized it as Melissa's.

"Hi, Melissa," Roy spoke compassionately.

"I'm really sorry," she trembled.

"Please, it's okay. I'm not here to judge you." Roy could hear her softly weeping at the other end. "I'm worried about Zac in that house, and Maxwell. Something seems, well, odd, to me."

"What do you mean?" a vague composure penetrated her voice.

"I don't know. I'm really hoping you could fill me in a bit. I'm honestly not judging you, but I am surprised by what Zac claims you did." As with all the characteristics Roy possessed to present himself as a well-oiled policing machine, an uncanny knack to ascertain trustworthiness and character was continuously functioning. He comprehended Melissa was not deceitful. She did not lie, nor hide her true self behind a bogus persona. "Please tell me about it."

Melissa, whilst apprehensive to divulge to Roy about such a wounding incident, now realized she shared Roy's trepidation. It was not something she had actively contemplated, but Roy had struck a chord in her head. Something was undeniably amiss. In fact, now she reflected on it, countless occurrences appeared wrong about her short stay with Maxwell Taylor, Alex and that house. Impulsively, she spoke words she had only intended to think. "There was more going on there than Zac and I were aware of." She fell mute.

"Tell me what happened," Roy encouraged.

"Okay," Melissa sighed. "It was weird. We were so isolated. I know that probably doesn't sound very odd, but it was. It's hard to explain, but the man who … erm … he kind of well, played me." She caught her thoughts for a second or two. Roy waited. "It's almost like Alex, the man …er … well you know, was trying to make this happen, right from the start. God, I've been so stupid. He played me and I never saw it, not till now."

"We all make mistakes," Roy offered.

"Yeah, I know, but this was such an awful, terrible thing to do to Zac and now he hates me."

"I'm sure he doesn't hate you, he's just shocked and angry. Give him time to calm down. Trust me on this one. I know," Roy reassured, before getting the conversation back on track. "So, what else was strange?"

"Well, all sorts. Alex was Maxwell's swimming coach and handyman, but it's not like Maxwell swam all day. And the house

123

was in such great condition, there really couldn't be much handy work to do. I don't understand why Alex lived there and how he justified his jobs."

"Alex lived there?" Surprise was evident in Roy's voice.

"Yeah."

"Did he do the gardening or something as well? Clean the house maybe?"

"Not that I'm aware of and there's no garden."

Roy pondered the information. "Yes, that does seem a little weird." he agreed.

"Oh, and something else." Melissa's temperament was significantly improved. "Maxwell made us do loads of psychological tests for background data to use in his computer program." Melissa divulged to Roy in detail about everything. Roy was stunned. Undoubtedly the entire situation was bizarre.

After completing the call, Roy walked to his bed and sprawled out on it fully clothed. His head whirled with all the information in it. Previously skeptical and wary, he was now convinced. But convinced about what? Maxwell was unquestionably up to something, but what? And to what end? Why with Zac? Where was the motive? None of it made sense.

Ten minutes passed, nothing changed. Roy yearned for a computer in his rudimentary, meager apartment. He didn't even own a smartphone. His cell phone was a dinosaur by modern standards. He very rarely turned it on and used the landline for his calls. He wasn't a man for texting, who would he text anyway? Only Zac. Now it was a source of frustration. He could have googled Maxwell Taylor, to investigate him and his reported affairs. He would have to undertake an excursion to the library to accomplish that objective. An alternative thought steamrollered through his mind. He got up, opened a wardrobe door and peered inside. From the back Roy hauled out a hefty storage box. He lifted the lid to unearth a mountain of documents and newspaper clippings. Cautiously he meticulously lifted out stacks and placed them carefully on the bed. Headlines on the clippings heralded numerous courageous acts and acclaim of a police officer. Roy. He did not glance at them. Subsequently he lifted out a file and tenderly opened it. His wedding certificate rested on top. Roy's finger traveled along the name of his deceased wife. A lump appeared in his throat. He lifted the certificate to reveal Amy's death certificate. The lump choked him.

"Oh, Amy," he murmured to nobody. "I still love you and I still really need you. Come back to me," Roy implored, in vain. Eventually he closed the file and positioned it sympathetically on the bed. Finally, he removed the box file he was searching for. Within was every newspaper article and document he managed to photocopy relating to James Stoneman, the child he had killed on that fateful night. With a deep breath Roy sifted through the entire lot, scanning for names. Names such as Maxwell Taylor or even Alex, but nothing stood out. No correlation that he could ascertain.

Roy studied a black and white newspaper picture of James's innocent smiling face, running his fingers gently over the grainy image. The blurred memories of that fateful night played in his head.

Roy responded to a call for a bar fight. Gene his partner was driving, he always did now, he knew Roy was frequently inebriated while on duty. As they pulled up outside the bar the squabble spilled out onto the street, two intoxicated men wrestling each other to the ground. Gene had already jumped out from the vehicle commanding the men to stop the altercation. As Roy clumsily stumbled out of the vehicle, events unfolded fast. He observed Gene jump back behind the car pulling his firearm screaming "drop your weapon". Suddenly one of the men smashed straight into Roy, knocking him to the ground. The other man, with the gun complied throwing the gun out in front of him. "Down on the ground" screamed Gene. Still disorientated Roy withdrew his gun as he clambered back up. He failed to realize the runner was unarmed and without measure, coherent thought, or sufficient aim let off a single shot toward the disappearing man. A smash of glass could be heard, the screech of car tires, then the screaming, but the man kept running. The screaming, the screaming within the stricken car. The screaming Roy would take to his grave.

He closed the file and packed it all in order neatly away. Then he returned to lying on his bed.

Roy desperately wanted to call Zac back and warn him of Maxwell but knew he could not. At the very least he would have to confess to phoning Melissa. Zac would indisputably be incensed by Roy's actions. Even then, what could he tell Zac? That he suspected something was amiss, although he was not sure what? No. He required evidence, something concrete. That wouldn't be straightforward, certainly not whilst he was residing in San Francisco, on the opposite coast. How was he going to poke his nose in and detect from there? The internet, it appeared was his chief and solitary option at the present time. On that consideration he arose from the bed, slipped into some shoes and departed for the library.

CHAPTER 22

Although Zac was surviving on practically no sleep and his relationship with Melissa was in ruins, he was staggered to be generating the finest work of his life. Not certain if it was a particular consequence of all the recent havoc or whether now in genuine employment he had unpretentiously stepped up to the challenge. Four days had passed since Melissa's rapid exit. Zac presumed the shock had not yet worn off. Nevertheless, the consistency in his concentration and absorption was unsurpassed.

Every day Zac started early and finished late, scarcely pausing to eat or breathe. He produced decidedly complicated sub-routines and algorithms for the program, abiding by the constraints and parameters determined by Maxwell. Any objective Maxwell wished Zac to accomplish he completed with ease, structuring the programs in logical natural paths, triumphing over conundrums without breaking sweat.

At night he spent time with Lisa. They would talk for hours, occasionally about somber topics like Melissa. Predominantly they merely had fun, chatting about nothing in particular. Laughing, joking and getting drunk. Zac was appreciative of Lisa. Coping with his personal reality at the conclusion of each day would have been much more grueling without her. Especially at night when he was aware the demons would come. At present between working and Lisa, he did not have a quiet minute to contemplate his real feelings. By the time Zac actually dragged himself to bed, inebriated and exhausted, he would pass out instantly. Then Zac would get up early the following day to do it all again.

Only a single issue concerned Zac. Maxwell. Or to be

precise, the lack of Maxwell. He was in effect a ghost, merely popping his head in to set Zac with work and objectives, and nothing else. For two foremost reasons this was perplexing. Firstly, Maxwell's role undoubtedly comprised a more taxing and time-consuming workload than Zac's, yet he had not witnessed Maxwell sat at his workstation for a greater period than ten minutes in a day. Not since that dreaded day when he had sent Zac down to the pool. Of course, it was feasible he was working from a computer in his private quarters, but why then build a state-of-the-art office in your house and never utilize it? Did that make sense?

Secondly, Maxwell possessed awareness and comprehension of the trauma in Zac's life. He had engaged in counseling him during the preliminary psychoanalysis, signifying that Zac ought to persist with it on a frequent basis. So, after witnessing the love of his life sleeping with another man, then as a consequence virtually killing him, he reasoned Maxwell would be especially eager to persuade Zac to come in for another session. Yet he offered nothing. Except for the short times he did stop by, Maxwell gave the impression he was not comfortable being in Zac's company. On such occasions Maxwell would be relaxed and open in his body language. He made a point of complimenting Zac on his programming and emphasized that he needed to keep up the same standard, setting challenging deadlines. He showed no concern for the amount of time Lisa was spending with Zac, or the fact she had elected to extend her stay at the house to care for him.

It all seemed a bit strange to Zac, although it was not anything he pondered on for long. Not until he received an email from Roy, enlightening him to some unnerving truths he had dug up that Zac was not aware of.

Knuckles rapped on Lisa's bedroom door.

"Come in," she yelled. The door opened and Maxwell

entered. Lisa was lying, fully clothed, on her bed watching something on television. She was endeavoring to enjoy a low-budget cookery show, but the naïve ability of the director, and the oversized ego of the chef were crushing any possibility of that. She flicked the television off without a second thought for the climax of the dish in the making and the contentment of the conceited chef presenting it to camera. "Hi, Maxwell."

"Hi Lisa. How's it going with Zac?" he asked reservedly.

"Yeah. Good, I think. He trusts me and likes me a lot."

"Yes, I've been observing, and I have to agree. You definitely have his trust. The only current problem is although his head is playing ball, his heart is still fixated with Melissa. If we're gonna get some kind of rebound action out of Zac, we must step things up a notch or two."

"In what way?" Lisa enquired.

Maxwell rubbed his chin in an unhurried fashion, and then produced some paperwork. He swiftly studied the sheets, scanning through his own work. After satisfying himself everything was correct and feasible, he handed them to Lisa.

"Thanks?" she uttered in a puzzled tone.

"Study these," Maxwell explained. "They're slight alterations to your personality and ways in which to treat Zac to make it all happen as we planned." Before she had even glanced at them Lisa shot Maxwell an aggravated expression.

"Alterations? Weren't you right before?" Her tone was raw.

"Slight alterations," Maxwell corrected. "Don't worry. It's just some fine tuning. Helping to guarantee we achieve the objective."

"But you think we will? Achieve it, that is?"

"I don't think, I know," Maxwell reflected confidently. "Just stick to the modifications in your persona. Sorry, slight modifications, and everything will run smoothly." He dusted his hands and gave Lisa a smug grin, although she never saw it, already engrossed in the papers before her. Maxwell left without another word.

CHAPTER 23

A week had passed since Melissa's departure. For Zac life had taken a peculiar new steadiness. He had established a post-Melissa lifestyle which ran smoothly, but not without the expectation of a sudden terrifying downturn. Zac was waiting for the day when the unmitigated magnitude of the dramatic breakdown of his relationship with Melissa would paralyze him and rupture his soul. Every day he waited, yet it never seemed to manifest.

It was early evening, or so Zac guessed. He was suffering a rare moment of writer's block, in all probability from fatigue and lack of concentration. His mind blank for the first time in days, he elected to take a break, leave the computer early and chill out, more than likely to attempt to sleep before meeting Lisa.

Prior to leaving he checked his emails, an action Zac performed countless times daily back at home, whilst living in populated society. It was a curious modern phenomenon; this need to be incessantly contacted through the medium of the internet. Zac practically self-judged his own popularity and status by the rate at which he received email. He had shied away from social media with so many school friends knowing everything that had transpired in his life, he could see no benefit in staying connected to them. But through emails he had engaged in new contacts, especially during his time at MIT. That had been a new world for Zac offering him the obscurity to start a new life, be a new person where people didn't talk in hushed whispers as he walked past, where people didn't stop and stare at him. At that time checking his emails had reached a point where a sense of humiliation transpired when, more often than he would have wished, no new activity had taken place. The genuine irony of it all was, when Zac was in effect uncontactable, out in the isolation of Maxwell's house, with inadequate cell phone signal, he had not bothered or even felt the desire to check his email for days.

As soon as it appeared on screen the subject of one email caught his eye. "Important. Read this." Sent from his father. Zac could scarcely recall Roy ever sending him emails. He lacked interest in modern communication techniques, opting instead to actually talk to people. Face to face was his ideal or, failing that, a telephone conversation was next on the list. He failed to comprehend the whole idea of texting on cell phones, going back and forth. Taking twenty minutes to cover a conversation that could be spoken in two. Zac had to admit he could identify with the logic in that idea. Least favorite of all for Roy was email.

The few occasions he had been obligated to use it were fraught with wariness and paranoia. Wary that the intended recipient was not in possession of his sent message, leaving the prospect of a purchase order or document floating aimlessly around the vastness of cyberspace seeking a home. By speaking to someone, Roy immediately had the reassurance they were in possession of the information in question. Through email, nothing was assured until the conformation reply came, which might be days away.

Despite these facts, an email sent from Roy was nestled in Zac's inbox. If any clues could be perceived from the title it was certainly significant in context. Zac clicked on it. Up came a short text and two documents to download.

Hi Zac,

I hope you're well?

Please don't think that I'm interfering, but I did some research on Maxwell and came across these newspaper articles Thought you should read them, I'm sure they will be of interest. Love you, son,

speak soon,
Pa.

To say Zac was intrigued was an understatement. As he clicked on the first document and waited for it to download, Zac queried what he himself knew about Maxwell. Not much. Sure, he was aware of his groundbreaking computer release but so were many other people. That really was about it, he had not even googled his name. Yet here he was, employed by Maxwell, living in his house, attempting to kill his other staff. Hmmm?

The opening document completed its download. Zac opened it. "Broken Mind? Broken man," the headline read. Zac continued to study the article.

"Maxwell Taylor, creator of Self Diagnose, who became an overnight multimillionaire as a result of record sales of his genius and widely controversial computer program, was last night declared bankrupt. It was directly due to his not so astute addiction to the flashing lights of Vegas."

Zac's breaths became shallow as he reread the word bankrupt. He read on.

"While on the casino floor Maxwell showed no self-control, a subject he taught to numerous patients over the years. He bet wildly with copious amounts of money, merely to lose everything."

Before reading further, Zac could not help but consider his wages. He had not been paid anything at present. How could such an impoverished man finance his healthy salary? How the hell does a bankrupt man own a house like this? And fill it with opulent cars? This did not add up, quite literally.

The article continued on to elaborate on Maxwell's erratic betting habits. "Single bets at the blackjack table of $1,000,000." It went on to divulge about all-night benders where Maxwell became a casino owner's dream – drunk, loaded and desperate, endeavoring to win back his losings by throwing an average man's lifetime earnings away in a single hand. The harrowing account of one man's downfall, culminating in the concluding retort.

"How could a man so astute at interpreting the thoughts and feelings of any and every man around him, have such inadequate understanding of his own specific weaknesses and vices? The mystery of mankind."

Zac had meticulously read every word, yet failed to take in any of the context, his comprehension marred by his bewilderment at the information's allegations presented in front of his eyes. Just as baffling was why Roy had unearthed this article. Zac soon appreciated he could only have been specifically looking for it, probing for dirt on his new boss.

It was fair to say Zac was aggravated by his father's actions. In his mind, Roy had no right or business to interfere in his life, certainly not unless invited to. Should the roles have been reversed and Maxwell had researched Roy, a whole catalog of damning articles would have flooded out, like some unforeseen freak tidal wave, splashing everybody in the face. People in glass houses should not be throwing stones. In that instant something occurred to Zac. Maxwell could well have done just that. After all he approached Zac about the job offer. How could he have known about him without doing some investigating first? Is it possible he could have dug a little deeper and unearthed all the horrors of his childhood? When he broke down in the psychological analysis and spilt his heart out to Maxwell, did he already know everything that had previously transpired? There was no way to tell. Zac clicked on the second file, and it commenced its download.

Zac was anticipating another newspaper article, but it was not. To Zac's astonishment it was an FBI document. The top of the page read: "Confidential File. Level 5 Clearance or above only."

What the hell had Roy forwarded to him this time? Zac reasoned he must have got hold of it through one of his friends at the precinct, if he had any friends still at hand there. No, that could not be right. This was an FBI document, a classified one at that. Zac concluded he probably did not want to know where his father had obtained this. Zac read the file with his mouth wide open. The paper was the account of an FBI informant, a nark against the Mafia. The M-word iced Zac's blood instantaneously. The account revealed that Maxwell had serious debts linked to the Mob. His gambling addiction had not ceased at wiping out his ample fortune. Its hold on him had extended to throwing Maxwell to the lions. The informant did not state the actual amount he owed his less than forgiving acquaintances, only testifying it was a frighteningly large amount of money. The nark affirmed the unscrupulous loan sharks now wanted a return on their investment. They desired payment, and soon. The unnamed informant concluded that due to the vastness of the arrears, failure to pay would result in very grim consequences. However, those consequences had certain complications. In the worst-case scenario, the call for a hit on Maxwell would not be plausible as the Mob would not tolerate losing so much money. Death for him would be an easy escape. They needed at least some of their money back, but ideally wanted to recover all of it with interest. A dead man could not pay.

Zac's brain was ahead of his conscious thoughts and scanned the document for a date. Nothing was shown.

Before he could throw together one rational thought about the context of the document in front of him, an immediate threat surfaced in his mind. Anything downloaded on his computer would also be duplicated and stored on the master computer in the network; the reason so many rogue employees are caught and sacked for looking at inappropriate web material in offices all across the world.

"Holy shit!" Zac exclaimed in panic. Without further thought he deleted everything he had recently downloaded off his hard drive. Zac jumped up and bounded over to Maxwell's computer, the primary computer in the network. Zac was confident the download history & document duplication stored on his hard drive would be backed up here. Before clicking on it, Zac hesitated and stared silently at the door. No sound. He clicked the computer on at the monitor. A nauseous sensation flooded his body as he held station for a few seconds while the screen lit up. After what seemed a lifetime Zac was able to get underway. Luck was on his side in a considerable way, the hard drive was not password locked. Zac was able to penetrate its contents immediately. As feared, a backup of both documents did exist. He hastily deleted them, cleared the download history, then speedily checked for any further trace of the downloaded data. Nothing. After returning everything back to normal he flicked the monitor back off and flew back to his own workstation.

"Jesus, Pa, what the hell are you trying to do to me?" he solicited to the heavens. Only now could he embark on processing the information he had received and ascertain what implications it might have on him and his well-being.

CHAPTER 24

Lisa was halfway through getting ready to meet Zac for their now daily get-together, when the intercom buzzed.

"Lisa, can you come to my private quarters immediately?" Maxwell's voice crackled through. Even with the feeble sound quality Lisa identified the aggravation in his tone.

"Okay, give me five."

"No, now. Things have changed." his response was immediate.

"For Christ's sake, where's the fire?" she asked boisterously without pressing the button. Straighteners unplugged and her hair half complete, she raced out to see Maxwell.

"This had better be important," she declared, bursting in through the door, with a nonexistent knock.

"I'm afraid it is. We have a problem," Maxwell replied motioning to his computer, the genuine master computer. "Look what Zac has received from Roy."

Lisa joined him at his desk and scanned through the text on the screen. "This is gonna make things much more complicated," Maxwell remarked as Lisa worked her way through the incriminating information. The antagonism she had felt quickly dispersed. Zac was not supposed to know this. Many questions occupied Lisa's head, but her mouth remained motionless.

"Look, don't worry. We can sort this," Maxwell encouraged. "It's all about damage limitation. If we can find a way to broach the situation with him, we can put a positive spin on what he now knows. If we do it correctly, I'm confident our objectives should remain unharmed and achievable."

Lisa finished speed reading and turned to face Maxwell.

His face divulged more than he was suggesting. He appeared stressed and anxious. "So, what's our next move?" Lisa finally posed.

Maxwell's frown metamorphosed into a reflective expression. He rubbed his chin and let out a long meditative sigh. "Right, first of all, he can't know that we know about these emails. Therefore we require for him to offer up the information without either one of us raising the subject. Next, it's important he discusses this with the one of us he trusts the most. After what he's just read, I'd say it's a dead cert bet, it's gonna be you."

Lisa slumped dejectedly in her chair.

"Don't worry, you can do this," Maxwell encouraged. Lisa bestowed a despondent look in return.

"How?"

"Tonight, meet him as normal. I know him, he'll be really edgy. Not able to hide there's something on his mind. Keep asking him what's wrong. For a while he'll deny there's a problem. Keep questioning but be careful not to back him into a corner, or make it sound like an interrogation. When you think you've exhausted the question, actually withdraw yourself from him. Act as if you've put emotional barriers up around yourself. Turn the situation on its head. Get him asking you what's wrong, but don't reveal anything. Tell him you're about to leave early and go to bed, even go so far as suggesting you might leave the house. When Zac is suitably panicked, reveal to him you already know what's wrong with Zac. Tell him you know it's yourself." Maxwell paused, allowing Lisa to take in the scheme.

"At the thought of losing you, the only person he trusts in the house, he'll break. I'm sure of it. It's in his interest to. He requires more information about what he's recently learnt and you're his only real option. Plus, as a bonus side effect it will further cement your relationship, and his need in you."

"Okay." Lisa deliberated it in her mind. "I can do that, as long as you're confident it'll work, but what do I say when he does bring it up?"

"Hmmm. That's a good question." Maxwell closed his eyes

and explored his imagination. With minimal delay he popped up in his seat, eyes wide open and a smug grin on his handsome face. "Got it," he reveled. "When he tells you what he knows, be surprised, but act like it's no real secret. Tell him the newspapers exaggerated the debt to give the story additional spice. Explain to him a large corporation wanted the rights to Self Diagnose, so they bought me out and fronted the budget to develop Self Help. Say it was enough to pay off all my outstanding debts and pay Zac his wages. Say it was all kept very quiet as the corporation didn't want to be tied to my name, say something like their Ethicacy Director was explicit on that matter. He should buy that. Trust me, he needs reassurance more than the explanation."

Lisa considered the plausibility of the excuse. "But what about the FBI document?"

"I honestly do not expect him to even bring that up once he's been told all my debts have been paid off. It would be difficult for him to explain how he knows about that. Should he mention the informant, suggest he had every logical reason to exaggerate, in your opinion. Suggest he was saying anything to get whatever charges they had against him dropped, or at the very least was just telling the Feds something they wanted to hear. End any doubt by suggesting that out of common sense I'm likely to have paid off any outstanding debts to bad people before going out and buying nice houses and cars."

"Yeah, that's good, Maxwell. I can do that. I'm certain he will buy it." With that Lisa suddenly realized she needed to finish straightening her hair. Plus, she still had to apply her make-up. This was not the night to be late. "Right, I've got to get ready, Maxwell," she said, getting up hastily.

"Sure you're happy with what you have to say?" Maxwell asked.

"Yep, no worries," verified Lisa. "Gotta go." With that Lisa disappeared from the room.

CHAPTER 25

A shower had cleansed Zac's body, but not his emotion. His mind was cluttered like a child's bedroom. He judged himself unable to process his own misgivings and tackle the deep concerns lodged in the pit of his stomach. With a profound burden on his shoulders, Zac made his way down to the main kitchen. Lisa had arranged to cook dinner for them both. Like a split allegiance both mind and body labored for differing priorities. He wanted nothing more than to enjoy Lisa's company, laugh and joke without a serious thought entering his head, to leave all his stresses at the door; Melissa, work and now Maxwell. To enter the room a liberated man, the shackles removed. Yet in truth, at best he had only managed to loosen the shackles. Since the death of his mother, they had always lingered, prepared to tighten at a moment's notice. Currently they felt as if they were strangling, stifling the life out him.

Now what? Did Lisa know about Maxwell's situation? What would happen if he told her? Either way it did not matter. With advice and comfort she bestowed about Melissa and work, Lisa was independent. Apart from being Maxwell's niece she had no direct connection with any of it. For this latest situation she could not be considered independent. Either breaking this news to her or telling her something she was already aware of would only lead to an indefinite number of complications. Yet keeping quiet and sitting on this volcano was no alternative, at the very least Zac needed to know if he would get paid for all this toil that had cost him his relationship. Taking precedence, though, was the incredibly foreboding concern of whether Lisa's life and his own were actually in danger?

Upon entering the kitchen Zac's nostrils were filled with

an abundantly agreeable meaty aroma.

"Hi, Zac," Lisa welcomed, approaching him with radiance and vitality. Lisa flung her arms around Zac, without invite. He matched the embrace. For a few seconds he felt only the warmth of her body against his. The briefest of respites, it was a warm blanket being tossed around his shoulders on a cold day.

"Hmmm, smells good," he complimented as they untangled. "What are we having?"

Lisa took his hand and led him to the table. "It's a family recipe, spicy meatballs in spaghetti, Taylor style."

Zac inhaled again. He could not recollect meatballs ever smelling as alluring. He suddenly realized he was starving, as yet again in pursuit of excellence in his work, Zac had neglected to eat. For the moment food was exclusively on the agenda. All the other crap could take a backseat. He was a man after all.

Half an hour later, his stomach satisfied, Lisa and Zac had progressed to the couch. The wine was flowing, the music chilled. Zac felt tranquil and serene. It did not endure. Anxiety, drip-dripped back into his body. Muscles tautened little by little. The conversation fragmented, ceasing to flow. Lisa detected the minute changes. Not ordinarily something she would pick up on, but normally she was not waiting for it. Not scrutinizing every sign of tension in someone's body.

"Is something wrong?" she asked, in the most innocent tone she could muster.

"No. What makes you say that?" Zac's tone was particularly defensive.

"You just seem … I don't know? A little preoccupied?"

"I'm fine. Honestly."

They sat in silence for an uncomfortable length of time.

"Something is definitely wrong. I thought we were able to share everything."

"Nothing is wrong, Lisa."

Lisa looked him in the eyes. Zac could not hold it; he moved his gaze to the ground.

"I knew it," Lisa muttered under her breath. She rose from

the couch and walked back into the kitchen.

Zac surveyed her as she loaded the dishwasher. Eventually he followed into the kitchen area. "I should do that after the meal you just cooked."

"I'm doing it now." Lisa's voice was spiky and foreboding.

"Why are you upset?"

"I'm not," Lisa answered. Her tone and body language did not coincide. Zac stood awkwardly like a child lined up with others waiting to be picked for a team in sport, desperately not wanting to be last.

"Come on, Lisa ..." Zac's sentence trailed off as Lisa shot him an angry look. She completed loading the dishwasher and started the cycle. The she washed her hands with her back to the stricken man who stood watching.

"I'm off to bed now, I'm feeling tired," she announced in a hollow voice.

"Jesus, Lisa. Tell me what I've done."

"Nothing." Lisa dried her delicate hands, still facing away from Zac. Suddenly her hands froze. "I think I might head back tomorrow," she said quietly.

"What?" Zac's mouth dried up. "You mean leave the house?"

"Yes." Her voice was blunt and unforgiving.

"Why would you want to do that? I thought we were having a good time. I don't want you to go." His voice developed into the needy child of the sports team line-up.

"I thought so too," Lisa retorted. "I'm not stupid, something is definitely wrong with you. Don't deny it, I can tell. If you won't talk to me about it, I can only conclude it's me."

Zac took a chair at the kitchen table, a little bewildered.

"No, Lisa, you couldn't be more wrong, you're my only saving grace, and without you I have nothing." His voice overflowed with sincerity.

"So?" Lisa encouraged as she took a seat opposite him. "Tell me. If it's not me, what's wrong?"

Zac held a long silence, looking at his beautiful new-found

confidant and savior. He sought to evaluate all the pros and cons of coming clean to her but was unable to manage it. His mind ran blank.

"Okay," he irrevocably conceded. "I found something out about your uncle."

Lisa's face registered surprise.

"I read a newspaper article about him gambling himself bankrupt."

Her face changed from surprise. Zac interpreted recognition in her eyes. "Wow," she whispered to herself. "Where did you come across that?" she asked.

"You know about it?"

"Yep."

"It was emailed to me," he confessed.

"By who?"

"A friend. It doesn't matter. Is it true?"

Lisa took a second to answer. She smiled to herself and shook her head. "Right." She grabbed Zac's hands and held his eyes. "This stays between these walls, okay?"

"Sure."

"Yeah, Maxwell had a real problem. It'd been building for a long time before Self Diagnose, but with all the success came a rather large bank balance. It gave Maxwell a sensation of financial immortality. His mindset was like an invincible God, he couldn't lose. If he lost a bet it didn't matter, he always had plenty more money to replace it."

"His addiction exploded, he was betting larger and larger amounts to actually make it mean something, just to find the thrill. Basically, he gambled away everything he had. He was on the verge of bankruptcy when a newspaper got hold of the story. In their urgency to print it they didn't actually wait for Maxwell to file for bankruptcy, yet just in the nick of time appeared his saving grace. He was approached by a large software company who offered to buy the rights for Self Diagnose. I don't know how much they paid him, but as you can see Maxwell is far from bankrupt." Lisa gestured around the room with her hands. Zac gazed at their surroundings.

Lisa continued. "The software company also owns the rights to Self Help and is paying Maxwell to develop it."

"So, he's on the payroll just like me?"

"Er, yeah, but you cannot tell him you know. He wants everybody to think this is his baby, he's still a proud man."

"Of course," Zac obliged.

"The software company is more than happy for Maxwell to be the front man. Due to the controversy, they don't desire or need all the hassle that comes with the programs or Max's reputation for uncontrollable betting."

"Just the money?"

"Spot on," Lisa grinned.

Zac took her hands again while he thought it through in his mind. Everything she had just said did actually make sense. He considered raising the subject of the FBI informant, but instantly decided mentioning it could only lead to trouble. Zac was convinced Lisa would not know anything about that one. She would certainly ask Maxwell about it, and then he would want to know exactly how Zac came across that particular segment of information. The newspaper article was in the public domain and easy for anybody to find. A classified FBI document is not the sort of thing you just come across on a Google search.

"Does he still gamble now?" Zac enquired, attempting to get the full picture without revealing his knowledge of the document.

"Absolutely not, he's a new man these days. Much nicer to be around, hence my visits out here. He throws his competitiveness into swimming now. Maxwell got the help he needed. The software company took care of all that. After all he had become their investment."

Maxwell must have paid off all unwanted debts with the Mafia when he was bought out, Zac told himself. It seemed all of Roy's digging was a touch out of date. There was nothing to worry about. Lisa's explanation made total sense. Only one topic remained to be questioned.

"Lisa, would you join me back on the couch, because I really need your company?" he conceded with a sheepish grin.

"Sure, why not?"

Maxwell rose from the monitor and walked around his private office. Lisa had certainly done an admirable job. Everything she had said sounded plausible. Better than plausible, it was truthful and frank. The entire plan was back on track. All ready for the next phase. The only concern was Roy. He was creating unnecessary anxiety in Maxwell. The resourcefulness of the information he passed on to his son had unquestionably surprised him. Maxwell did not enjoy underestimating people. He prided himself on having an unerring ability to judge the capabilities of anybody. If Roy continued to dig and warn Zac that all was not as it appeared, it would become more and more difficult to keep this train on the tracks.

Already dressed only in his swimming trunks, Maxwell grabbed a towel. He needed to swim, to clear his mind and regain control of his thoughts and the current situation. Just before leaving the room he allowed himself one quick look in the mirror. His eyes implied worry, all red and puffy. The shallow lines of age in his face had deepened and the skin surrounding his discolored eyes was much grayer than normal.

"Shit, this is taking a toll on you, Maxwell," he told himself. "But don't worry about Roy. After all, in a few days he will be dead." After a half-hearted grin, Maxwell then stared an empty look into his reflection. It was more than the exhaustion, pressure and stress projecting themselves on his face. Something much darker. But there was no way out. He was as trapped as Zac; the only difference was he could see the bars of his own undesired confine. He left for the pool.

CHAPTER 26

The world gradually filtered in through Zac's senses. Without clear thought he silenced the ever-intrusive alarm clock in the tried and trusted "press as many buttons as you can in one go" technique. Immediately silence descended upon the room; the technique never failed. Zac lay in a frozen state, caught in the no-man's land between the sleep world and the real world. Thick with sleep, his eyes only managed to take blurred images, like an out-of-focus camera on auto shot mode. His brain was trying to fire up, but not all the cylinders were able to run yet. He managed to drowsily establish he was waking in a familiar location, his bedroom.

As his body made the progression to consciousness other senses started up their day. Now he could hear Melissa's breathing in his ear. He could sense her arm pressed against his. A sensation of warming comfort laced his body like riding on a gigantic marshmallow floating in an exceptionally oversized cup of hot chocolate. Zac lethargically turned his head to bestow a kiss on his love, when bang!

The marshmallow promptly melted causing him to plummet into molten chocolate. It was not Melissa who lay next to him. In a flash a deluge of information crashed through his mind: everything that had recently transpired with Melissa, Alex, Roy, Maxwell, and the young woman asleep beside him. Lisa.

He replayed the previous night's events in his head. A hug had led to a kiss, to heightened passion. To, well, here. Unexpectedly a congenial delicate feeling spread throughout his body. Now fully awake Zac recognized contentment. He continued to take the kiss he had formerly tried for. As his lips tenderly pressed against hers, like a bee searching for nectar lowering onto a petal, Zac was consumed by an electric desire. His lips amplified their pressure.

Without opening her eyes, Lisa kissed back, with even greater force. The craving it seemed ran throughout both of their young and abundantly sexual bodies. Melissa had been the only woman Zac had previously slept with. She was gentle and loving, timid in her passion. Lisa was not. She dominated and took exactly what she wanted. She gave lots back simultaneously, but only what she allowed. At times Zac felt like a passenger, Lisa was at the wheel. He knew not where she was taking him, but all the same he adored it. He was partial to her wild temperament and aggressiveness. He loved her confidence to acquire exactly what she wanted, and then some.

Roy phoned Maxwell's house again, for the fourth time that morning, each time hearing the same recorded message. He had not heard back from Zac since before sending the emails. Roy got up and paced anxiously around the small lounge while waiting for the opportunity to leave a message.

"Hi, this is Maxwell Taylor. I can't take your call right now. Please leave your name and number and I'll get right back to you." Beep.

"Hi, Zac, it's Pa again. Please give me a call at home when you get this." He pressed end call and positioned the phone back on his cheap flat pack coffee table. He did not like this one bit. Surely Zac had read the emails. Roy had checked his email on his way home from work as the library opened that morning, but no reply there. Now he had no answer from anybody on the phone at the house.

He reviewed the situation. It was possible Zac was in grave danger, yet far more likely he was completely fine. Until he got in contact with Zac it was impossible to tell. So Roy considered his options. He could go back to the library now and recheck his email, but if Zac phoned back while he was gone, he would miss the call. He could always just fly out to the house. What then? If Zac was fine, he definitely would not appreciate a surprise visit to save the day.

"Zac is a bright lad. He's got bags of common sense. If he were in danger, he'd know just what to do," Roy told himself. His only real option was just to wait for now. Sit it out for one more day. If Zac didn't contact him by tomorrow morning it would not seem so ridiculous for Roy to call the local cops and ask them to check it out. Not satisfied with his decision, Roy grabbed the phone one more time and hit redial. It rang, then as before the answer phone clicked in. This time he left no message. Taking the phone with him, he headed for bed.

Maxwell listened to Roy's latest message before unemotionally pressing the message delete button. All calls to the house were being diverted to his private study. No chance for Zac to be distracted by his interfering father. Not when everything was so tantalizingly close. The previous night Maxwell had taken immense gratification in watching Zac and Lisa cavorting sexually through his voyeur-style monitor. Not in any kind of perversion, though, the plan was far more important than any homemade porn movie. Lisa successfully completing her obligations in the very near future was imperative. Getting it together with Zac was vital. It was the preliminary part of the next phase, the full devastation of the plan depended on it.

CHAPTER 27

For once, Zac's day dragged. He found maintaining concentration on an infinite number of mind-numbing sub-routines intolerable. His only desire was to find Lisa and receive yet more punishment at her hands and body. They had arranged to meet at eight. Lisa was going to cook for him again, but it wasn't the food on Zac's mind. Previously the end of the working day would arrive all too soon for Zac, but not today. He plodded on unenthusiastically.

Meanwhile upstairs Maxwell and Lisa discussed the next step.

"So you're clear on everything?" Maxwell asked.

"Yeah, I'm clear." Lisa's tone lacked interest.

"It has to be tonight," he warned. "I have an early flight booked. I can reach Roy as he gets home from the nightshift. If he gets home and still hasn't heard from Zac, he might do something stupid, like call the cops. That would ruin the whole plan."

"I'm clear, Maxwell." She gritted her teeth for added effect. "I told you. Don't overstep your mark. Are you clear?"

"Okay, Lisa. I'm clear," he apologized, backing down.

Zac could not wait for his usual knocking-off time. A good hour before the arranged meeting time, he left the office and headed upstairs for a long refreshing shower. He searched his wardrobe afterwards for a favorite shirt to wear. The truth was it was slim pickings. He had already been dressing in his best items, ever since Lisa and he had started meeting every night. Granted, the arrangement had not been in place long, but the trendsetter Zac was, he did not possess numerous first-rate shirts. He pulled out the best of the rest, just as there was a knock on his front door.

Zac wrapped himself in a towel and walked to the door. After opening it, Lisa stood before him. She wore a thin lace blouse accompanied by a black knee-length skirt. She wore no shoes, just bare feet. Zac had not seen Lisa in a skirt before, but he sincerely liked what he saw.

"Wow," he mouthed.

"Hi, Zac," she whispered with a cheeky smile. Her foot lifted and seductively rubbed up the back of her other naked leg.

"I thought we were meeting at eight?"

"We are, but I want to ask a favor first. Can I come in?"

Without answer Zac pulled Lisa in through the doorway and kissed her in a longing and impatient manner.

"Wait for it," Lisa commanded, backing off and regaining control. "I want you to do something for me."

"Anything," Zac panted, running his eager hands all over the outside of her clothes.

"Calm down a minute," she laughed, leading him to the couch.

Zac gathered some composure and took a seat. "What do you want me to do?" he asked keenly.

"Well," Lisa looked up to the sky, her cheeky grin working overtime. "It's a bit embarrassing ... er ... I have a fantasy I'd love to act out." She threw out a childish laugh.

"What?" Zac smiled. "You mean role play?"

"Yeah, sort of."

Zac gave a perplexed face.

"Oh god," Lisa buried her face in her hands.

"Come on, tell me. I'm game for it," Zac reassured her.

"Okay." Lisa straightened her face. "I know this sounds really weird, but I'd really get off on us acting out you raping me." Zac's face dropped and his eyes opened wide like saucers. "Does that sound really bad?" she followed up.

"No, I can't say it's what I was expecting, to be honest."

"I'm sure it sounds really odd, but I just know I'd enjoy it."

"So, what would I have to do?" Zac could not hide the apprehension in his voice.

"I do have it sort of planned out. Wow, that really did sound bad, didn't it?" The cheeky grin once again returned, and Lisa leant in towards Zac. She rubbed her hands up his bare thigh, slowly creeping up the naked flesh, until she reached the bottom of his towel. Her hands started to slip underneath the towel, but then simply to torment him, she stopped. She moved her head towards his, until her mouth was against his ear, proceeding to gently whisper her instructions.

"When eight comes, come into the kitchen as planned. Don't talk to me or make your presence known. I'll have my back to you. Sneak up to me and grab me from behind. Force your hand over my mouth to stifle my screams. Pull me to the ground, rip off my clothes, and I mean rip, then well, you can guess the rest. Don't stop even if I cry or scream. I'm just acting. If I want you to stop, I'll say a code word. Let's say, er ... abort. When you're finished leave me lying on the floor and walk out of the room. Don't come back in for five minutes. It's important to me that you leave straight away afterwards and stay completely in character until you've left the kitchen."

"Bloody hell, Lisa," Zac gasped back in shock.

"I know, but if you do this for me, I'll make it worth your while. I promise." With that she jumped off the couch and headed for the door. As she turned the handle Lisa added one more thing. "Oh, and don't worry about Maxwell hearing anything, he's just gone out and won't be back until tomorrow evening. I'll leave Buster up here in case he decides to come to my rescue." She blew Zac a kiss and with that she was gone, leaving a shell-shocked Zac on the couch.

At eight Zac hovered apprehensively at the door of the kitchen. To say he was feeling dubious was an understatement. The metal of the stainless steel handle felt cool against his sweaty hand. For an instant he froze, attempting to summon up the courage to open the door. He cherished Lisa's proactive approach in the bedroom and craved to please her, but this? He could not help considering he was a little out of his depth.

Even so, he pushed down on the handle and permitted the door to silently open. Like an explorer discovering a never before entered cave, Zac peered into the unknown. Lisa stood in clear sight, her back to him as promised, washing her hands at the sink. Zac gazed up and down her feminine figure. He wanted her frantically, and no role play was required for that. Slowly he crept toward her, with each step he slipped more faithfully into his dark role. A sense of power and masterfulness ran through him.

Before Zac knew it, he was upon her petite frame, his sturdy arm reaching around her face. He snapped his hand over her mouth in an instant. Her body tensed; Zac felt a rush of hot air burst out of her mouth against his confining hand as she endeavored to scream. Lisa tried to push away and escape out the other side. She had no chance, Zac's other formidable arm flanked her and dragged Lisa dominantly in toward his body, quickly overwhelming her like a constricting snake. With that Zac allowed his body weight to pull them both to the ground. Lisa fought to withstand the weight but was powerless to cease her own descent. Once on the ground Zac turned her body to face his. All her limbs flailed frenziedly. Zac wrestled to maintain control as she thrashed about, all the time keeping his hand locked securely over her mouth. At that moment his eyes met with hers. They were filled with undulating terror. Panic began filling his body. Was he actually hurting her, or was this all part of the act? As a reflex Zac released his hand from her mouth, in anticipation of hearing the code word, contemplating he had taken it too far, been too physical. Only a blood-curdling scream emitted from her vocal cords. Immediately he stifled it by replacing his hand. Unsure of what to do next he glanced back at her eyes, pleading for advice. For just a split second the revulsion deep within dispersed and she winked at him, then the horror returned as abruptly as it had departed. She was okay. Relief charged through Zac and he resumed his role.

His breath was hasty, panting like an animal. Feeling like an animal. With his free hand he grasped her blouse, wrenching it open along the buttons, lacking any finesse. The thin cotton ripped and tore, exposing her stiff young womanly breasts to the open. Her body arched as she writhed, but Zac could tell she was enjoying it. Next with might and single-minded intent he forced her legs apart using his own stronger legs. Her feeble resistance was no match for his complete supremacy. He moved his hand down to her panties, wary not to hurt her, found a weak spot and tore them open.

Within an instant his jeans were undone and pulled down to his knees. Her body presented new vigor as he forced himself on her. Her hands pawed at his face. Zac could tell Lisa was being careful not to scratch him, without losing the realism of the event. Zac also became conscious of the actual gratification he was obtaining from the act he undertook. Reality hit him with a thump. This was all too real, all too appalling. He needed to stop, and stop now. Quickly he jumped back off her.

"I'm sorry," Zac panted as he gasped for air. Gracelessly he rose to his feet and pulled his jeans up. He glanced back at his victim but could only make out a blur of flesh and clothes. With that he ran out of room, slamming the door behind him.

The relief of exiting the room overwhelmed Zac and he collapsed on the floor, fighting for breath and clear thought. The other side of the door Lisa lay in a heap sobbing for a couple of minutes. Then as if nothing had happened, Lisa got up and straightened her clothes as best she could. She swept her hair into something like its usual position and opened the door. Zac lay on the floor feeling confused.

"Are you okay, Zac?" she asked calmly, with a smile.

"Er, yeah. Are you?" His voice shaky.

"Of course. I loved it. You did a great job." She held her hand out to Zac. He grabbed it and Lisa helped him to his feet.

"That was kinda intense," she added.

"Kinda?"

"Come on, stud, let's fix you some food." With that, she led him back into the kitchen.

Although both Zac and Lisa were in plain view, Maxwell no longer watched the screen. Now he possessed exactly what he required. Whilst downloading a copy of the recently recorded footage to a flash stick Maxwell found time for a quick double-check of the flight time and his ticket. He removed the flash stick and with it tucked safely in his coat pocket he discreetly left the house.

Next stop San Francisco and Roy.

CHAPTER 28

Roy returned to his shabby apartment in the cold first light of morning. The air had an earthy crispness to it, which ran in contradiction to the ground, dampened by overnight rain. Appropriately, the clouds were now broken open to expose those precious first rays of light from the early sun. All of this nature's wonder was lost in the eyes of Roy. He did not observe any of it. He had still had no reply from Zac. He now knew something was most definitely wrong. But out of the murkiness of yesterday came clarity more powerful than the sun and its first light offerings. Roy had a plan. He reached his apartment's communal doorway. His cop instinct was still able to function when required and he was aware he had been followed for at least the last few blocks. He opened the door without delay and headed up the stairwell to his place. The outside door swung gradually closed on its ever-recurring journey back to shut and locked. Only this time the door stopped midstream. A hand intervened. Within the blink of an eye a figure slipped inside.

Once inside his apartment, Roy listened, ear to the door. He could hear the footsteps climbing the stairs and then stop outside his door. Roy tried to peer though his old grubby spy hole. His sight obscured by the grime, he could not make out any telling details, just the lurking silhouette of his stalker. Already prepared, Roy held a loaded and cocked handgun. Without giving the mystery guest a chance to think about his next move Roy speedily swung his door open making sure to keep the gun out of sight behind it.

The surprise tactic worked as the figure that Roy could now make out to be a middle-aged man jumped back and almost fell back down the stairs.

"What the hell do you want?" Roy fired at him before the man could regain balance and composure. He did not answer, just shot Roy a filthy look, fire raging behind his eyes. He obviously did not appreciate the shock welcome. Tired of waiting for his answer Roy revealed the gun from behind the door. "Now answer me. What do you want?"

"Hi, Roy. I'm right, you are Roy, aren't you?" his unwelcome visitor spoke in a somewhat condescending tone.

"Who wants to know?"

"I'm sorry, how rude," he patronized. "Where are my manners? I'm Maxwell Taylor but call me Maxwell." Maxwell extended his hand. Without conviction Roy shook it, following the act by un-cocking his gun. Maxwell's eyes turned to the weapon. "Maybe I should have called ahead," he jeered unpleasantly. "May I come in? We need to talk."

Without a word Roy opened the door wide and stepped back to allow entry. Maxwell promptly did so.

"What's going on, Maxwell? Why are you here?"

Maxwell glanced at Roy but failed to respond. Then turning his attention to Roy's basic and cramped home, he browsed through it in a pretentious and arrogant manner. "Wow, Roy, what a lovely home you have here. You must be very proud."

"Get to the point, Maxwell. What's going on? Is Zac okay?" Roy had long since lost his patience and this added real bite to his voice.

"You're obviously not a man for small talk, are you?" Maxwell sighed, staring out the window. "Well at least the view is quite good. I suppose."

Roy took at hostile step toward Maxwell, who raised his hands in mock surrender. "Okay, okay," he conceded, "you win. Take a seat and I'll tell you exactly what's going on."

Roy hesitantly lowered himself down on the couch. He gestured for Maxwell to join him, but Maxwell ignored the offer and remained standing. For a few seconds both men just looked at each other, as if sizing up the threat, like in an old spaghetti western film.

Maxwell finally broke the stand-off and turned his eyes back out of the window, back to his analysis of early morning San Francisco. From his fourth-story observation point he scrutinized the many people out and about just beginning their day, rushing to take their place in society, an essential and yet pointless role in the rat race. Maxwell reflected back on that life he once knew so well. He did not miss it, as just one of the masses, everybody giving so much individually for an insignificant contribution to civilization, all for their meager reward. Although salaries varied, everyone struggled to get by all alike. A culture of people living beyond their means, purchasing houses, cars and lives they could not quite afford, endeavoring to demonstrate to everybody, including themselves, their own success and attainment. Behind closed doors was a nation of people fretting about mortgage payments, car loans and bills. It was a needless stress of modern life, keeping up with the Joneses on steroids.

With sincere revulsion Maxwell recalled that life. But those days were long gone, he had progressed that extra step for personal glory, and climbed above his fellow man with wealth and a lifestyle beyond their trivial dreams. No way was he going to step back down into the colony of ants that he had left so gladly behind. He could not let that happen, even if he had to sell his soul to avoid it. It was cheap at twice the price.

Without taking his eyes off the scene out of the window, Maxwell finally readdressed Roy. "There's something you have to do for me, Roy. It's not something you're going to like, but you've got to do it. It's for Zac's sake."

At the mention of his son Roy jumped up from the couch. Maxwell did not even flinch. "Tell me what the fuck is going on," Roy aggressively stipulated. He was geared up to grab Maxwell, when he said something to make Roy freeze in his tracks.

"Zac could be in really big trouble." Maxwell heaved a sigh and turned to face Roy. "I think you'd better watch this," He withdrew the flashstick out of his coat.

A blank-faced Roy took the memory device and gawped at it as if he had never seen one before.

"Oh come on Roy, surely you have a laptop? You can't be that far behind the times, can you?" Maxwell jeered.

"No. What has Zac done? What is this all about?" Maxwell gave a patronizing sneer.

"A tablet?" Roy opened his mouth to speak, slightly confused he hesitated. Max took the opportunity to belittle him some more "The electronic kind, I mean. Not for a hangover Roy."

"I know what you mean." Roy Snapped back. "I haven't got one."

Maxwell withdrew an iPad Mini out of the inside pocket of his coat and fumbled around through the other coat pockets until he located a lead to connect the flashstick to the device. The whole time he kept a disdainful expression on his face. Roy's patience was wearing thin.

"Just tell me what's going on" He demanded. Max continued getting the contents of the flashstick ready and ignored Roy's command as if he hadn't spoken. Eventually Max gave a small nod to acknowledge the device was ready and handed it Roy.

"Watch this, then we'll talk."

Roy grabbed the device. He could feel a knot in his throat swelling. Whatever was on that screen, he was convinced it was going to be detrimental, both for him and Zac. Roy observed a video cued ready to watch. He pressed play. Maxwell promptly returned his eyes out of the window. He really did not care to observe the footage again.

Roy was presented with an image obviously recorded from a closed-circuit television camera. He witnessed a beautiful young woman washing her hands at a sink. For a brief time, the status quo was maintained. Then another person crept into shot from the side. Roy recognized Zac instantly, as he moved with stealth-like capabilities towards the woman. Then with immeasurable revulsion he watched as Zac launched his assault. Observing in horror, Roy momentarily glanced at Maxwell. He was stuck fast to the considerably less sickening view out of the window. Roy returned his eyes to the screen, his mouth open and dry. Every single part of his being wanted to stop the video and terminate the visual torture. But Roy watched on. He had to continue, to somehow establish this was not real, not actually what it appeared to be. The girl though, illustrated that it was. Her distress was unmistakable, it was nauseating to witness. Was this aggressive animal really his son? Have I turned my sweet, sweet boy into this monster? Roy deliberated.

Abruptly Zac ended his violent attack. As he pulled himself off the traumatized woman, Zac spoke. "I'm sorry." The audio was clear. Roy dropped his head and a tear rolled off his cheek onto the floor with a gentle thud. Now Roy could just hear the muted sobbing of the girl. He forced himself one more look. The girl lay half-naked with torn clothes on the floor. Her body trembled in anguish. The recording ended.

"This can't be right; it can't be real." Roy spoke as if he had been choked. He placed the tablet on the table in front of him as if it was itself polluted by the content within.

"I'm sorry you had to watch that." Maxwell's tone was for once genuine in his apology. Both men held their positions and remained silent for some time. Maxwell eventually snapped back and recaptured himself. "Roy, just answer me this one question. What do you think of your son right now?"

Roy's response took a second or two, yet he still spoke without any real consideration. "I've just watched my only son, my only real reason for living, commit a sickening rape and to be honest, right now I don't know if I want to lock him up or kill him."

"So you would agree the evidence is as clear as day?" Maxwell posed.

"Yes." Roy lowered his head and voice further still.

"If this recording was passed to the authorities along with the victim pressing charges, they'd literally throw away the key?"

"Yes."

Maxwell finally turned back into the room and looked down at Roy. It was not Maxwell's intention to feel pity for Roy, but it was impossible not to. He had just caused this man intolerable suffering and yet from his hand much worse pain was to come.

"Roy, look at me. What I'm about to say is important."

Roy peered up. For a man with a magnitude of the harshness of life ingrained on his rugged face, his expression reminded Maxwell of a small child, innocent and trusting, so vulnerable to an adult's will and desires.

"I'm going to tell you something but understand that if you attack me or do anything detrimental when I tell you this, that woman, along with a copy of this will be going straight to the cops."

Roy gave a perplexed nod of acknowledgment.

"Roy, you need to know that all of what you just watched was a set-up." Maxwell paused for effect. Roy did not budge but sat frozen like a tormented statue. "Zac didn't actually rape that woman. She asked him to do it as a kind of kinky role play fantasy." Roy remained motionless. "Now let's be clear on this bit. Yes, it was faked, but it appears real. The woman in question will lie and press charges against Zac if need be. Let's be honest, if that happens, real or not, it's gonna be a very, very long time before Zac ever sees freedom. If ever. *Capiche*?"

"Then we have to consider what might happen to Zac in the can. A rapist? An attractive young rapist in there, living amongst the real animals of society?" Maxwell began to pace, relaxing back into his patter after a few moments of doubt. "Dear, oh dear. Just imagine the special treatment he'd receive from his fellow inmates. I'm sure they'd been lining up around the block to offer some quality time, so to speak."

Finally, Roy presented a visible reaction, sitting back in his seat and rubbing his face with his hands.

Maxwell persisted in painting the gruesome picture of

Zac's possible future. "What's gonna happen when his new friends, the inmates, find out dear Zac the rapist has an ex-cop for a father? Hmmm, you just know those guys love cops. Ha ha."

"Enough," Roy demanded.

"I'll bet you could do with a drink right now, eh?"

The word sliced through Roy. But not the drink word, something else Maxwell had said, "bet." Roy glared at Maxwell, weighing him up. "If I'm reading this correctly, Maxwell, you're about to try and blackmail me. I hope for all our sakes it's not money you're after, to pay off your gambling debts." Roy lifted both hands to gesture to the flea pit apartment within which he resided. "As you can see, I don't have a pot to piss in."

Maxwell gave Roy a rewarding smile. "That's very good, Roy. I'll bet you made a damn good cop, that is before you began killing innocent wives and kids."

Roy almost flew at Maxwell for that one, but just managed to keep his control.

"Yes, you are correct. I do want something from you to buy your son's freedom. As for money? No. Please don't worry yourself with my finances. I can assure you that's all very much under control, but thanks for the concern all the same."

"What the hell do you want from me then?" Roy's temper and patience had frayed like an old lady's carpet.

"Roy, keep your voice down and I'll tell you." Roy simmered silently. "Okay this is a difficult one, but here goes. The young boy that you killed whilst drunk and shooting your gun like it was the forth of July has finally come back to haunt you."

"Oh shit." Roy's head pounded with the abrupt resurrection of James Stoneman and that horrific memory. The grave sensation that had haunted him relentlessly for years afterwards raged inside his body.

"Oh shit indeed. It's time for pay-back, I'm afraid, my friend."

"Who was he to you? He's not your son." Roy was desperately striving to recall all the names he knew connected to the case.

"My relationship to him is of no importance or even relevance to you here and now. The only thing important to you at this precise moment in time is that you're in a position to actually be able to save your son's quality of life. Am I safe in the assumption you would do anything or give anything in your power to do that?"

Roy quickly got back on track and assessed his options. "Yes, you're correct, I would."

"Good. There are two things you are going to do so the recording and victim never turn up at the cop shop. Firstly, you're going to kill yourself."

"You're mad. You're crazy. You're an insane ludicrous bastard," Roy spoke quietly, shaking his head. Almost as if he was saying it to himself rather than Maxwell.

"I may be all of those things," Maxwell replied in a soft, yet commanding voice. "But I'm serious."

"No. Fuck you!" Roy blasted out of the blue.

"Sorry, but it's poor innocent Zac's only hope."

Roy started to creep forward off the couch, this time he truly was prepared to fly at him. Maxwell noticed the movement and reacted promptly.

"Don't even think about it, Roy. You touch me and any evidence of my visit here is left then all bets are off. Zac will go straight to the slammer. Remember, this is only a copy." Maxwell waited a second until Roy was once again coherent. "Okay, Roy, this is what you're going to do. Firstly you have to complete my other demand, which is to write a suicide note to Zac. You will say everything is entirely his fault. Your wife, his mother, only died because of the camera he placed on the car's parcel shelf. The journey itself was his fault because it was a trip for his birthday. You must tell him everything that subsequently went wrong was as a result of that day, including you taking your own life, and therefore he is ultimately to blame for all of it. After sealing it within an envelope addressed to my house, you are to climb into your bath and slit your wrists. I'll wait until you're dead or at least too far gone to save yourself."

"Maxwell, how does this help? Why do you want to punish Zac for what I did? It was nothing to do with him."

"I've already told you; my reasons and motives are not your concern." Maxwell looked Roy dead in the eye. "Roy, start writing. You can't bargain with me or make a deal. Either do as I've requested, or Zac goes down."

Roy thought about it. As entirely absurd as it was, Roy was struggling to think of any way out of the situation. As much as he wanted to believe the system would work, he knew the evidence against Zac, no matter how false, was effectively completely damning. He recognized he could not risk putting his poor son through the prospect of that future.

"For Zac, maybe I could kill myself," Roy thought out loud. "But there's no way I could blame him for anything in the suicide note. It would destroy him."

Using his psychological expertise Maxwell rapidly detected something in Roy's persona. He realized quickly he had effectively talked Roy into killing himself, but not into writing the note. He confidently distinguished from the other man's body language and tone that Roy would never complete a letter blaming Zac. To persist in persuading and threatening would be pointless.

However, the suicide note was an imperative part of Maxwell's highly structured and elaborate plan. It would threaten the success of its final stage. Maxwell had to think fast and modify his plan of attack, rather than persevere with the blackmailing angle. Despite this, Maxwell's concentration was contaminated by exasperation at himself. He knew there and then he had let himself once again underestimate Roy. Before this encounter Maxwell had only envisioned Roy as a weak, submissive man, not someone prepared to fight, yet to his annoyance when he read between the lines, all the evidence was in clear view. Prior to the day he had killed his wife Roy was regarded as a local hero. A cop all other cops looked up to and idolized. Roy might have completely derailed like a train, but his tracks still remained. He could get back on them at any time. Nowadays Roy had quit drinking and begun to rebuild from the destruction of his personal derailment. He was forming a fresh new relationship with Zac, and even digging the dirt out on Maxwell. He could have kicked himself. Maxwell did not like to be mistaken or underestimate. Then Roy brought Maxwell out of his self-centered anger and gave him an in.

"Look, Maxwell. I'm the one who's completely ruined my son's life. All of it was my own fault. I made a promise to myself to only do things to help him in his future. Now I'm prepared to take my life to save my son's, but not if it means leaving him riddled with guilt. To put all of this shit on him would be as bad as doing nothing."

In what Roy said, Maxwell unearthed his new assault. He prayed inwardly it would work.

"Roy, I think you've entirely misunderstood my intentions. It's my fault, I didn't explain myself properly. My dispute is with you, not Zac. Sure, I've used him to get to you, but only that. I'm a psychiatrist and I've profiled Zac in great detail. Once you're dead, my vengeance will be complete, and as I won't actually have murdered you, I will have no fear of going to prison. I will have no further use for your son. I know he's absolutely innocent of all this, so afterwards for my own conscience I don't wish him to suffer any more than he has to. Now from the profile I've compiled, if you take your own life and blame yourself, or worse still give no reason, Zac will automatically begin to consider all of it is ultimately a consequence of the camera and he is to blame. He will allow it to eat him up and begin to self-destruct, much like yourself. I know the only real way to avoid that unwanted result is for you to actually blame him. He will regard it as a cowardly act. His perception of your suicide will be that you just tried to pass the buck for your failings. Subconsciously he will fight back, bypassing any route of self-blame or guilt. After anger will come acceptance, and he will be able to move on. He will sense a feeling of closure, that you're gone and can't hurt him anymore.

Okay, it means your legacy is somewhat unhealthy, but his future will not be."

Maxwell waited for Roy to call his bluff, but the other man did nothing. He could tell Roy was considering his options, attempting to contemplate the consequences of writing the note. Maxwell could not quite believe Roy might actually buy it. He opted to fan the flames a smidgen more.

"If you're serious about only wanting to help Zac get on with his life and be happy, then you'll write the note. The price you pay is he will hate you forever, but not himself. I'm afraid it's what you have to do."

Roy stared coldly at Maxwell, still trying to read him. Maxwell recognized it and put on a face of integrity and honesty.

"How do I know that you're telling me the truth? You're obviously a twisted fuck. For all I know you could be out to hurt the whole world. What reassurances do I have that this ends with me?"

"Please stop with the compliments, you're embarrassing me," Maxwell quipped before returning to his serious resolute tone. "Look, it's true, I can't offer you any guarantees. I can only reiterate that my goal was to destroy your life in the cruelest way imaginable. Just like you did to that poor child. Zac was a tool I used, but only that. I wish him no further torment."

Roy felt far from convinced, but with a lack of options he sensed he had no alternative but to succumb. "I'll do it, but I hope you go to hell for this, you son of a bitch."

Like an ocean wave, Maxwell felt the reprieve wash over him. It was this part of the whole plan that was the hardest sell. It promoted his already oversized ego, bestowing him a nigh on divine-like impression of his status amongst the inferiority of mortal men.

"I do have one request, Maxwell, which for all you've asked of me I'm sure you can permit."

"Go on?" Maxwell said suspiciously.

"I do have alcohol in the apartment."

Hmmm, Maxwell thought, maybe Roy's not as strong-willed as I gave him credit for.

Roy stood as he spoke. "Look, if I'm going to do this, I don't want to slit my wrists."

"So?" Maxwell was intrigued.

"I've got a large bottle of vodka hidden in the cupboard and loads of prescription tablets. I'll take them all with the whole bottle of vodka."

Maxwell rubbed his chin as he considered this. "You'd better start writing your final letter."

CHAPTER 29

As Roy completed writing the most sickening letter of his soon-to-end life, Maxwell stood over him going through every sentence like some obsessed school teacher. He sought to ensure it carried the gravity required to affect Zac in the manner he desired. Roy read it back in his head. Tears streamed down his face, not out of fear for his own life, but in anticipation of the suffering Zac would go through if and when he read it.

Maxwell was becoming concerned at the progression of the time. He had a flight back to catch and with the letter taking much longer to complete than anticipated, time was now of the essence.

"Come on, Roy, let's get moving. Put it in the envelope," he ordered, as his impatience began to manifest itself.

Roy slipped it in and sealed it. "What's your address, Maxwell?" he asked somberly.

"Don't give me that crap, Roy. I know you've been checking up on me. You already know my address."

Without further word Roy began to write it out from memory. "You know, Maxwell, if I could find your address this easily, I'm sure anyone else could do the same. Perhaps someone you owe money to? Maybe a gangster, who'd cut you up like a fish?"

"Well yes, that is correct, but as I don't owe anyone, including any gangsters, money anymore it's not really a concern for me. In any case the movies give those guys a bad name. Trust me there's far worse people out there than them. More ruthless than even us two."

"Really? Even you?" doubted Roy as he fixed the stamp. Maxwell pointed to the tablet on the table.

"Grab that, Roy, and give it to me. I'm sure you don't really want the cops to find that here when you're gone."

Roy handed it to Maxwell. "Okay, let's get to the main event," he said grimly.

Roy left the letter on the table and walked into the bathroom. He collected a concoction of half-full prescription tablet bottles, a whole range of antidepressants and pain killers. He carried them in his arms back into the lounge for Maxwell's inspection. Maxwell refused to touch anything, so Roy had to hold them up one by one.

"Wow, that's quite the mini drugstore you've got here, Roy," he remarked. Although Maxwell was not a pharmacist, he was trained in medicine. Back when he was a practicing psychiatrist, he'd had to prescribe drugs. He certainly knew taking that collection with a bottle of vodka was more than enough to snuff out the life of his victim. Roy took the pills back into the bathroom without comment and lined up each bottle open on the rim of the bath. A quick trip to his minuscule kitchenette provided a large bottle of vodka, almost full.

"Tut, tut, Roy. I'm almost disappointed in you," Maxwell criticized.

"Well, it doesn't really matter now, does it?" Roy replied. He got into the empty bath fully clothed and began.

Maxwell stood outside, near the doorway of the bathroom. He was cautious of entering, being wary not to leave any unwanted evidence of his trip. Any investigation would be concentrated primarily in the bathroom. Not the place for Maxwell to drop his calling card.

He watched almost inquisitively as Roy placed pill after pill in his mouth and washed it down with the vodka. Suicide, an act not often witnessed, triggered a morbid fascination in Maxwell. It was something which in his career he had battled hard against his patients ever reverting to. Now here he was, watching it happen like it was a training video. Roy appeared emotionless, cold, with robotic-like qualities performing a repetitive everyday procedure. It was monotonous and almost dreary, but to Maxwell it was that very aspect that made it interesting. The psychiatrist in Maxwell could not refrain from speculating whether people undertaking overdoses of their own free will were all this tranquil in the actual act. Did the person's own realization of what they were actually doing in taking a decisive step to end their pain offer them a composed serenity, an inner peace of acceptance?

"They're all gone, Zac. Maxwell, I mean, they're gone," Roy garbled, the effects of the tablets obviously already taking place. He was practically unconscious, but still able to continue drinking away to the bottom of the bottle. The dedication of an alcoholic, discerned Maxwell.

When the last drop was consumed, Roy let the bottle drop on himself, now too weak to hold it. The bottle rolled down him and into the bottom of the bath with a loud clunk. As Maxwell monitored consciousness slipping away from Roy, he embraced mixed emotions. On one hand he experienced a God-like persona, all powerful, entirely in control of the will, fate and life of another. Yet conversely, he felt horrendous pity. Roy looked so helpless. In this man's heart was only good. Only bad decisions had brought him to Maxwell, not dire intentions. Maxwell experienced a sudden rush of remorse. It was not this man who was the bad guy. Maxwell knew he exclusively held that title.

"The evil that men do," he whispered to himself. After another twenty minutes had passed, Maxwell walked back into the lounge. Covering his hand with his sleeve he picked up the letter and placed it in his pocket next to the tablet. He then conducted a comprehensive check round the room with only his eyes, searching for any possible indication or evidence of his visit. He could see none. He had been careful to a professional standard. He had not touched anything or sat anywhere. Satisfied, he walked back towards the bathroom. Roy remained in the bath, his life slipping down the plughole.

Maxwell froze. Was Roy actually dead? He could not be definite. He wanted to check his pulse, but under no circumstances could he do that. It would almost unquestionably leave the kind of clue the cops would jump all over. He wanted to avoid even walking in the room. It was just too risky, although he had to check, just in case. Maxwell glanced at his watch. Not good, he should have left for the airport at least an hour ago. It was going to be challenging to make the flight even if he left right now. Missing it really was not an option.

As if walking on eggshells Maxwell crept in. He hovered over the bath. He could not see Roy's chest moving. All appeared dead still. The bitter vodka smell was noticeable. Maxwell leant over and positioned his ear above Roy's mouth. No breathing of any kind that he could detect. This close the pungent fragrance of the vodka was overpowering and obnoxious.

The plane. Maxwell had to leave right now. He abandoned Roy in his cast iron death bed and slipped back out of the apartment. Roy was gone now, and so must he. The letter would be posted nearby and then this grim task was concluded.

CHAPTER 30

That evening Zac was located in the office beavering away at his customary remarkable pace. His life may have been once again ripped apart as a consequence of this opportunity, but the fact that it was the career chance of a lifetime nonetheless remained. He still had a responsibility to generate the goods for Maxwell. No boss in the world was going to pay such a substantial salary and not insist on results. Zac had imagined Maxwell would have been chained to his desk day and night, forcing him to work frantically by hysterically cracking the whip. Yet since the fateful day Zac had caught Melissa with Alex, he had not witnessed Maxwell at his workstation for longer than a few minutes at a time. It certainly appeared strange to him. A two-man team was hardly sufficient as it was. He could not help but wonder what Maxwell was up to, especially after apparently leaving the house yesterday evening without word to him and not yet having returned, to his knowledge.

Zac was feeling a little neglected. In the beginning Maxwell had recommended regular sessions with him to help Zac deal with his past. Yet it was not happening. It seemed Maxwell had got the information for the program data and without delay had become a total stranger. He could at least have popped his head in from time to time to check my work, or after Melissa, check me, Zac thought to himself. He leaned back from his computer. The modest rant inside his head had broken his concentration and flow. Zac took a glance at his watch.

"Damn it," he cursed, looking at the time. "Quarter to eight." He had as usual arranged to meet Lisa at eight. For more normal relations this time, he considered with optimism. Time for a quick shower still remained. Speedily he packed up his work and left for the elevator.

As he called it, he observed it was situated at the garage level. It arrived with a ping. The doors slid open revealing an unexpected figure inside, Maxwell complete with overnight bag.

"Hi, Maxwell," Zac welcomed him enthusiastically.

"Zac," Maxwell returned the greeting.

"Just got back?" Zac asked, looking at the overnight bag as he stepped inside. Maxwell gave a simple nod by way of an answer. Zac noticed his boss seemed slightly aloof. He looked shifty and did not appear pleased to be caught in the elevator. "Where did you go?" Zac wished he had not posed the question as soon as he asked it.

"Just some business to take care of," Maxwell muttered, looking at the door as if he could not wait for it to open. Zac recognized these signs. Whatever Maxwell had done or was up to he was definitely trying to hide it. He certainly did not want to discuss it with Zac. He could tell from the body language and speech tones. If living with an alcoholic teaches you one thing, it is how to spot someone hiding what they've been up to.

Finally, the doors slid open at the living quarters' level. Maxwell stepped out of the elevator as if anxious to abscond from his temporary imprisonment with Zac.

"See you tomorrow, Zac," Maxwell said at his door, not even turning to face him. Zac watched Maxwell go and slowly exited the elevator. Zac felt positive about where Maxwell had been. He surely had been gambling again.

At just after eight, Zac entered the communal kitchen. He was surprised to discover nobody else was in the room. Usually, Lisa would be present preparing a meal for them both at this time. He had never asked her to cook for him. It was merely a routine they had fallen into. Zac contemplated that Lisa might have been held up by Maxwell's return. Maybe she also suspected his behavior was questionable. Right now, she might be giving him the third degree. Lisa was an assertive, resilient woman. She would categorically give Maxwell a piece of her mind if she assumed he was gambling again. Zac smiled to himself at the contemplation of Lisa telling Maxwell off.

Zac elected to cook the meal tonight, as she was held up. After all it was about time he took his turn. After a fleeting browse through the fridge, he plumped for cooking chicken in pasta and vegetables, mixing it with tomatoes and garlic and then placing it all in a dish, and finally grating a thick layer of cheese on top to bake in the oven.

He got underway by pouring himself a substantial measure of red wine to benefit from while he worked. It was a long time since he had last had the time and opportunity to cook a nice meal. His spirit was adventurous, and Zac experimented with an assortment of herbs in the sauce. Then his buoyancy was somewhat dulled when it occurred to Zac that the last decent meal he had cooked was for Melissa just before they left together to come here, a meal to celebrate their new life together. Zac recalled how happy he had felt at that time, for once in his life he was without a care in the world.

Sure, he considered himself really comforted by and fortunate to be with Lisa. She was remarkable, but he would give anything for Melissa to have not done the things she did. For them both to still be together, looking forward to their combined future and expectations. Zac shrugged off the sentiment and continued to cook.

Lisa had failed to arrive at the stage when Zac was loading the bake into the oven. The time had progressed to twenty to nine. This was not right, if she was unable to make it down surely she would have let him know by now? He opted to use the intercom system to quiz Lisa on her absence. Zac was apprehensive, feeling intrusive as he pressed the call button for Maxwell's private quarters. Something had to be going on for Lisa to be this late without a word. Undeniably he would be interfering in whatever they were both up to. He was certain they would fail to appreciate the interruption.

He lingered by the intercom for a long time waiting for a reply. His finger hovered above the buzz button. Should he press it once more? One of them must have heard it already. No reply must suggest they're busy, persistent buzzing was not going to help the situation.

Zac was ready to give up all anticipation of a reply, when suddenly the intercom crackled into life.

"Hello?" Maxwell's voice was casual, but at the same time was not exactly welcoming.

"Hi, it's Zac. Lisa was supposed to be meeting me at eight, but I haven't heard from her. Is she there?" Zac over explained to substantiate his intrusion.

"One second," Maxwell replied, then silence. Zac presumed he had gone to find her. With a stood-up-on-a-date look on his face, Zac waited impatiently, attempting to hide the embarrassment and discontent from himself. Finally the crackle arrived in advance of a forthcoming transmission. Regrettably for Zac was not Lisa, but Maxwell once more.

"Zac?"

"Yes," he replied, pressing the speak button.

"Sorry, but Lisa isn't feeling too good. She's asked if she can take a rain check tonight?"

Zac's fragile heart fell heavy with the news. "Yeah sure. Is she okay?" His voice sounded light and trivial, but it was obvious he was endeavoring to conceal his disappointment.

"Yes, yes. Don't worry. I'm sure she'll catch up with you tomorrow."

"Okay. Good night, Maxwell."

"Good night." And he was gone.

Zac walked solemnly back to the oven and pulled out the pasta bake. Its cheesy top had browned nicely. Zac himself was surprised at how agreeable it appeared. Shame nobody else was here to witness his accomplishment. After dishing himself out a portion he sat at the kitchen table and steadily worked his way through it. The dish was pleasantly flavored, but Zac scarcely noticed. He was unable to understand why Lisa had not even shown the courtesy of notifying him she would be absent tonight. Surely, she could have come down in the lift, even if she was ill, just to let him know. Or at the very least, what was the problem with just calling him on the intercom?

Zac could not determine if he was angry or concerned. Maybe, he considered, he was just blowing this all out of proportion. Perhaps she was merely ill, had gone to bed and not woken up until Maxwell informed her Zac was buzzing, asking for her? Then she may have just passed on the message and returned to her slumber? It seemed reasonable. Zac cursed himself for developing into such a paranoid person. The onslaught of pain and anguish in his short life seemed to be prejudicing his judgment. Not everything is a terrible event waiting to happen, he told himself, while pouring and speedily consuming another generous glass of red wine.

After covering the leftover pasta bake with tinfoil and loading the dishes in the dishwasher, Zac left the kitchen. He took a walk into the great room. As the gliding doors whirred open, Zac was reunited with that most delightful view, stunning enough to steal his breath away, every single time he was fortunate enough to gaze upon its exquisiteness and splendor. As he entered, Zac rolled the doors closed behind him. The momentum carried them together as one with a subtle thump. The moon was full tonight. Its indescribable brightness illuminated everything caught in its path in a decadent, alluring silvery radiance. The shimmering water was dancing in a sequined dress, reflecting back numerous shots and pockets of light. As if watching a large crowd within a football stadium taking thousands of pictures with flash photography, Zac stood immobile in the darkness of his elaborate observation tower, drawing in the hypnotic stimulus before him.

Eventually he switched the light on. The resultant unsympathetic glaring neon upsurge overwhelmed the view, stealing it from Zac's eyes and replacing its majesty with a reflection of the room and Zac stood within, alone, forlorn in a state of solitary vulnerability. Feeling demoralized he swiftly returned the room to its darkened tranquil majesty.

It came to him with a bang. The might of the torment within his body erupted in crescendo of anguish. The break-up of his relationship, up till then masked and postponed, now surfaced, seething and bubbling akin to molten lava. Zac broke down. Falling to the floor he wept and wept. His body twisted and arched as monstrous quantities of heartache struggled to find a way to escape. Zac's body was unable to release its pent-up anguish rapidly enough. White hot torment surged in hysterical releases, hardly allowing him to breathe. Zac suffocated on backlogged tears as he unchained the layers of concealed misery.

CHAPTER 31

Zac lay motionless in bed, wide awake, silently waiting for his alarm to ring. It was only minutes away. This was the first night of his life he could recall getting absolutely no sleep at all. Sure, he had suffered through many bad nights when his mind refused to settle, lying awake for hours, getting more and more frustrated, but he had always eventually managed to obtain some small measure of sleep. Throughout this night, though, Zac had declined the option of even attempting to sleep. The need for sleep was secondary to the requirement to stay awake and calmly work through the incessant feelings roaring in his head. As a result of the breakdown the day before, Zac now realized he had been completely unaware of the level of grief he had suffered through recent events. His objective was now to take some time out and truthfully consider what he wanted. Was it to make a new start with Lisa and form a substantially more serious relationship? Or on the other hand, he deliberated, perhaps he should give it another go with Melissa? Zac remained bitterly angry with her for the incident with Alex, but now appreciated that he missed her desperately. For all Lisa's amazing qualities, she lacked the magic which Melissa possessed. He could not be certain if that magic would emerge and intensify with Lisa if they stayed together, or whether it was exclusive to Melissa.

After a whole night of pondering, Zac was no closer to an answer. The other consideration was to actually choose neither and go it alone, just to give himself time as a single man to heal, before beginning once more. However, pursuing the single option appeared a scary prospect. He doubted his own capacity and strength for a trip down that road.

Zac sat up and switched off the alarm a minute before it was due to sadistically cut away the gentle ambiance. He tenderly touched his eyes. They were puffy and sensitive from the outburst of emotion the previous night. He rose from the bed, walking to the mirror above the bathroom sink and examined himself. Zac soon regretted it when he viewed himself. His appearance was terrible. His eyes were much worse than touch suggested. He filled the bowl with cool therapeutic water and proceeded to scoop it up in his hands and splash his face, over and over. It was a vain attempt to calm the swelling and revive himself. It was futile. Zac was a sunken void, as if a black hole was sucking him up, totally consuming him, leaving a hollowed-out man. He lacked the sadness of upset, or the anger he knew he should feel. His only feeling was a sensation of total dread, lodged deep in the pit of his stomach. Only that declined to abate. He felt nothing else. A vacant numbness, akin to a soul trapped between two dimensions, unable to prevail in either. All Zac could manage was to stare forlornly at his sodden pitiful reflection in the mirror.

The numbness dwelling within was new to Zac. Previously his life had been a rollercoaster of peaks and troughs. There had been periods when he suffered as much sadness and distress as any man could, which contrasted with great happiness and satisfaction, but never this oblivion, never this nothingness. Feeling sad was much healthier.

After his emotional outburst, after getting it all out of his system, Zac was expecting to now feel brighter and more optimistic. But no, the dread remained, knotting his stomach up, a sensation everybody feels for short periods when things are exceptionally amiss, or in anticipation of an appalling event. Much like a child feels when in trouble, sitting outside the principal's office, helplessly waiting for their destiny. Except for Zac, this was not a short-term occurrence. The sensation held strong, refusing to wither, consuming him painstakingly slowly, until he could choke on it.

His legs felt weak. He clumsily lowered himself to the

floor, lying there helpless and lost, reverting to a baby-like form, unable to move, exploring the room with only moving eyes.

"I wish I was dead," Zac whispered quietly to himself as he unwitting slipped into a state of severe depression.

Meanwhile Maxwell's position was not a great deal healthier than Zac's. The previous day's events had also repeated over and over in his mind throughout the night. Before yesterday Maxwell was at ease, positive he could handle the possible remorse to arise from the darkest elements of his evil plan. Sure, after having ripped Zac's life apart he had felt twangs of guilt, but the achievement of success easily outweighed it. The awareness of power from planning out accurately everything he intended to happen, all the things he desired his subjects to do and then watching them undertaking it exactly as intended was ruthlessly addictive. As a callously proficient puppet master he could control them at will. Although yesterday with Roy had been a big ask, he had slickly and even at times spontaneously manipulated him into following his bidding.

This morning while swimming unaccompanied, no sense of achievement or pride surfaced. Only a single question recurred. What have I done? He appreciated his responsibility was to see the concluding part of his inventive scheme through to its grisly climax, for his own well-being if nothing else, but he could take no pleasure from the final act. The whole thing had gone too far, like a runaway train hurtling down the hill. On paper it seemed extreme, but at that time Maxwell had only had his eye on the prize. He had failed entirely to consider how it would affect him as it played out, instigating these heinous acts.

Swimming was the single activity Maxwell could ordinarily undertake with an unequivocally clear mind. It was his freedom, his escape from all the burdens in life. Yet today his mind was working overtime, occupied with regret and apprehension. His conscience implored him to stop immediately, but the wheels were inescapably set in motion. Things were now out of his control. If Maxwell terminated his involvement at this stage, nothing would actually change. Except that he would also be in the shit. He had cleared a path for the boulder on the hill and had begun pushing it down the slope. If he ceased pushing now, the boulder would continue to roll by its own momentum and the force of gravity. If he attempted to get round the boulder and hamper its descent, it would certainly flatten him as well.

Zac made it to his desk, although later than intended. During his fruitless struggle to pull himself together, he had at least managed a shower and to dress himself. Nobody else was about. Zac was quite frankly relieved. He needed to get himself collected and composed. Certainly, Maxwell would be in attendance in the office today. How would he react to his highly paid and prized employee wallowing in this state, unable to produce work or even think clearly? Furthermore, Zac required time for supplementary self-assessment before he spoke to Lisa. He was truly unsure about their relationship at present. He did not feel confident about it now. Zac was not yet ready for another serious relationship. It was just too soon, yet he desperately did not want to be on his own. Emotional support was a vital requisite if last night was anything to go by.

Zac looked blankly at the computer screen. How the hell was he supposed to work in this state? He tried to focus his mind on his most applicable abilities, but all to no avail. His mind ran as blank as an empty piece of paper. Eventually he gave up on flogging the dead horse and walked to the kitchen to make himself a coffee, blindly hoping it might awaken or invigorate something in his despair. Subsequent to the boiling of the kettle, Zac opened the fridge to grab the milk. He froze at the sight of the leftover pasta bake. It yielded an upsurge of flashbacks that almost suffocated him. Yet simultaneously the numbness reasserted itself. It was odd, Zac appreciated he should be currently awash with strong emotions, but again nothing, like a hollowed-out tree. Only that knot in his stomach slowly rotting him out.

The coffee made, Zac returned to the office. His head lowered in self-pity.

"Good morning, Zac," a voice said, taking him off guard. Zac almost dropped his coffee, just about saving it with only a few droplets plummeting with suicidal force to the ground. Zac looked up to see Maxwell sat at his workstation. "Sorry, did I surprise you?"

Zac faked a smile. "Er, yeah," he replied sheepishly and placed the offending drink down on his desk. "How is Lisa feeling?"

Maxwell immediately appeared anxious, as if he had been asked a difficult question. After a squirm in his seat and a brief uncomfortable pause, he wheeled the chair back slightly from the desk and lent back in it, placing his hands behind his head.

"Zac, I'm afraid Lisa left the house last night."

Zac was taken aback. "Left where?" he asked in confusion.

"She's gone home, Zac. Lisa's not coming back. I'm very sorry."

"Why?" Zac's voice was strained and croaky.

"She left you a letter explaining why, Zac. I slipped it under your door before I came down. I didn't realize you were already down here. I feel for you, I know you'd grown quite attached to her since Melissa left." His voice was faint and concerned.

"I don't understand," Zac stated quietly, almost only to himself. Then he just stood there, reminding Maxwell of a little boy on his first day at school, not wanting to be left.

"I think it'd be better if you go up and read the note," Maxwell advised.

Zac skulked off without another word. As he waited for the elevator, he tried to make some sense out of what Maxwell had just told him. No palpable thoughts arrived, but the elevator did. Zac stepped inside and rode it up to the next level in a zombie-like state. His persona forsaken and soulless.

After unlocking and opening his door, sure enough he was greeted by an envelope on the floor. Zac picked it up and walked to the couch. Before sitting down, he took a few seconds to look at the ominous paper shroud, delaying the revealing of the letter he was dreading inside. He sat, and for a minute or two just twiddling it from the corners, round and round with his fingertips. In the fullness of time, he eventually plucked up the courage to open it and read the letter's handwritten contents.

Dear Zac,

I know this is a really shitty thing to tell you in a letter, rather than face to face. For that I'm sorry. I only intended to offer you support during your break-up with Melissa. I just wanted you to have a shoulder to cry on.

I really didn't want this kind of relationship with you. I guess I let my sympathy allow things to go too far. It's not that I don't like you, but just not in that way. I hope you can forgive me if I gave you the wrong impression.

I know if I told you this face to face it would be really awkward so I suppose that is my reason to let you down in a letter. I decided it would be better if I left the house as well because I don't want to create an atmosphere. I hope you can understand, and that everything works out okay for you.

Thinking of you
Lisa.

Zac stared blankly at the letter. What the hell was that? he mused, at long last sensing muted feelings awakening inside his muffled mind. Anger rose up within him. He felt cheated, as if hoodwinked by her. Lisa did all of the chasing, Zac thought to himself. She was the one intent on spending so much time together. It was she who had decided to remain at the house, after initially intending to stay only a few days. Lisa was the one instigating everything, requesting sexual role plays. Yet now she had the front to insinuate she never really sought any of it. A third party reading that letter, Zac considered, would come to the conclusion he was the one advocating any development in their friendship. The reality was anything but.

Zac was currently consumed with anger and rage. How dare she fob me off with this spineless letter, he thought, which ultimately neglected to give any real reasons or answers for her abrupt disappearance. He sat there and read the letter a second time. By the time he had finished his anger was already subsiding, diluting away in the oversized vacant lake within his head.

After all his recent debating on whether he wanted a relationship with Lisa, Melissa or neither, he had overlooked the possibility Lisa might not want him. The last flakes of self-confidence Zac possessed wilted and died, right there and then.

"She didn't want me," Zac whispered in a defeated tone. He faced the demons of rejection, heightened by the cold and impersonal way Lisa had chosen to end their fling. Had there been any signs? Anything at all he could recall? Zac thought back to their last few nights together. Okay the role play was a bit odd but did not offer a hint or clue that she would opt to do this. Now self-loathing flowed through his body. Zac theorized he must have done something wrong. Whatever it was, it had changed her perception of him swiftly. Perhaps he had said something to upset her without realizing. Maybe he had talked about Melissa too much. Did it make her feel inferior? He asked the questions, but no answers sprang to mind.

This was nonsensical. Zac knew he had to speak to Lisa. The letter was ridiculous in way of explanation. The contents were a poor excuse for a rationalization. It was clear that whatever reason she had for leaving the house and him, it was not divulged in that letter. If he had done something wrong, he needed to know. Zac could not be satisfied leaving it like this. To find the truth, Zac had to overcome one significant predicament. He had never actually gotten around to recording her number in his phone. Living in the same house, this was the first time he had required it. His only real option for overcoming this quandary was to convince Maxwell to pass it on to him. This was certainly a problem in itself. Maxwell would almost definitely be able to shed some more light on the situation, if he were so inclined, but for him to give Zac her number without permission was unlikely. His loyalty would and should lie with her, she was family after all. Zac the employee and former boyfriend of the girl who cost Maxwell his handyman and swimming coach would not be able to compete. The blood thicker than water analogy sprang to his mind. Yet Zac prayed Maxwell could be persuaded to sympathize at her inadequate explanation. He was his only hope to find out the truth.

Zac stood up to take the letter down to Maxwell and convey his position, but his legs weakened yet again, and he reverted back to his sitting position. In the subsequent few moments, the anxiousness diminished, all but the knot. His mindset returned to its former numb state, an inescapable web fusing itself within him. All Zac deemed himself capable of was just to remain sitting on the couch. It was such a peculiar sensation, as if he no longer retained control of his limbs, thoughts and feelings. By now he did not even care about going back down to the office. His natural inclination, to push through this for the sake of his job and career, was now ineffective, they no longer concerned him. At this point he bizarrely lost interest in even Lisa or the letter. Zac remaining breathing, but from his own perspective he was dead inside. He slowly lay down and adopted the fetus position on his couch, staring into the oblivion.

CHAPTER 32

Zac awoke with a start. For a couple of seconds, he could not ascertain exactly where he was. In due course he realized he was still on the couch. Only now it was dark outside. Zac's last memory was lying down there at mid-morning. He searched in a flustered state to locate the current time. His eyes met the clock on the wall. Through the darkness it revealed the time was just gone six. Zac hardly dared consider what Maxwell would be thinking about his unanticipated absence. Zac reasoned that Maxwell was aware he was very fragile and being dumped out of the blue would have a detrimental effect, but surely he would have expected Zac to return to work within a reasonable time frame, or if not, at least ask to take the rest of the day off. This was hardly justification to go absent without leave.

Zac provided his eyes with a quick rub to clear away the bleariness. He felt more with it than before, but hardly alive and kicking. His lack of sleep had been impairing his ability to function. However, by no means did he feel normal, but at least well enough to locate Maxwell and endeavor to express regret for this misdemeanor. He encountered heaviness in his body as he rose, his lethargic legs struggling to carry him to the elevator.

In what seemed no time at all, Zac was at the office door. He was unsure if Maxwell would still be in attendance, but at least if he was, Zac could meet him on more neutral ground. He did not relish the idea of knocking on the door of Maxwell's private quarters. Maxwell apparently was guarded of his personal space and the only other option of contacting him through the intercom, was even less favorable. It was not an appropriate mode to convey this kind of conversation.

He opened the door and peered round hesitantly. Sure

enough Maxwell was present.

"Hi, Maxwell," Zac expressed weakly as he crossed the threshold.

Maxwell completely failed to acknowledge him, continuing to tap away at his keyboard, eyes transfixed on the screen. It was as if Zac was an invisible mute. Uncomfortably he walked over to Maxwell and lingered shamefacedly for him to look up. After what seemed an eternity, he did. Zac was suddenly stuck for words. Maxwell just looked at him, showing no sign of throwing Zac a lifeline.

"Maxwell…" he stuttered nervously. "I'm sorry for missing today. The letter kinda took me by surprise. I needed some time to get myself together. I didn't sleep well last night, and I guess I just shut my eyes for a second and unintentionally fell asleep."

Maxwell nodded with a stern face, before returning his eyes to the monitor and recommencing his typing. Zac just stood awkwardly waiting for a response. Maxwell hung him out to dry for some time before countering his excuse.

"I'm sure you're fully aware of the pressure I'm under to meet deadlines for this project." He continued to type as he spoke. "Lisa informed me you're now aware we have backers for this venture. They are the ones calling the shots. They say 'jump' and we say 'how high?' If we get behind the schedule they're not going to be interested in our excuses. Certainly not in our personal problems, are they?"

"No," Zac limply agreed, his head hanging down in shame.

"I think it's fair for me to expect a level of consistency from you, no matter what else is going on in your life, considering the large amount of money I pay you." Maxwell's voice was cold and authoritative. "Do you agree?"

"Yes."

"Okay. Let's not dwell on what's done. Get back to work and try to recover some of the time you lost today."

"Sorry, Maxwell," Zac walked back to his desk feeling Maxwell had been a bit over-the-top.

He did actually manage to direct his concentration on his work. Not anywhere near full capacity, but certainly better than nothing. Maxwell toiled away in silence at his workstation. Zac desperately wanted to enquire what he knew about Lisa's abandonment. But as impatient as Zac was feeling, now was not the right time to be asking awkward questions and trying to extract guarded information. Zac could sense the tension within the room. It was emitting from Maxwell, something was unquestionably distressing his equilibrium. Zac discerned there was more to it than losing an important employee for the day.

Zac could not help but ponder this. He deduced two possible explanations. One, Maxwell had been gambling again and lost heavily. Or two, Maxwell and Lisa had had some kind of bust-up, which would have doubtlessly contributed to her leaving so abruptly. Then just as likely, a combination of the two. Zac sustained his typing, but every so often shot Maxwell a fleeting look from the corner of his eye. There was definitely something wrong with him. Now Zac was aware of it, the signs were clear and comprehensive. He was not his normal faultless self. His smoothness protracted to reveal corners and sharp edges.

Then with a metaphorical slap a much darker consideration hit him. If Maxwell had bombed on an illicit gambling trip, he would be undeniably angry and irritated before returning to the house. He was hardly whistling a tune when Zac had encountered him in the elevator. Lisa might well have realized he had been gambling and Zac was sure she would have confronted him about it. Then what? Maybe they had one almighty fight? And then?

Zac ceased typing as his blood ran cold. Lisa had not made it down for dinner, not even to cancel their prearranged meeting. She had neglected to even speak on the intercom when he called her. Then the subsequent day, for no reason whatsoever, she left the house, apparently never to return, dumping Zac in the process, again as far as Zac could deduce, with no rationale. Her only attempt to contact Zac since

Maxwell's return was the handwritten letter. In spite of that, it occurred to Zac that he did not actually know what her handwriting looked like. In reality anybody could have written the letter.

Zac looked yet again at Maxwell. He appeared at odds for sure. He was incontrovertibly failing to disclose something, something big. Zac returned his eyes to the screen. He had to be mistaken, surely? The consideration vigorously bouncing around in his mind seemed so far-fetched. Was all his misfortune clouding his judgment and playing games with his mind?

Zac took a moment to gather his thoughts. He determined on reflection these were just a collection of random suspicions. To even entertain such wild theories, he needed more to go on. He elected to obtain a sample of Maxwell's handwriting to compare to the letter as his first line of enquiry. Zac sifted through some printouts by his desk. They were a collection of sub-routines that needed plotting into the main program body. Zac had set them aside a few days ago to invite Maxwell to jot down his desired locations for them. Without further contemplation he jumped up out of his chair and grabbed some of the sheets.

"Sorry, Maxwell, do you have a second just to route these for me. I need their locations to insert them into the main program. I need to test it'll work in the way I think it will before I can proceed."

Maxwell could not have looked any less enthusiastic about the request. "Okay, Zac, pass them here," he grumbled. Zac handed them across quickly, before he had time to change his mind. Maxwell looked impassively at the jumble of letters and numbers. "Right, what's this one?" Maxwell asked pointing at the first homeless fragment of computer jargon.

Zac had been set a mountain pile of work by Maxwell, writing these monotonous routines, instructing the computer on what it was required to do on any certain input. When setting the workload Maxwell had briefly described what he required each one to accomplish when activated. Zac would then complete the hard part and write a program to make it happen. Simply put, if the user of the program entered in x then y the computer recognized it was obliged to activate z; in reality, a very complex flowchart. Zac explained to Maxwell which subroutine was which. Maxwell then noted down the specific location of the flowchart it needed to be incorporated into.

When Maxwell had finished, Zac expressed thanks and sat back down. He commenced studying the recorded locations. Not for arrangement purposes, but to see if he recognized the writing, to examine its equivalence to the text in the "Dear John" letter Zac had received that morning.

It was hopeless. Zac was attempting to evaluate it from memory, but he had read the letter in such a state it could have been written in hieroglyphics for all he could recall. The letter was upstairs, on the couch of his living quarters. The only way he could sensibly compare the two was to have the printout notes and the letter both together.

If Zac had been shrewder, he would have determined his only real option was to wait patiently for Maxwell to finish off whatever he was doing and retire back to his living quarters. Only then could he complete his comparison without raising suspicion. Unfortunately, Zac was not a patient man. He acted on gut instinct, reacting there and then. Often it was directly in the heat of the moment, sometimes for better, but often to his detriment. For now at least his inner numbness had abated. Zac was engaged in purpose. He had a mission to focus on.

Zac checked the time. It was just gone eight. He looked over at Maxwell, it did not look as if he was going anywhere for some time to come. Discreetly and with caution Zac folded up some of the printouts and, keeping half an eye on Maxwell, he slipped them into his trouser pocket. Maxwell did not look round or appear to notice Zac's undercover actions.

"I could do with a coffee before I get into this. Do you want one, Maxwell?" Zac lied as innocuously as he could manage.

"Er, yeah. Thanks."

Zac got up and walked out of the room, shutting the door behind him. He dashed into the kitchen, filled the kettle and turned it on. Next, he hurried to the elevator. He was thankful to find the elevator car on the same level. The doors slid open immediately he called it, buying him a few extra precious seconds. Upon reaching the living quarters he rushed into his complex. With steely determination etched on his face, Zac unfolded the letter together with the printouts. He stood in his room astounded. For no handwriting expert was required to attend this examination. The two sets were a precise match.

CHAPTER 33

Zac carried in the two coffees. He tried to feign casualness, but in actuality was nothing like it. Maxwell had discovered his poker face was not infallible, but Zac appeared as if he had gone "all in" on a jack high. Maxwell made the distinction immediately.

"You look like you've seen a ghost," he observed as Zac handed him his drink.

"Do I?" Zac panicked, looking for an excuse. "Sorry. I guess I'm still upset about everything," he covered, trying to disguise his awareness of his own assumptions.

"It's not your fault, you know." Maxwell spoke in a much softer voice than his earlier address.

"I don't understand why she has gone. The letter didn't really explain anything," Zac baited Maxwell, looking for more cracks in the lie.

He rubbed his chin. "It wasn't the best way for her to tell you, I must admit. I'm really disappointed in her."

"What did she say to you, Maxwell? Did she explain to you the reasons?" Zac waited impatiently to hear Maxwell come up with an excuse.

"Take a seat," Maxwell instructed. Zac did so. Maxwell sighed before continuing. "Lisa revealed to me she had accidentally gotten into a relationship with you. She had the intention of trying to look out for you and be a good friend. My opinion is that her leaving in this fashion was cowardly, but the fact remains, she doesn't want you in that way. Even if she were present it would still be so. I'm sorry. I know that's never a nice thing to be told. To be honest with you, Zac, she should have told you face to face, but I think it's a good thing she's gone. Apart from the obvious development of an atmosphere, it would do you both no good to be in each other's life, especially when I need you and your work to be at the top of your game."

Zac did not trust a word of it. He knew Maxwell was lying. However, he was beginning to doubt his own worst suspicions, they just seemed too extreme. It was just that at present, those qualms were the only avenues that made sense to Zac. He needed to compile more evidence but had no clue how to obtain it. He elected to bide his time for the moment. It was not as if he could just point his finger at Maxwell and straight out accuse him of murdering his niece. That was not an option until he was wholeheartedly certain. It was not the kind of accusation they could just move past if Zac was wide of the mark.

"Okay, Maxwell. I understand," Zac dully replied, turning back to his computer and continuing his work. Zac once again simulated working, his mind was locked on more pressing issues.

A short time passed by without incident, when an unexpected sound broke the muted clacking of computer keys. A dog was barking. In fact, Buster was barking somewhere within the house. Zac and Maxwell turned to look at each other.

"Buster?" Zac asked him in a bemused tone. Now Maxwell was the one who looked like he had seen a ghost. Zac watched him, waiting for a response.

Maxwell squirmed and took his time about it. "Yes, that's Buster," he stated as if the dog's presence was no surprise.

Zac started to get up from his seat. Maybe he had got it all completely wrong. Lisa had come back. Perhaps she had changed her mind and realized she did want Zac after all. Zac had entertained doubts himself overnight, but after losing her, he would now cross hot coals to get back with her.

"Sit down, Zac," Maxwell sternly instructed.

Zac froze, half out of his chair. He looked Maxwell directly in the eyes. At that moment he grasped Lisa had not returned. He sat back down and waited for an explanation.

"Lisa left Buster behind. She said you needed a friend here. She thought you'd benefit more from his company than she would." Maxwell hesitated for a few seconds before continuing. It was obvious to Zac he was just struggling to fabricate his next untruth. "I was going to tell you after you'd read the letter, but, well, you didn't come back down."

Zac had serious misgivings about the entire rationalization. "So why didn't you tell me when I did come back down? It was nearly three hours ago." Zac was determined to fully utilize this unanticipated development.

"Because I needed you to do some work. If I told you as soon as you'd finally reappeared, you would have gone straight back up to see him." If Maxwell was spouting spontaneous propaganda, he was doing a good job. Zac could not argue with his reasoning, but he tried anyway.

"So, Lisa just left her dog behind? Who she loves, and who loves her back?" Zac's tone came across with a degree or two of cynicism.

"Yes, she did," Maxwell replied firmly. "She's not as attached to that dog as you think, Zac. She's left him here several times before. Her customary reasoning is because she's worried about me being lonely. The truth of the matter is she likes being a dog owner, but then gets bored with all the responsibility of it. So, every so often she offloads the poor pooch onto someone else with a valiant reason, but it's really just so she can have a break."

"Oh right," Zac answered, mildly convinced. The explanation did seem sort of plausible. Yet that was not the case for Maxwell's immediate reaction. The panic in his face when Buster bestowed a tell-tale bark was indisputable and Zac knew it.

"He's still in my quarters. Looking at the time and his vocal efforts I'd say he's well overdue for a walk and some attention. I guess that's what he trying to tell us," Maxwell said, attempting to lighten the mood. "Stay here a minute and I'll go and fetch him."

Zac nodded in agreement and then Maxwell left.

He must have killed her, Zac thought to himself. He was definitely lying about her non-attendance. It seemed the only explanation for him to need to concoct this fantasy story. What was he going to do now? Zac thought. He could call the police, probably not the most cunning of his options. He had no actual hard evidence, only circumstantial. He was not in the position to give them anything credible to go on. Their only option would be to interrogate Maxwell about it, and Zac knew he would effortlessly lie his way out the situation. He would probably be able to turn it around to make Zac look like he was a barmy ex-boyfriend making unfounded accusations.

Another realistic alternative was to enlighten Roy of his suspicions. Yet this might also worsen the situation rather than actually help. From the emails Roy had sent him, he was obviously undertaking an operation to bring Maxwell down. Zac speculated that Roy now felt inadequate as a father-figure in his life and bringing Maxwell down would kill two birds with one stone. He would eradicate the competition and redeem himself in the process.

Attempting to inform him of this grave, but loosely presumed event would certainly encourage Roy to jump in with both feet, single-minded in taking Maxwell out in a blaze of glory. It was reasonable to suggest Roy was more than qualified to handle a matter as delicate as this with tact and astuteness, but Zac had to doubt his father's mental stability. Trying to cope with the torrent of retaliation Maxwell would categorically throw back might be beyond him at the present time.

Zac ardently did not want to be responsible for propelling his father back over the edge, causing him another breakdown or sending him back to the deathly enslavement to the bottle. Maxwell was an extraordinarily formidable and dominant man in mental strength. Guilty or not, any kind of threat offered by Roy would cause him to come out fighting. Zac's confidence in his father's ability to cope under such a fearsome reprisal was slight, any way he looked at it, the option just did not stack up.

The final choice open to Zac was to work alone, seeking to unearth some concrete irrefutable evidence all by himself. He would have to keep his mouth shut for now. He evaluated it in his mind. He was confident Maxwell did not yet suspect he was on to him. Zac recognized this advantage in terms of his opportunity and flexibility to snoop around and locate whatever was available to find. Zac settled on this; at this point in time, it was the best option.

The office door opened and in burst an excited Buster. He knew it was "walkies" time and was adorably carrying his lead in his mouth.

"Hello, boy," Zac cheerfully greeted his canine companion. He vigorously stroked him before taking the lead and giving him a cuddle. Maxwell stood in the doorway watching them both.

"Take good care of him, Zac, and don't let him distract you from your work tomorrow. Okay?"

"Yeah, sure," Zac replied as Buster attempted to lick his entire face.

"I'm calling it a night. I suggest you give Buster a walk and then do the same, so you're fresh for tomorrow," Maxwell instructed with a light tone, but Zac was aware he meant it.

"Okay, Maxwell. See you tomorrow."

"Good night, Zac." With that Maxwell was gone.

The night air was freezing. It hit Zac the moment he left the garage side door, as he was led along by the ever-eager Buster. The poor dog had already been forced to wait an extra twenty minutes while Zac swiftly rummaged around Maxwell's workstation. He had failed to uncover anything, but the search was light. Zac was petrified of moving too much around in case Maxwell noticed the next day.

A more intensive search followed in the garage. Zac did not know what he was looking for. Blood maybe, or a concealed weapon? A body wrapped in a rolled-up carpet? Nothing transpired but sexy cars and an empty space where Lisa's used to park. Zac even attempted to enlist the assistance of Buster, hopeful he would sniff out the make-or-break piece of evidence in a Lassie-type scenario. However, this was not the movies, and upon Zac's command to "go find," Buster provided him with a baffled look, finally walking to the outside door, subtly hinting he had business of his own to take care of.

The moment Zac stepped out into the cold he could see his breath in front of him. The chilliness hung unnervingly in the air, until it was pushed along with sporadic gusts of wind. Walking down the mutely lit driveway, Zac had to blow into his hands to protect them from the acute temperature variation until they acclimatized.

Zac took the decision that a quick walk down the drive and back would suffice. That was all Buster was going to enjoy tonight. As they took to the steepest part of the decline down to the road, Zac noticed an inconspicuous turning off the main driveway disappearing around a lofty group of trees. He had never noticed it before, but then before he was not looking for the inconspicuous. The track was gloomy, moving away from the serenity of the drive lights which only bathed their intimate vicinity in cool inoffensive radiance. The supplementary light from the near full moon sporadically filtered through the trees giving the path a sinister, threatening appearance, as if its shadowy bleakness came straight out of a stereotypical horror movie. The further Zac advanced past it down the drive, the greater his vantage around the wooden obstructions increased.

Yet before he had moved along enough to distinguish anything of significance the trees on the other side of the track began passing into view and frustratingly his line of sight waned away. Zac and Buster soon reached the bottom of the drive which opened out onto the deserted highway. Again, but for the assistance of the moon's silvery glowing carpet, nothing would be visible. Not a chance of finding the civilization of streetlamps out here in nowhere. Zac gazed left and right. Nothing. No sign of life of any kind. Unmitigated silence only eliminated by the whirl of the wind and the hypnotic rustling of the trees, whispering their hushed secrets. Zac sought to acquire a tranquility in the delicate swish, but in reality, it unnerved him.

Turning back up the hill he headed toward the house, picking up his pace slightly as his already heightened senses became spooked. Several times he looked over his shoulder, half-expecting Maxwell or someone to jump out of the trees wielding a large spade. Soon Zac returned to the opening of the track. It intrigued and terrified him in equal measures. The rational part of his mind understood the potential merits of investigating it further. All that was missing was the huge flashing neon sign reading "vital clue this way." The remainder of his psyche was absolutely freaking out, urgently wishing to return to the protection and safety of the house. The irony being, if Zac's suspicions were correct, he was irrefutably out of harm's way here in the darkness and the shadows.

From nowhere a surge of courageousness engulfed his body and he took confidently to the rocky track, leading to, god knew where? Even Buster seemed reluctant, sensing Zac's quickly restoring uneasiness. No longer tugging constantly on the lead, he walked tentatively as close to his new master as possible, almost tripping Zac up a few times. In next to no time Zac's view of the lit driveway completely disappeared, as the track rounded the trees leading him into complete isolation. Zac considered if he were a killer stalking an innocent dog-walker this was the point at which he would launch his attack. But seconds after Zac had abandoned sight of apparent safety, a concealed building began to come into view. Swallowing the lump in his throat, Zac pressed on towards it. On closer inspection he could distinguish it was a large wooden lockup. The white paint was flaky and old, completely in contrast to the house. It was rightfully hidden away, like a scar on this exquisite development. As Zac approached the large access doors, a bulky padlock was visible, securing them shut. He still gave the doors a half-hearted tug, but they were more rigid and unyielding than the impression this dilapidated and oversized shed conveyed.

Zac froze suddenly. He thought he heard something. Was it a branch breaking in the surrounding area? He attempted to search around, moving only his eyes, remaining assassin-like silent. Buster, however, did not oblige, sniffing the ground and ambling around apprehensively. Zac could not see anything or anyone, and reasoned that Buster would have at least reacted, if not barked if someone was approaching. He was desperate just to run. To go at full pelt back to the house, but he had to see this through.

Tensely he wandered around the building. No more doors existed, but he located a single small window. Peering through, even with his eyes trained to the darkness it was near impossible to make anything out. The window itself was grimy, encrusted with smudged dirt. To make things worse, the glass was covered with a tightly meshed wire that further hampered his line of sight. Its position barely permitted any of the silvery moonlight through into the unknown. After another momentary check around his vicinity, Zac cupped his hands up against the tarnished glass. Something large was definitely in there, but Zac was unable to make it out. It did not appear to be Lisa's jeep; its height and shape was wrong. Zac placed his coat sleeve on the window and rubbed it firmly. Upon resuming his portal through cupped hands, he tried again. The view was slightly improved, and using his mind's natural shape recognition capacity, he finally determined it was a speed boat.

"Shit," Zac cursed under his breath. Then his eyes caught something else, just beyond the speed boat. Once more it was large, but even more difficult to make out. This time its general shape could be a match to Lisa's jeep, but something was different. Zac continued studying it, repositioning his face up and down the glass. For a time even his fears of the surrounding darkness abated, his full-blown brainpower locked on deciphering the faint unlit object.

Then all at once it came to Zac. It was a car-shaped object, only covered with a thick dark tarpaulin. Its silhouette outline was the correct shape to be the jeep, but for all Zac's efforts it was impossible to be sure. Buster began to let out a whiny cry, evidently the sinister environment was becoming too much for him to endure. Zac offered the surrounding trees a final scrutiny. He too, had reached his limit. He hauled on the lead and commenced a gentle jog back to the sanctuary of the driveway. Buster needed no encouragement and led the way.

Zac took one last glance at the remote ominous boatshed as it disappeared from view. He would come back tomorrow, when the alleviation of daylight would aid his exploration. Zac had to know what the unsolved covered object was. He genuinely hoped he was mistaken, and it was not Lisa's jeep. In fact, he wished to be completely wrong about everything. Although the likelihood of her ever reoccupying his life was slim, he at least wanted to know she was safe and well and, at the very least, alive.

CHAPTER 34

The next morning Zac awoke with a jolt. The alarm was boisterously ringing. Zac got up and made his way to the bathroom. He did not feel agreeable at all. Zac had experienced anxiety even when getting back inside the house the night before, eager to get to the deceptive safety of his living quarters and lock the door behind him. Once there, for the briefest of time he found respite. But fear had soon caught up with him as it occurred to him that Maxwell would surely have several sets of keys for his living complex. Even the marvelous Alex had had a set whilst he was employed at the house, allowing him access to replace groceries and see to Melissa.

Zac did have to concede that Alex had done a good job with the groceries. The fridge was always stocked full, and everything was fresh. Now it was nearly bare. Lisa had taken care of the communal supplies but overlooked Zac's kitchen. The few pitiful items remaining in the fridge were now stale or perished. Zac had cast his mind back to the pasta bake in the downstairs fridge as he endeavored to lodge a chair up against the door handle as a security measure. Then he considered all that had gone wrong since cooking it. After that Zac no longer craved it. So, with no appetite and a lack of food inside him he had regarded his best prospect of getting some sleep that night was to sink a bottle of wine before bed.

It had worked admirably then, but not so much now. His head felt full of rocks. Every time he moved, they all banged about. At the top of his agenda was a large drink of water and two pain killers.

Zac checked the time. Experience told him they would take a good twenty minutes to fully activate and begin to alleviate his self-inflicted symptoms. Although to function entirely normally at least half an hour was required. The time was half past seven. That was fine, he could allow himself half an hour to chill and have breakfast, then give Buster another quick walk up and down the drive, using the opportunity to reinvestigate the mysterious large object inside the lockup using the luxury of daylight in his quest.

Zac took a fleeting shower, literally for the purpose of freshening up rather than cleaning himself. After dressing he made his way into the kitchen and started making a coffee. He was beginning to feel more human, the tablets taking effect already.

Soon Zac was sitting down in front of the television with a bowl of healthy cereal and in direct contrast, his caffeine benevolent beverage. He was not really watching the television; his mind was reconstructing the events of the last few days. Everything that had occurred in that time frame was abnormal and severe. Zac knew he could do without all the hassle and dejectedly wished he could just have a quiet and uneventful life. Yet it never seemed to work out that way. Something, usually out of his control, always transpired to thwart it.

Reconsidering his suspicions of Maxwell, Zac contemplated what might have happened to Lisa. In the cold light of day, yesterday's theories all seemed somewhat far-fetched. He reminded himself he was not living in a movie. This was real life. He contemplated all the issues making him skeptical. Everything but the handwriting on the letter now materialized as coincidental. Like Maxwell's expression of culpability when Buster unexpectedly revealed his presence with his bark. He could simply have looked guilty because he had not mentioned the dog, which by his own account he was instructed to pass onto Zac's care. Furthermore, if Maxwell had actually killed Lisa and then taken all this effort to fashion her just leaving of her own accord, why would Maxwell leave her dog in the house to give the game away? He would have indisputably taken care of Buster as well.

The only sincerely damning item in the story was the handwritten letter from Lisa which appeared to be in Maxwell's handwriting. How could that phenomenon have occurred? Zac measured the possibility that they had very similar handwriting, but it was stretching things, and he knew it. The handwriting was an exact match, the probability they had exactly the same style was too much of a coincidence to even consider. It had to be Maxwell who had written it, but for what possible reason?

Zac finished his cereal and placed the bowl on the table. For a few brief moments he took in the show on the television. A group of teenagers were attempting to water ski. It was clearly their first go at the skillful sport as they were all falling into the water as soon as the speedboat launched them off the jetty. They plainly loved it, despite repeated soakings, laughing and joking, all of them persistently smiling through drenched faces. Zac encountered a twang of sentiment. He longed for his teenage years to have resembled theirs, having a good time messing around, learning all about the world and sharing it with friends.

The sentiment washed away, Zac returned to the here and now. It was believable to contemplate that Lisa had been set on leaving without offering him any explanation of any kind. Maxwell might have perceived it was too cruel and elected to forge a letter, allegedly from her, just to give Zac an explanation of her disappearance. It materialized as a prospect, yet it did not entirely fit. If Maxwell truly did write the letter, why express the letter in such a negative light toward Zac? Surely, he could have indicated the rationale was Lisa's own problems and shortcomings, rather than his?

Even with that consideration, the potential remained that Maxwell had written it to benefit Zac, but felt honored to only replicate her actual reasons, therefore minimizing the deception. The reality was Zac was only speculating. At the present time he could probably conjure up a thousand different reasons for the who, why and when. Zac had to return to the deserted lockup and get a second look through the window.

Buster was ready for his walk, so Zac quickly loaded the bowl and cup in the dishwasher and took his canine companion down to the garage. Zac stepped out into the cool crisp fresh air. Inhaling deeply and then releasing the breath in a measured consistent flow, observing the clouds of condensed moisture harmonically float away and disperse in the sky. Even though the painkillers were now fully activated his head was nonetheless still feeling fuzzy and unpleasant. But the refreshing air seemed to be rejuvenating and with every breath he moved closer to his usual self. Buster keenly led the way, pulling tightly on his lead. Zac felt regretful for restraining him, but the road at the bottom, although quiet, was also very fast. The odd vehicle passing usually did so at a remarkable speed. He certainly did not want to be responsible for any harm coming Buster's way.

The morning winter sun was low in the sky. Zac had to place his hand over his eyes to protect himself from a direct view of its formidable rays. Wearing a pair of sunglasses would have been the sensible option. He pressed on, dazzled. As Zac approached the opening, he could understand in the cold light of day why it was so easy to miss. The entrance was exceptionally tight, with closely neighboring hefty and oversized trees either side. Unless you were looking across adjacent to the insignificant break in the tree line you would be unable to see it. Before or after the turning, the trees appeared to follow each other without interruption, swallowing the existence of the track completely. Viewing the trees from a car moving at speed, it just would not be noticeable.

Zac and Buster began walking up the track. Everything looked familiar, yet in daylight unrecognizable from the previous night. It still had its overwhelming impression of comprehensive isolation, but it had lost its threatening and bleak edge. The upshot was Zac walked along with a sense of safety and reassurance, not the trepidation he had experienced the night before.

Soon enough the large white building came into view,

albeit calling it white in daylight seemed charitable. More a green-come-gray, where the weather and dirt had taken their toll. Zac approached the small window. As anticipated, it was much lighter inside, largely due to the scruffy dirt laden glass portal. Even with the obstructive grime plastered on it, the sunlight poured through, almost fashioning a searchlight inside. The beam was assisted by an array of cracks and holes in the warped wood, permitting small specks of light through. Although insignificant individually, their aggregate effect was more than adequate for Zac's purpose. He put his hands up to the window and peered through the glass. To his absolute disgust, he could see that something had dramatically changed inside.

CHAPTER 35

Zac peered through the clouded glass in a state of distress. The speedboat remained in its former position, nearest the window. It emerged impressively now Zac was afforded an enhanced view, but the tarpaulin that covered the vehicle, if that is what it was, had been roughly folded on the floor leaving an empty space in its place. Whatever it had been concealing had vanished.

"What the hell?" Zac questioned himself. His primary disbelief was now being substituted with frustration. There was no way to know if it was Lisa's jeep. Zac had lost his only lead.

He hastily looked around the remainder of the shed in the hope of unearthing any more clues, but there was nothing else of interest. He peeled himself away from the glass and walked back around to the doors. The padlock was securely locked. Then glancing down at the muddy track, Zac found a consolation clue. Fresh tire tracks. Although the ground was mostly dry and frozen solid, sporadic patches of wetter soft mud remained. One considerable patch directly outside the door had the imprint of tire marks in it. There was no way for Zac to determine if they were caused by Lisa's jeep, but at least he now knew for sure it had been a vehicle under the tarpaulin. Someone must have taken it between the time that Zac was here last night and before he had returned. The question still begged, who, why and when?

Assuming it was Lisa's jeep, and it was Maxwell who had moved it, he must have carried it out because he was frankly worried Zac would see it. Did it then signify Maxwell knew he had been up here snooping around last night? Had he been following him?

Zac rapidly returned to the previous night's state of high

alert. He nervously looked all around him and listened for any unidentified sounds. Whatever had happened here, Zac chose to make it a priority to get back to the driveway immediately. He did not feel at all safe in this total seclusion. Tugging Buster into following suit he actually sprinted until he was safely on the solid ground.

Once within his self-elected protection zone he caught his breath. Zac was still suffering and feeling far too delicate for full-pelt running. Although only a short distance the acute exertion was sufficient to give rise to a nauseous sensation. His mind was beleaguered by the awareness of being watched. He looked back at the house, half expecting to spot a dark mysterious figure at the window staring back at him. Only nobody was there. Once more Zac looked all around himself. He could see nothing untoward, but his escalating paranoia screamed at him that there were many positions to hide in the surrounding overgrowth and trees. Yet again he gawped back at the house, this time vigilantly checking each window individually. The reflection on the glass hindered his view and obstructed him from being sure. He squinted, attempting to focus his sight beyond the obscurity. Still nothing. Yet he just could not shake the feeling.

Then suddenly in the window of the communal kitchen something shifted. Zac only caught it in the corner of his eye, but a shadow had disappeared, moving back into the room from the glass. He stared intensely at the window but could see no further movement. Doubt began creeping into his mind. Had he seen a shadow? Was it just his intellect playing tricks on him?

Eventually his mind was pulled back away from the house. Buster was tugging hard on his lead, obviously having grown bored of waiting. He had decided to make the point by practically throttling himself, choking on the collar as he yanked with all his might. Zac accordingly obliged and started walking down the drive, looking back at the house for moving shadows with virtually every step.

It rapidly became a fruitless task. Zac realized he had now

moved too far away from the house to distinguish anything shifting about. Zac centered his interest back on his immediate area. He continued to look for clues, something, anything, that might help.

Upon reaching the road a new-found source entered into the equation. The post box had received mail. Zac wandered over and released its small metal opening exposing a bounty of correspondence. The metal spring-shut door was unpleasantly cold to touch. Frozen drips of condensation clung to the metal box like miniature transparent leeches. Zac pulled out the substantial stack of letters. He sifted through it, not precisely sure what he expected to find. The majority of correspondence came in regular bill form, typed addresses exhibited through clear plastic windows. They were unlikely to churn out anything of consequence.

After filtering through a third of the mail Zac came across a handwritten letter, addressed to him. The handwriting was instantly recognizable. He seemed to be progressing into being an expert on that subject. It was, without a doubt, his father's. A glance at the postmark from San Francisco confirmed it. Zac pulled it out and placed it separately under his arm. He hurriedly checked through the remaining letters and placed them back in the box and returned his attention to the only letter of interest.

Without hesitation Zac ripped the envelope open and pulled out the letter, imagining it would be supplementary scandalous filth on his boss. He trusted nothing relating to his current suspicions, but at the present time anything giving Zac a more complete picture of Maxwell was welcome. Unfolding the paper, he began to read its grizzly and macabre contents. Like a sudden darkness looming overhead he took in the words of his father. The self-loathing of his life, of all the torture and grief his only child had caused him. How it had reached the point where he could see no alternative but to end it all.

Zac read the whole letter. He calmly placed it back in the envelope and began walking quietly towards the house. Buster merrily trotted beside him, unaware of the harrowing information his temporary master had just received. Inside Zac, his brain had switched to a form of safety mode. It did not permit this new information to be processed. He continued up the driveway as if everything was normal. Zac shielded himself with shock. His body remained functioning, but nobody was driving at the wheel.

He reached the door into the garage. Once he opened it, Buster ran through. Zac staggered inside letting go of the lead and subsequently collapsed to the floor. It was now beginning to take effect. His breathing became forced, his stomach started to contract. For a few moments he had the urge to vomit. Slowly the inclination faded. Zac lay, devoid of thought and function, in a heap just inside the doorway. Somewhere in him a function tried to obtain influence and regenerate his rational coherence. To try and manage this written account his father had submitted to him. However, the overwhelming predominance inside him squashed it down to nothing. It resulted in Zac lying crippled on the cold hard floor gasping for air. He was finally brought back by Buster who had returned to investigate Zac's collapse. The dog licked his face. Zac initially pushed him away, trying to save himself from the slobbery confrontation. Isolated thoughts progressively began to filter in. It was not real, Zac told himself. The letter is not real. Somebody faked it, just like Lisa's letter. His pa must still be alive, on the case, locating the dirt on Maxwell and ready to bring him down. Zac laughed hysterically. This was not true. His pa was still very much alive.

"He's not dead," Zac told Buster optimistically while still lying on the coldness of the floor. "My pa is okay. He doesn't blame anything that happened on me." Buster listened intently, but without a clue of what Zac was saying. For all he understood Zac might as well be reading out the shopping list. "My pa is back on the road to recovery, you know. He's had a bad time, but he's out the other side. He just wants to get by and give his son some support, like any good father would. It's not too much for him to ask for, is it?" Zac sat up and pulled Buster in, furnishing him with a hearty embrace.

Already the denial phase was coming to an end and beginning to degrade. Zac started to sob, with his head still buried in Buster's fur. For a fair amount of time Zac lacked any conscious thoughts, but soon enough the realization of the truth began to trickle in. The trickle turned into a small stream, enough to make his heart pound so loud he could hear it in his ears. Before long the stream had become a flood, a raging waterway ripping away at the walls Zac had quickly built up in his mind. He knew this time the letter could not be forged. Zac knew his father's handwriting well. He tried to comprehend where any of this had come from. Roy had not been building up to the moment. There was no substantiation of a slow decline to rock bottom and ending it all. If anything, the complete opposite was true, Roy was presently in the best mental and physical shape he had been in since Amy had died all those years ago. Why would Roy go through the intense personal hardship of pulling himself out of the gutter and recovering his life to just go and commit suicide out of the blue?

Zac reread the letter, trying to ascertain some reasonable motivation for his timing. The first time Zac had read it, all he had been able to take in was his father telling him he was ending it all. The remainder of the text was only read on autopilot and none of the content had sunk in. Now though, on his second attempt the full horrendous subject matter, pointing the finger of blame squarely on Zac's shoulders, was hard to take. Zac experienced a mixture of feelings. Hardened anger at acquiring unmitigated blame, blended with acute guilt, contemplating he was unequivocally responsible for killing yet another parent.

Zac's anger raged. Was this really how his pa had felt? He had always insisted none of the appalling incidents that had occurred was Zac's fault. In reality Zac did not fully believe his father bore no blame towards him, but the reassurance he took from his father saying he did not attribute culpability to him was an overwhelming reprieve. Nevertheless, the issue had often haunted Zac. He just could not get past his involvement in his mother's death, no matter how indirect it was. He was the reason for the trip to the zoo and it was he who had placed the camera on the back window shelf. That was the catalyst for every single grave event that had followed.

Following his session with Maxwell, Zac had come to the conclusion he would never get past blaming himself, but was able to live with that condemnation, purely because he his father never cast blame on him. Now though, it was all turned on its head with the last confession of a dying man. Why would his father throw this on him? Had he been experiencing this revulsion all this time? Burying it deep inside, until it besieged him and detonated in this rant and act of sheer hatred, all directed like a focused beam of light straight at his son.

The fact remained, if this letter was authentic, it meant his father was dead. It became too much for Zac to tolerate. His head spun, while his stomach contracted. The force of the nausea escalated, until the only thought Zac could manage was, he was going to throw up. Incapable of standing he just turned his head away from Buster and let it spew out onto the floor.

For several retches Zac could not breathe or even focus his eyes. All he heard was a slurred and distorted version of his bile splattering on the concrete. The physical vomiting soon ended, but the wooziness continued. Zac managed to focus briefly, only to be presented with partly digested cereal all over the floor and himself. After that came nothing but blackness. The warped sounds of Buster's panting slowly melted away. Zac collapsed backwards, smacking the back of his head on the cold hard unforgiving floor, passing clean out.

CHAPTER 36

Zac opened his eyes. He was lying on a couch in the communal kitchen. He spent a minute trying to recollect how he arrived there. It was soon deferred, as a more immediate throbbing pain at the back of his head became perceptible. Zac brought his hand round to touch it. The wound was bloody and sore. He felt a towel placed under his head, he guessed to soak up the blood and protect the injury. He delicately felt his way around the gash. It appeared to be quite big, but he could not be sure.

Zac sat up, feeling dazed and confused, his head pounded even more with the small exertion. Before Zac was able to summon up a clear thought about how he got here, Maxwell approached him. He had been in the room the whole time, but only now made his presence known.

"Hi, Zac, how are you?" he asked in a concerned voice.

Zac just looked back at him vacantly. "What happened?" he asked instead of answering the question. His requirement to understand was dominating all his thoughts. Maxwell pulled a heartfelt expression and sat himself on the broad arm of the couch Zac was sitting on.

"I found you passed out, just inside the garage. Despite your head injury you were still breathing normally so I took you up in the elevator and cleaned you up a bit." As Maxwell finished the sentence Zac became aware of the strong pungent smell of vomit on his clothes. He could not recall being sick though.

"I passed out?" Zac asked, screwing his face up in confusion.

"You'd just had some bad news. Don't you remember it?" Maxwell probed.

Zac thought for a while, but everything was hazy in his

mind. Then all at once it flooded back to him as if a tidal wave had broken, crashing his brain back into full function. It signaled the activation of a catastrophic storm within Zac's head. Maxwell scrutinized the glazed frozen look on Zac's exterior, recognizing it was concealing torture of an apocalyptic scale transpiring from within him.

"You remember, Zac?"

"Yes," he whispered back as his outward façade began to crumble. His eyes began to well up and his body started shaking uncontrollably. Maxwell placed a reassuring hand on Zac's shoulder.

"I'm very sorry, Zac. I read the letter when I found you. It is such an awful thing. I phoned the San Francisco police department and told them what Roy had claimed he'd done. They said they'd send a unit straight out to check his apartment. They'll phone back here as soon as they can tell us anything."

The phone was sitting on the table in front of Zac. Neither said anything further for a while, they both sat motionless, staring at the phone. Eventually Zac picked it up.

"I'm going to try phoning his apartment just in case…" Zac did not know how to finish the sentence. He nervously dialed the number and waited. As the phone began ringing Zac located an inner confidence, he really believed his father would pick up the phone. Considering the present point of time in the day, and the fact that his father was working nights, he was sure that he would be greeted by a sleepy hello. With each unanswered ring of the phone his confidence diminished. Finally the answer phone kicked in. Zac felt his heart sink. Not only as his father failed to answer the phone at the time of day he was most likely to be home, but also because Zac was suddenly listening to his voice on the greeting message. The voice of his father, who he did not know was dead or alive. This was possibly the last time he would ever hear his voice. Then before Zac knew it the beep sounded. Zac became stuck for words, but finally managed to throw out a sentence.

"Hi, Pa. When you get this message can you ring me back

at Maxwell's house immediately?"

Zac put the phone back down on the table with a thump. He glanced at Maxwell, who gave his shoulders a shrug. There was not much he could say. Zac looked down and re-examined his clothes. Not a pretty sight. He sought after a shower to clean himself up and wash his stinging wound. At the very least, to get out of his defiled clothes. But Zac could not leave. He needed to be there when the police phoned back.

Some time passed before Zac broke the silence.

"You read the letter?" he asked.

Maxwell sighed and got up off the couch arm. "Coffee?"

Zac nodded.

Maxwell walked over to the kitchen area and turned the kettle on. He then leant across the adjacent counter to face Zac. "That was a horrible letter, Zac. There's no denying that."

Zac nodded again and looked out of the window. Maxwell resumed making the coffees. Zac was struck by the view out of the kitchen area down the driveway. He could have easily been observed disappearing off it and heading toward the boatshed, even from where he sat now on the couch. He had not previously studied the immediate view out the window. The vista was just so biased to the awe-inspiring lake. He tried to look for the roof of the shed, but the trees proved too dense around it. Maxwell returned with the coffees in hand. After placing them on the table he took a seat across from Zac this time.

"Pa said everything was all my fault." Zac's voice trembled with the gravity of the declaration.

"Yes, he did. I'm very sorry for you that he wrote that, but you have to realize it may well not be true."

"The letter?" Zac blurted out.

"No. Sorry, not the letter. I meant the reasons he gave. Firstly, when someone is in such a terrible state of mind, they have often lost sight of reality. They may say things they don't actually mean."

Zac gave Maxwell an unimpressed look, he was not buying that.

"Okay to put it in another more blunt and detailed way, if someone is prepared to kill themselves, they will be trapped in an entirely self-centered world. When that far gone they are past even caring about their closest loved ones. They have way too much shit going on in their head for anybody else's concerns or feelings to matter. Now to be clear, this doesn't apply to the cry for help suicide attempts where people want to be found and saved. In that situation their mind is in a completely other place. When someone is genuinely suicidal their perspective is limited to and only focused on themselves. If they allowed themselves to consider others and how the act would affect them, there is little chance none but the most unfeeling of people could go through with it." Maxwell paused and took a sip of his coffee.

"Pa isn't callous," Zac voiced in his father's defense.

"Exactly. If he was on that dire route to ending it all your father would have to cut all his mental and emotional ties. As we've spoken about previously, you're really all he had left in this world. It would be extremely difficult for him to sever that tie with you. I'm certain the only way your father was able to achieve that was to attack your relationship in his own mind. Give himself a reason to hate and remove you from his conscience. To do this he chose to blame all of the past shit directly on you. Do you see that?"

Zac hung his head down and nodded. "I guess so," he murmured.

"On top of that fact another consideration applies. You've stated Roy was a strong and proud man."

"Yes."

"Right, well if he desired to take his own life so badly, which he would judge as a weak and cowardly option, he would require more than desire. He would need a motivation, something to take the prominence off his own spineless decision. So he made the reason you, he made himself hate the only person he still loved. He falsely created you in his mind as the person who drove, even forced, him into this horrible act. Basically, he used you, nothing more and nothing less. It wasn't that he actually held you responsible for it all, in the real sense of the feeling."

Zac considered this. It was hard to be convinced his father would use him in such an abhorrent way, but at the same time, everything Maxwell had just laid out on the table did in reality make perfect sense.

Zac was about to offer a response, when the phone began to ring. It startled Zac, anticipating this was the call that would confirm his worst fears. He looked at Maxwell, who gestured with his eyes to answer it. Zac was thrown into a state of apprehension. He desperately wished to pick the phone up and answer it, but was held back, displaying an odd trait of human nature, that it was almost better to torment yourself with the uncertainty of not knowing, than to know for sure what you dread most.

"Answer it, Zac," Maxwell encouraged.

It then occurred to Zac it might be his father safe and sound responding to his answer phone message. Swallowing a large lump in his throat, Zac picked up the phone and pressed the answer button. "Hello?" he shakily asked after a short delay.

"Hi, is that Zac?" a voice responded. Zac was agonized. It was not his father's voice. However, the voice did sound familiar, Zac vaguely recognized it from somewhere.

"Yes, speaking."

"Hi, this is Gene." That was the voice he had acknowledged. It was Roy's last partner when in the police.

"Gene?" Zac was confused as to why Gene was calling him.

"Yeah, I transferred to the San Francisco police department a couple of months ago. When this was reported I requested to phone you as we know each other," Gene enlightened him. "Some of my colleagues went to check out your father's apartment, after... er ... I think it was your boss ... had informed us of the letter. The apartment manager had a key and let them in." Gene paused a second. Zac discerned a pause was not a good sign. "I'm very sorry, Zac."

"No," Zac whispered back down the phone.

"I'm afraid we found your father inside. It appears he took an overdose. He's been gone a few days. There was nothing we could do." Gene's voice trailed off.

"My pa?" Zac sobbed quietly. Although prepared for this news, it still hit him with an immense pulverizing thump. He could almost see the last remaining tower of sanctuary in his life crumbling away all around him. Only blackness appeared on the road ahead.

"Zac?" Gene asked.

"Yeah?" he delicately replied.

"I want you to listen to me very carefully. I don't want you to do anything for the time being. I'm going to come and get you myself and bring you back here. I'll help you with all the arrangements." Gene's voice was caring, yet stern and commanding at the same time.

"What? Why?" Gene's generosity seemed a bit excessive.

"Look, there's more you need to know. Just sit tight and wait for me to get to you, okay? All will become clear then. Don't speak to anyone about this, not even Maxwell. Just trust me on this and please don't do anything stupid."

"I don't understand." Zac was now distraught and totally confused by the ambiguous comments Gene was making.

"I will explain. In the meantime, promise me you're not going to do anything stupid."

"Okay, I promise," Zac believed he understood what Gene meant by anything stupid. All the things he said were very peculiar. And explain about what?

"Is your boss there, Zac?"

"He is." Zac looked up at Maxwell, who sat leaning forward on the couch trying to understand the one side of the conversation audible to him.

"I want you to put him on the phone."

"Okay."

"And, Zac, once again just sit tight and wait for me. Everything will be okay, trust me on this."

Zac said goodbye and passed the phone to Maxwell, who

looked confused he was being offered it. Zac sat in anger and resentment at the suggestion everything would be okay. What did he know? Nothing was okay. It never would be again. Who was he to suggest otherwise?

"Hello?" Maxwell nervously answered. Zac watched him from his private strop. Maxwell did not really say or ask anything, he only responded with a series of yes and no answers to whatever Gene was saying to him. Then Maxwell read him the address of the house, obviously for Gene to get there.

It was somewhat bizarre that Gene was going to come all the way to the house and get him. Surely, Zac thought, he was capable of getting on a flight unescorted. However, he really did not care about such minor details. They diminished into nothing as Zac became trapped within a personal bubble of grief.

CHAPTER 37

Zac lay on his bed wrapped only in a towel. After the telephone call he had immediately returned to his living quarters and removed his soiled clothing. The bump on the back of his head was tender and had left lumps of dried blood in his hair.

The shower had facilitated the cleaning of his body but had done nothing for his soul. The numbness had returned. Zac now lay frozen, devoid of thought and emotion. No outward outburst or even a tear came. He was limp and lifeless.

After a while haphazard and unsystematic thoughts began popping into his head. What a mess, he pondered. My whole life is a complete fucking mess. Why has Pa done this to me? With each thought and consideration, Zac's numbness waned, and anger and frustration crept in. Buster lay on the floor beside Zac. He turned over on the bed to peer down at his only ally.

"It doesn't matter what I do, Buster," he told him, with a tear of aggravation beginning to well in his eye. "Everything in my life turns to shit." The lone tear wound down his cheek. "I'm cursed. I can't go on living with it constantly happening. Jesus, I wish I was dead," he softly implored, now with a current of individual tears streaming down. "If I died now, who would miss me?" Suitably timed with the comment, Buster lifted his head and looked back at Zac. He let out a tearful laugh. "Okay, you would." He reached out his hand and affectionately patted him on the head.

Zac sighed heavily, then rolled back into the middle of the large bed and patted the mattress. Buster did not require a second invitation and inelegantly jumped up next to Zac.

"I guess Melissa would as well, but that's it. Lisa doesn't

care and I'm only Maxwell's employee. He only cares because I'm an investment. Our relationship doesn't bridge beyond that." Zac briefly recalled his suspicions about Maxwell and Lisa, but in the current climate far-fetched notions like the one he had entertained now faded into insignificance. Zac's plate was more than full with his own problems.

Besides, at present he was particularly appreciative of Maxwell. Without his justification of why his father blamed everything on him, Zac would have felt far worse. It is a horrendous affair to learn your father has taken his life, but that is small potatoes when compared to learning it is entirely your fault. This was not to say Zac totally believed him, but the explanation did make more sense than Roy suddenly revealing this was the way he had always felt about Zac and had concealed it entirely all this time.

Furthermore, if his father had been harboring all this resentment, it was surely not possible they could have come so far in rebuilding their relationship, after Roy had quit drinking and become a reasonable person. At that point it was Roy who had done all the running and bridge building. Initially Zac had been reluctant to accept his advances, truly fearful of being hurt again. His father was a persistent man and had worked hard at mending old wounds right up to the point where he had killed himself. After all that, could he really have been clandestinely holding Zac accountable for everything? Yet the further Zac considered these aspects, the more problematical it became for him to understand why Roy had killed himself. Something was missing to make the equation add up.

It was still too soon for Zac to grieve. He had not yet reached that stage. For now, he needed answers. To have a chance of figuring out what was absent, Zac decided Maxwell's help would be his best option. Maybe in his expert capacity, he could determine the missing piece of the enigma.

Zac got up off the bed, leaving Buster there to doze and hastily got dressed. Clothes on, he stroked Buster, then left to find Maxwell and hopefully fill in some blanks.

CHAPTER 38

Zac searched the office first. Nobody. He walked across to the kitchen. It was empty. Finally, he tried the great room, but again, no sign of Maxwell. Zac returned to the elevator and headed down to the pool.

Sure enough he heard the sound of water splashing as soon as the doors opened. He peered around to observe a fish-like Maxwell cutting through the water. Zac decided it was not the best time to disturb him. Besides the fact that Zac did not feel at ease in this room after what had happened, he understood Maxwell had problems of his own. Yesterday, after clearly spelling out to Zac the pressure he was under from his investors, Maxwell was about to lose his only employee.

Of course, Maxwell had neglected to mention this it in light of the situation, but he would surely be worrying about how the fallout of Roy's actions would affect him. Maxwell would be anticipating Zac to return after the funeral and continue working, but how effective he would be was a different matter completely. Especially as they would immediately be playing catch-up on the few weeks lost out of the schedule.

Zac stepped back into the elevator and returned to the office floor. He entered the kitchen and paced around for a while, not really knowing what to do with himself. He was unsure when Gene was going to arrive, and all this waiting was driving him mad. Eventually Zac decided he would have a go at completing some work. It might help take his mind off things. Besides, anything he could achieve now would relieve pressure on him when he returned.

Zac entered the office and clicked his computer on. Whilst still standing he glanced over at Maxwell's workstation. By the keyboard a file was open. Zac could see the exposed sheets of paper were filled with handwritten text. If only by way of duty to his concern for Lisa's well-being, Zac decided to take a look.

He promptly stepped over to the door and verified he was alone. The hallway was deserted. With no further hesitation he crept stealthily over to Maxwell's desk and without touching anything began to read.

What Zac had discovered to his horror was a written account of everything Maxwell had explained to Zac concerning the reasons for his father's claims. How in his father's perception Zac was responsible for all the tragedy in his life and then ultimately, the motivation for his suicide. Maxwell's inscription continued. He was fearful of Zac's ability to manage the gravity of the information. After explaining that the rationale detailed in a suicide note was often the only accurate indication of why someone actually killed themselves, especially if they were trapped in a web a denial, it went on to read:

... the suicide note is frequently the only time the victim can be strictly honest, principally if it results in implicating someone very close to them, a person who the sufferer could not bear to know the truth if they were still alive. It is more of an act of confession than an explanation.

Zac read on again with his heart pounding so loud it was thumping in his ears. Maxwell had written:

Clearly Roy completely blames Zac for instigating a chain of catastrophic events. Without question the governing basis for his alcohol abuse stemmed from endeavoring to block out the revulsion he subsequently held for his son. It is apparent from Zac's earlier testimony that alcohol was a direct contribution, if not the solitary cause that Roy shot an innocent child dead whilst on duty. Roy would have been unable to avert his anger and loss from magnifying the notion of blame towards his son.

I suspect the net consequence of Roy recovering from his alcohol dependency was that he became incarcerated with his perception of abhorrence towards his son. I seized the opportunity at a vital early stage of his acceptance to convince Zac his father did not in reality hold him responsible, and the suicide letter was not a true reflection of his attitude. This step was imperative as I personally fear if Zac understood the reality of the situation he might well be at risk of a total breakdown, manifesting itself in self harm or even as an upshot, becoming suicidal himself.

"You're not wrong," Zac uttered at Maxwell's printed qualms. Now he knew the truth and it had hit hard. He walked out of the room without any further consideration.

Zac found himself outside the house, all alone and walking down the driveway. He was unaware of his destination, and incapable of controlling the self-loathing and guilt speeding around his head like race cars on a track, each car representing an array of appalling self-deliberations, such as hate and fury. They constantly battled to take the lead and to have control of his thoughts. Any wishes of reason or hope were either stuck in the pits or had crashed out of the race in a dramatic fireball a long time ago.

He reached the bottom of the drive and crossed the road without even looking. He no longer cared. If he was fortunate enough to be hit by a truck, splattering him all over the road surface, it would be all over. He would be liberated from his despondent life of misery. Even if he went to hell for the suffering he had caused his father, Zac did not care. That place could not offer anything worse than this life had bequeathed him.

Soon he had negotiated the steep banking and was once again reunited with the flipside of the trials and tribulations of life – its occasional unremitting majesty. In this case, the awe-inspiring lake before him. Despite one of nature's best shots, Zac's steel casing of dismal self-aversion did not even dent. At the top of his voice, he screamed out a terrorizing cry. Water birds floating on top of the icy oasis directly took flight, spooked by the power and volume of the exclamation. Zac continued down the gentle decline, back to the bench where he had first met Lisa. He helped himself to the empty seat and stared out, expressionless, across the lake. This time no reprieve could save him. Here he was, all alone, unhealable and inconsolable. But still ready to take his destiny into his own hands. To just swim out into the freezing lake would be so easy. The icy water would quickly steal away his breath and strength. Its speed was a welcome virtue, to exhaust him quickly. Then finally the arctic liquid would overwhelm and consume him.

Zac had read somewhere that the only unpleasant element in the act of drowning was fighting the urge to breathe. Once you have permitted the fluid into your lungs it becomes painless and serene. Slowly, you slip away into unconsciousness and ultimately death. Zac did not expect to fight it when the time came, he would welcome the watery invasion to defeat his breathing capabilities. Sitting on the bench he relished the prospect of conquering fate's power and control in destroying him in this life.

Maxwell shut the file that had done so much damage. He hoped and prayed it would be enough. This role he was undertaking had been a dire commitment since Roy's death. It was going too far, and he longed for no further part in it. Yet at the same time he was aware he had a responsibility to finish the job off. At the very least Maxwell did not want to contemplate the consequence to his own life if he did just walk away.

As much as he hated it, he was now trapped like a rat. His only reprieve being that the whole thing was very nearly over. Despite his reservations, Maxwell took solace in his competence in handling it beautifully, pulling the impossible out of the hat, yet again. He had been fully aware that the suicide note would arrive today. After all, he had posted it. He had ensured that Zac received the information in the most devastating way possible. The mechanism Maxwell used had been tailored for Zac, to maximize the damage of the incident, including the way in which Maxwell had explained it all away as not being Roy's real feelings and his father needing to blame Zac in order to enable himself to carry out the act. Giving him a lifeline, only to snatch it away by allowing Zac to discover the truth for himself. For him to then understand that Maxwell had only covered for Roy because he was so worried about Zac's stability. Putting him in a position where the end results left Zac with no doubt as to where his father's complete and unadulterated blame lay.

Maxwell had observed Zac reading the file. When Zac had checked for him down at the pool, Maxwell had been aware of his presence. In the water he had listened for the ding signifying the elevator doors were to open. The moment Zac took the elevator back up to the office floor, Maxwell had vacated the pool and raced up the back steps to his private quarters to find the surveillance monitors in his private office. There, still dripping with chlorine-treated water, he had observed Zac reading every painstaking word from Maxwell's planted bogus report. He could almost feel the pain and anguish rising in his latest victim's body. After Zac had vacated the house, Maxwell watched him walking lifelessly and despondently down the driveway. Clearly, he was heading for the lake.

To Maxwell it was like completing a dark and disturbing, yet beautiful, work of art. He was torn between the significance of his accomplished masterpiece and haunted by its disconcerting content. However his emotions lay, he did not have any doubt the grand finale was imminent. If Zac unwittingly followed his plan it would be all over in more ways than one. The outcome would leave Maxwell free and clear, and able to get on with his life. To build himself a new one, a real second chance.

He identified he needed to take one imperative vow from this episode in his life – to never gamble again. He thought of Roy, the hopeless alcoholic. He could only look down at his decayed memory. Transformed from a highly respected man, a hero to the many people he had helped to protect all those years ago. At his concluding moment he had become a first-rate loser. A piece of trash, everything Maxwell despised in other humans, so weak and now – dead. Maxwell told himself he should not feel guilty. He was doing the world a favor, just one less of life's pieces of scum roaming the streets. Now he was dead, who would miss him? Zac would, of course, but not for much longer. Zac had mentioned Roy had a brother, so maybe he would miss the man? Or understandably he might be relieved.

Maxwell did not want to become that man. The contemplation terrified him, chasing him in his sleep. It was difficult to admit to himself, but in actuality he knew in his heart of hearts he already was. Yet now he had grafted, jumping through a series of ethical rings to earn himself a second bite of the cherry. To then go and throw all that effort away at the poker table, would in Maxwell's personal opinion make him indisputably worse than Roy.

All Roy had wanted was a second chance, but a quick fix option was not open to him. The only way back was a prolonged grueling climb, the accolade for reaching the summit was at best a subsidiary relationship with his only child. No wonder, Maxwell empathized to himself, Roy was once again drinking. Maxwell realized he also could never be strong enough to accomplish the ascent up that mental gradient to only fulfill a compromised goal.

Maxwell opened the bottom drawer on his desk, and while seated bent down to lift up a stack of paperwork. He proceeded to slide the incriminating file in under it. Now the evidence was suitably concealed all there was left for Maxwell to do was wait. Returning back up from the drawer he heard a click right in front of his head. He rose slowly to bring his eye level above the desk. Maxwell found himself staring straight down the barrel of a gun.

CHAPTER 39

In absolute horror Maxwell glared past the deadly end of the handgun, aimed directly at his head. The figure threateningly situated in front of Maxwell was the last person he had expected to ever see again, let alone aiming a pistol at him.

"Hi, Ryan," Maxwell said in a calm, affable tone. After one look in Ryan's eyes, which were still bruised from Zac's vicious assault, but healing, Maxwell determined he was in grave danger. Being able to read so much from a person's eyes gave him a chance to be a step ahead. A skill he first learned in his psychiatrist's office but perfected in the poker rooms of Vegas. Understanding the integral fashion in which they shifted and moved. The pattern of blinking, even the measure of time and manner they looked away after a period of direct eye contact. With many players, their own excitement of a favorable hand or their inward tension during a bluff was entirely decipherable in their eyes. Maxwell's forte was detecting diminutive pupil dilations during the revelation of the flop, turn or river cards. The chink in his armor was players who quite within their rights wore dark sunglasses to screen these tell-tale reactions. It robbed Maxwell of his advantage and he hated it. Having built so much emphasis on reading other players' eyes it would even affect his own game. If one player at a table of eight was sporting them and doing well, it was sufficient to throw Maxwell off his strategy, making him vulnerable not only to the player in the shades, but to the whole table. It was an Achilles heel that had cost him an awful lot of money.

In the present though, Ryan was stood before him, his eyes naked and there for anybody to read as they stared fixately at Maxwell. His eyes divulged only one intent. Maxwell knew unless he played this in precisely the correct way, he would end up getting shot.

"Ryan, can I ask you what the problem is?" His voice was open as if he had nothing to hide.

Ryan readjusted his feet slightly but did not answer.

"Ryan, how can I help you, if you won't tell me what's wrong?"

"I don't need help," he sternly replied. "Not from you anyway."

"Okay. Well, I'm guessing you're not back here for a job reference, so tell me what it is you do want." The entire time Maxwell spoke, his brain was whirring like a supercomputer, trying to establish Ryan's motive for this confrontation, whilst simultaneously endeavoring to plan several moves ahead, incorporating all possible permutations and variables. To bolster this process, he required Ryan to talk, buying him time and giving answers.

"I'm here because I'm putting a stop to this." Ryan's voice was filled with the conviction he had demonstrated to himself whilst rehearsing this confrontation in front of the mirror. Maxwell did not respond, as he wanted Ryan to continue. "I know more than you think, Maxwell. I know what you're trying to achieve. I'm aware you're planning to force Zac's father into committing suicide and then going to manipulate Zac into doing the same."

While Maxwell's outward response was unmoved, inwardly he panicked. How the hell could Ryan know this? Maxwell had only explained the part of the plan involving Ryan to him. He had departed in a battered state straight afterward. It was not possible for him to have acquired this information. Only Lisa and he knew the full extent of the significantly darker parts of the scheme that were to follow. How could Ryan have learned this? One possible leak was obviously Lisa, but Maxwell knew she would not have divulged this facet of the plan. Maxwell had absolutely no doubts about that.

On the plus side, Ryan appeared unaware Roy was already

dead, and Zac was about to follow suit. No matter how Ryan had found out about it all, his motive for this defiance was clear. He was here to save them.

"Why on earth would you suggest something so absurd?" Maxwell answered him in a patronizing fashion. It was essential for him to steer Ryan to reveal his source.

"I'm suggesting it because it's the truth, Maxwell."

"Uh huh," Maxwell replied in a child-like mockery. It was critical to frustrate Ryan, although he had to be cautious as a gun was pointing at his head. Maxwell could tell he had practiced what he was going to say, being watchful not to divulge too much. If he could pull Ryan off his self-manufactured tracks, it would make it easier to extract the elements Maxwell needed. He would almost certainly reveal far more if he had to justify his accusations. It was a dexterous approach, but it fell short of the grade, Ryan could see straight through it.

"I know what you're doing, Maxwell. You're trying to trick me into telling you how I know, aren't you?" Maxwell simply shrugged his shoulders. "Well don't worry. Seeing as I'm holding the gun, I'll tell you the mistake you made." Keeping the pistol trained on Maxwell, Ryan walked over to an empty workstation and wheeled a chair back over in front of his adversary and took a seat.

"After Zac rightfully beat the shit out of me for what I did with Melissa, Lisa tended to my wounds in your private study." Maxwell swallowed hard. "After she left me to recover and wait for you to sort out my flight back to LA, I got to feeling quite bad about the whole thing. I wanted to know how Zac and Melissa were, so I decided to use the hidden CCTV to check on them. Now, as you know, the access in my own room was limited only to the rooms Zac and Melissa used. The access in your private quarters, however, enabled me to view any room of my choosing. I ended up watching you and Lisa discussing the whole appalling strategy."

Maxwell shifted agitatedly around in his seat, angry at his own incompetence.

"Of course, I kept my mouth shut," Ryan continued. "I was scared for my own life. Initially I was just glad to get out alive, but soon enough I realized I could not permit you to go ahead and coax two people into killing themselves."

Maxwell's face became despondent. He had understood where Ryan was going the instant he mentioned being left alone in his private quarters. After a bout of early anger directed inwardly, Maxwell's attentions were then concentrated solely on discovering an escape route from this dispute. Somehow Maxwell had to shift the balance of power. Ryan had the gun and was firmly in control. He was the current chip leader. The odds were firmly stacked in his favor.

"Ryan, let me ask you a single question, if I may?"

Ryan nodded consent.

"Why are you here right now?"

"To stop you, Maxwell," Ryan answered, without hesitation.

Maxwell embarked on a risky strategy, he was going all in. "Ryan, I'll be honest, you're too late for Roy, Zac's father. He's already gone. An overdose, of all things."

Ryan, looking immediately flustered, returned his gun back to Maxwell's eye line, aiming directly at his head.

"However, you can still save Zac, but you need to be quick."

Ryan's body steadied, but Maxwell read the whole masked reaction in his eyes. "Zac is in a very concerning state right now. He walked out of here and down to the lake about an hour ago. He hasn't returned yet. Who knows, unless you reach him right now, he may never?"

Ryan was definitely wavering now. Even the hand holding the gun was shaking. Yet Maxwell was intrigued to observe puzzlement forming on the young man's face.

"You're lying," he retaliated angrily.

"Oh, am I? Zac found out about his father this morning. He left him a suicide note saying it was all Zac's fault. I don't think he took it well. I have to say I'm bothered about him being all alone with his thoughts at that lake. Aren't you?"

Ryan could make no sense of this but was aware he had to make a decision. Right or wrong, he needed to choose. Experience told him not to trust Maxwell. One thing he did know was that Maxwell was attempting to goad him into leaving and going to the lake. There was no way he would have divulged that, unless he actually wanted Ryan to wander off down there. Ryan decided it was a trap. He made his decision.

"I'm going nowhere," he informed Maxwell. But as Ryan looked back at his eyes, he could see something was amiss. Maxwell was staring straight past Ryan, at a point behind him. Ryan was nervous of investigating, knowing full well that it was one of the oldest and most desperate tricks in the book to try and distract your assailant in order to try and make a grab for the weapon. However, it was not that blatant deception Maxwell was endeavoring to throw. Before Ryan knew anything, it was too late. The tables turned full circle. It developed into Ryan's turn to sit under aim. He knew the second he sensed the cold metal object jab against the back of his head. A hand reached past and seized the gun from his grasp. Ryan now had the chance to sweat under the threat of lethal persuasion.

CHAPTER 40

Zac remained inhabiting the seat of the bench, before the watery edge. He was caught as a moon trapped between the two gravitational pulls of neighboring planets. On the one hand, swimming out into the icy lake as the sky darkened around him was an easy escape. On the other, taking into account others in his life, it was not the freely permissible option he wished. It had nothing to with Zac not being ready to give up on life. It lay further than that, in his inability to give up his own selflessness regarding the feelings of others, or more accurately, concerning just one other. At this point in time only Melissa counted to Zac.

He told himself over and over she did not care, how could she after what had happened? Yet all the self-convincing failed to alter what Zac knew was the truth. Melissa would be devastated if he did anything like this. He understood she still frantically wanted him back, to right her wrongs. For whatever reason she had for cheating on him with Alex, Zac had to concede she had immediately realized what a terrible mistake she had made. It was not as if she had chosen to leave Zac for him, she had simply misconstrued her own feelings. Plainly it would be devastating for her if Zac did kill himself.

He might have been angry with Melissa, but nevertheless he loved her dearly. Zac did not want to hang this mentally scarring injury on her person. At this point, out here, he was unable to construct a suicide note. If he took the preference of ending it all, he wanted Melissa to be certain in entirely unambiguous terms that at root she was not to blame. Without the presence of a note, Melissa would naturally shoulder it on herself. Zac would be liable to pull her into the same nightmare he was currently residing in. Yet deliberating on all these specifics did not induce a decision to go back. Zac had no aspirations about rejoining a life that gave only suffering in misfortune and took everything pleasantly enchanting. He no longer wished for any part of it.

Aside from Melissa, he had nothing to care about. He would be unshackled from all the current agony and all the anticipated grief he felt assured was to befall him. Yes, he even considered it a cowardly act, but what would he care afterwards, when he was dead? Zac would be free, either someplace else, leading a newborn existence in a new world or nowhere at all, his soul swallowed up in the great infinity. Whichever came to pass he would no longer be here.

Ryan had always envisioned showing strength and bravery in an armed offensive against himself. It stemmed from a local theatre production he had starred in back in his hometown. Ryan had played a gritty fearless cop, who had a villain pull a gun on him, just as at present. Within his character's persona he was courageous and decisive. Prior to the villain taking a strong position with his newly exposed firearm, Ryan had wrestled the gun clean from him. It was a theatrical challenge, to convey to the audience precisely what was occurring when contesting for the gun as soon as the outlaw had publicized its existence, yet as always Ryan had demonstrated the effortless ability to illustrate clearly to the audience the narrative's rapid sequence of events. But all that was acting. This was real life with real bullets, where he would be forever dead, not just until the conclusion of the scene. The prospect of valor in engineering a move to turn the tables materialized as a less attractive option. In actuality Ryan was in disbelief of the fear coursing through his veins. He was frozen like a rabbit caught between two headlights, incapable of moving a muscle. Ryan could only do nothing, the literal opposite of what he had envisaged himself accomplishing.

The unknown assailant gradually wheeled around into

Ryan's immobile gaze. He might have guessed who Maxwell's unidentified savior was.

"Lisa?" he questioned in bewilderment as she emerged into view.

"Enough with the fictitious names crap," she barked. "Call me Sarah. That's my real name." From her tone Ryan appreciated she was extremely angry. She obviously did not welcome his assistance in terminating this dark, psychotic free-for-all. "Why are you back here? You're going to ruin everything," she screamed so violently at him minuscule flails of saliva spurted out of her mouth.

"Ryan heard about the rest of the plan on the surveillance cameras before leaving. He has come to put a stop to it," Maxwell informed Sarah. Despite his tell-tale antics, his expression suggested nearly as much uneasiness as Ryan. Although petrified, Ryan managed to speak.

"Sarah, this man is insane. Yes, I did come to stop him, it's not too late. Please think about the seriousness of the situation." It occurred to Ryan that between Sarah and himself they could maintain control over Maxwell. As long as he was unable to get possession of a gun, Ryan was in reasonable safety. "Look, I can't let this happen. I'm sure deep down you do not want it to either. If it's getting paid you're worried about then you can have all the money I took for my part. I really don't want it after all this."

Ryan's plea plainly amused Sarah. She laughed in a shrill unbecoming cackle. "Oh, Ryan, you're so naïve. If you hadn't just completely fucked everything up, I'd probably feel sorry for you."

Ryan looked at Sarah bemused, then to Maxwell before returning his perplexed expression back to Sarah. He did not have a clue what she was getting at, but a feeling of missing background to all this grew within him.

"God, Ryan, are you really that slow? I'm not working for Maxwell, you idiot, he works for me." The words hit Ryan with such force they might as well have been bullets from the gun. He looked once more at Maxwell, who sat at his desk unmoved. At that instance Ryan became aware Maxwell was just as anxious and afraid. The reality hit, he was the weak and she was the strong.

"But, I thought Maxwell...?" Ryan stammered not even completing his own question.

"Yeah, but you thought wrong," Sarah answered to the issue Ryan was unable to query. "I let you think Maxwell was the one in power, purely because it suited the situation. I also have to award Maxwell full credit for the mightily evil plan. It was all his creation and I'm contented with his brilliance in compelling it all to happen. At this very second Zac should be losing consciousness in those icy waters across the way and that will be that. Finito."

"But why?" Ryan could not conceive of any motive for her macabre aspirations.

"Well," she started with a contemplating laugh, "Maxwell was a naughty little boy. He became very rich, extremely quickly. He had done very well for himself. Unfortunately, Maxwell here had a trivial vice. He liked to gamble now and again." She stopped and looked inquiringly at Maxwell. "Sorry, it wasn't trivial and now and again was it? More like unbridled and every day. Especially poker. I think Maxwell considered himself a bit of a pro at the table. Well anyway, because poor old Maxwell got himself very rich, he just couldn't achieve the same buzz from his poker nights. Winning or losing a few hundred or even a couple of thousand dollars just didn't mean anything to him anymore. To put it in perspective it was akin to you winning or losing twenty cents. No big deal?"

Ryan fleeted a glance at Maxwell. He witnessed the powerful figure shriveling before him.

"So Maxwell decided he needed to visit Vegas and play at the high rollers' table. He was pleased to discover it worked. He again enjoyed the high thrill of a big win and the crushing devastation of a massive loss. Unfortunately, the latter came about far more frequently, and soon rich Maxwell became poor Maxwell. But it didn't stop there, oh no. Maxwell knew he could win it all back, he just required some capital in order to do it. I think desperation led him to borrow off some very unpleasant men. Can you see where this is going, Ryan?" her voice crammed with sarcasm. What a bitch, Ryan thought to himself.

"Well, I'm sure you can work it out. He lost that money as well. Of course, these men wanted, no demanded, their money back, plus interest. They were about to take the measure of relieving Maxwell of some of his fingers, just to convey to him their earnestness in collecting the debt. He was in quite a tight spot, and that's where I came in. After my affluent tycoon father passed away to join my beautiful twin brother in heaven, I inherited his entire fortune.

Now Maxwell here, was in a position to offer me the unique service of his masterful manipulation skills, so I bought the debt off those depraved men. They didn't care how the money got paid to them, just so long as it was. So, after my life saving act, I could do with Maxwell as I wished. I made sure he understood right from the start, any failure on his part would result in me contacting the gangsters he used to owe the money to and offering them double to do their worst on him. I think he got the message." She laughed.

"You made him do all this?" Ryan softly spoke in disbelief.

"I instructed him to complete a mandate of directives. He had to make Roy and Zac's life a complete misery. Taunt and tease them, and eventually press all the correct buttons until one murdered the other, or until both took their own lives. Maxwell went for the latter."

Ryan cast Maxwell a disgusted look and shook his head.

"Yes, of course Maxwell refused," Sarah added, observing Ryan's reaction. "But he did not want to die at the hands of those animals. It's funny though, as Maxwell was completely broke, I offered him a nice financial sweetener on successful completion, just to seal the deal. I think being penniless concerned him more than the gangsters."

"Sarah, there is no need to divulge all this to Ryan," Maxwell nervously interrupted, significantly removed from his usual confident self. It was apparent who had the real power in their relationship. It was all there for Ryan to see.

"Maxwell, shut the fuck up," Sarah blasted back at him, only reinforcing Ryan's observation. Maxwell sank deeper behind his desk, as if it were a grotto of sanctuary, his hand raised presenting Sarah his palm outstretched to gesture compliance.

"Now, where was I?" she asked herself. "Yes, that's it. Maxwell finally agreed to come on board. My stipulations were that they must both be as emotionally hurt as possible and both must take their own lives, if Maxwell could not get one to kill the other. I did not want them to be murdered by a third party as a homicide investigation would plainly be unhealthy for Maxwell or myself. Plus, I fathomed, I would be adequately satisfied if they had suffered so much they reached that oh so desperate point to end it all. I filled Maxwell in on them both and requested he devised a strategy to make my idea come to fruition. This is what he came up with, and it seems to have worked a treat. Don't you agree?"

Ryan sat disorientated. He was ardently regretting his decision to be the hero, coming to the salvation of Zac and Roy. It had all blown up in his face, big time. Also, he was not getting any amusement from the gun waving around in front of him. Finally, Ryan gave a half-hearted nod.

"Now the plan wasn't without drawbacks. Chiefly it meant I had to have sex with and be nice to Zac. That's not an easy thing to fake when you hate his guts. However, it was small sacrifices in terms of the goal. Maxwell assured me it was necessary, and I guess he wasn't a bad lay. A little too submissive for my liking." She cackled yet again.

Although terrified Ryan could not help but consider how totally unappealing this girl was. She would have undoubtedly acted her part just as he did. He guessed she would have been sweet and charming, making Zac feel very special. Although outside of her character she was clearly an obnoxious first-rate bitch. Entirely self-centered and absolutely consumed with her own world and life. To boot, she evidently had the financial resources to have whatever she needed, whenever she wanted it. Ryan could not help but consider Sarah would fit flawlessly into a highbrow Hollywood lifestyle.

"So, I agreed to do my part," Sarah continued, composing herself. "Maxwell knew what he had to do, only leaving your part. Maxwell will agree with me that we were both deeply unhappy about involving a third party. It was unquestionably the weak link in the chain, and here you are demonstrating that point to its entirety. It was Maxwell's idea to audition desperate unknown actors. He assured me Hollywood was the best place to look. Hey, what can I say, I was just glad he didn't ask to look in Vegas. Seriously though, we had to find someone with the talent, charisma and looks to pull off the part. So well done, it was you who was the lucky candidate."

Ryan did not feel very lucky.

"Maxwell said it would be good to pay you a large amount of money. The idea being you'd be more likely to keep your mouth shut." She turned to Maxwell. "Note for future reference – should have paid a bit more."

"I don't want your money," Ryan objected, irritated at the suggestion his morals would be less affected by an even more substantial pay packet. "Have it back, all of it. I don't want payment for my regrettable part in your sordid scheme. It makes me sick I even participated in it."

"Whatever, Ryan. But it's a little late in the day for a turn of conscience. What's done is done, and to be frank if you didn't start snooping and learning more about the plan than you were supposed to, you could have returned to Hollywood set up with cash and blissfully unaware of its grizzly conclusion. Maxwell was very specific about what you should and should not know, but, well you had to go and ruin it, didn't you?"

Ryan sensed a distinct change in the atmosphere. The ambiance took on a particularly sinister focus.

"Ryan, I don't know what you wanted to achieve by coming back, it's not as if there's anyone left to save.

The only real detriment you've accomplished is significantly complicating my situation. I hope you understand I cannot let you leave, knowing what you do."

Ryan forcefully gripped the handles of his seat. He constricted the smooth plastic arms so tight he felt they could cut into his hands. Sarah stepped forward, emphasizing the gun pointing at his head.

"I did not want anybody to be murdered, but you've left me with no choice."

"No, please." Ryan squirmed in his seat as he begged. He blocked the visual threat by shutting his eyes and turning his face away. "I don't want to die. Please. I won't tell anyone," he implored.

"Sarah, stop this!" Maxwell shouted, trying to exercise authority in his voice, but his futile attempt was fooling nobody. The balance of ascendancy was swung firmly towards Sarah. "You do not need to do this. It's going to fuck it all up."

"Maxwell, I told you to shut up," Sarah snarled straight back at him, although this time her glare remained transfixed on her prey. The impression of superiority as Ryan writhed like a child within the confines of his seat was electric. He appeared so helpless and pitiful. Sarah had long since forgotten the meaning of pity. Any remorse and mercy had died along with her father and twin brother. Sarah fulfilled an almost sexual, tantric type moment as the pressure of her finger increased on the trigger. With a piercing bang the gun recoiled violently as the weapon ejected its awesome lethal power. In unison Ryan was thrown back into the chair, before slumping out onto the floor. The desk and computer behind were sprayed with a sickening mixture of blood and body.

Sarah gazed down at the consequence of her actions. She felt nothing. No guilt or regret, only a manner of self-assuredness, able to undertake whatever was required to continue on and prevail. No one could stand in her way. Much akin to the person her father once was. Although he would never have actually killed anyone, his fierce dominance and brutal ruthlessness in the boardroom kept him ahead of any pretender to his throne. No one stood in his way, ever. Progress, Sarah contentedly thought to herself.

Maxwell jumped up from his seat. "Shit, Sarah, what the hell have you done? We're screwed now. That's murder. We're gonna go down for this. You've ruined everything for the both of us."

"On the contrary, Maxwell, everything is going to be fine. This time I have the plan, but I'm afraid you're not going to like it."

CHAPTER 41

Maxwell walked over to Ryan's body. He lay still. The remnants of his formerly perfect manly face were imprisoned in the contorted expression he wore to his death. His body slumped unnaturally on the floor, his blood and brains splattered over every object behind him. It was an atrocious spectacle, which Maxwell wished he had never had the privilege to witness. Coaxing someone who was to some extent deserving into committing suicide left Maxwell with a nasty guilt-ridden footprint. Then to add misleading his son, who he knew really did not warrant any of it, into following suit, just for financial gain, was a mammoth weight to bear, pinning him into that footprint. So now where did this latest development leave him? Ryan was an entirely innocent young man, just trying to get a break in his acting career. He had never aimed to physically hurt anybody. After determining the truth, he had courageously attempted to impede their progress and bring the whole thing to a premature conclusion. He had informed Sarah with complete honesty his aversion to profiting from the scheme and had even endeavored to give the money back. It certainly made him a better man than Maxwell, and he knew it.

Maxwell had sealed Ryan's death when selecting him for the part. He had auditioned this promising young hopeful, with so much to offer the world besides his abundance of integrity and self-pride. Now, though, Maxwell absorbed the reality that he would have to live with Ryan on his conscience as well. He felt sick, averting his gaze from the deathly image, turning to Sarah. She stood looking impassively at her victim, as if his body were simply a broken packet of dried pasta on a grocery market floor. The kind of occurrence you observe as a shopper but pass by without a care and absolutely do not work to resolve the situation. Maxwell could only stop and stare in disbelief and horror at his psychopathic employer. Eventually she turned her detached glare to meet his. Maxwell read her eyes, expectant of locating some covert remorse. Regrettably Maxwell could only recover one solitary factor from the blue, dead, piercing windows to her soul. What Maxwell caught a glimpse of horrified him to the bone.

Sarah raised her gun to follow her glare, directly at Maxwell.

"Things have changed now, Maxwell. I need to cover my back and you're going to help me or end up like poor Ryan here."

Maxwell did not doubt the sincerity of her threat. "Sarah, please slow down. There's no need to start turning this into the Wild West."

"There's every need, Maxwell. All bets are off. Now it's about self-preservation, for both of us, but in very different ways. Before we do anything else, we need to go down to the lake to check on whether Zac has done the deed. Once we know the full picture, you'd better come up with a good plan, because I guarantee you won't much care for mine." She motioned with her gun for Maxwell to follow her. He did so, albeit confined within a petrified state.

Overcoming a normal man armed with a gun, such as Ryan, who valued his life and experienced culpability and repentance was fairly straightforward to Maxwell. When it came to the crunch, no matter how strong the desire, to actually pull the trigger and take that irreversible act was hard to carry out. To take such decisive action, to end another's life is a giant step in even the most motivated. Sarah, though, was an entirely different prospect altogether. She was a psychopath, in the broad sense of the word. Maxwell completely comprehended the dangers of a psychopath only too well. Back in his college days, bright and enthusiastic, schooling in psychology he discovered an extensive interest in the mechanisms of a psychopath's mind. His final thesis was based on the very subject.

His fascination stemmed from the directness and candor of their thoughts. To such a person, the world revolves around themselves. Other people are just incidental pieces, to be used for personal gain and satisfaction. Someone of this temperament neglects the concept that the people they share their lives with have individual thoughts and concerns. They are unable to experience pity or compassion to another, unless for personal benefit, most often to merely gain attention. As people are only perceived as tools, an unreserved psychopath would have no qualms in taking their lives, if need be. To the average person it is parallel to throwing a formerly useful tool straight in the bin after it has served its purpose.

Maxwell realized he was in significant trouble, if Sarah determined her best chance of walking away from this unraveling situation without reprimand was to kill him as well, he would be dead before the subsequent thought ran through her mind. He was certain her only motive for not sending him to join the expanding list of casualties was that she believed he might come up with a credible and convincing way out for both of them. Well, at least a plan surpassing her own. Maxwell knew Sarah would have a plan of her own. Psychopaths always did.

"Come with me," she instructed using the presence of the gun as leverage. She slipped the second gun, confiscated from Ryan, into the belt line of her tight feminine jeans. Maxwell led the way out of the office. "Into the great room," she directed with hostility.

"Why are we going in here?" Maxwell asked with puzzlement.

"I need to do something first. Sit here and wait. Do not move. Remember that I won't hesitate to kill you."

Maxwell slid the heavy solid wood doors apart and stepped in. Sarah abruptly closed them shut behind him. Still remaining in the corridor, she untied her shoe and slid the lace out. She then wrapped the lace around the firm metal door handles, crossing it up and under, securing the door shut. After tying it off, she attempted to open the doors. No movement whatsoever. Satisfied Maxwell was going nowhere, she walked back into the office to rejoin the corpse of Ryan.

Once Maxwell was confident Sarah had departed from the doors, he tried to open them. He pulled with all his might straining his powerful arms, but they refused to give.

"Damn it," he swore. Maxwell quickly realized he could not possibly escape in this fashion. The doors were sturdy solid oak. No man could have the strength to defeat such an obstacle. He turned his attentions to the rest of the room. Apart from the expansive window, no other options were available to him, unless he could walk through solid walls. He could not. Walking over to the huge stretch of glass it became immediately apparent he had a better chance with the walls or door. The window did not open. It was one section of curved impenetrably thick glass. He speculated that glass of that size would be toughened. Any futile endeavor to break it would only attract the attentions of Sarah who had so adamantly warned him of the consequences of trying to escape. Maxwell knew she would not hesitate to make good on her dire threats.

Meanwhile, Sarah was busy in the office putting in place the facets of her own escape plan. Pulling her sleeves over her hands, she unplugged Zac's keyboard from his computer tower and brought over and connected in one of the idle keypads from a vacant workstation. Not the one covered in Ryan's brain matter.

She concocted a fictitious suicide note from Zac. It declared he could not go on after his father's own suicide. It alleged he was extraordinarily angry and would take out his vengeance on the world for failing him before ending it all. It went on to disclose his intention to shoot Ryan for sleeping with his girlfriend and to gun down Maxwell because he detested his tyrant oppressor of a boss. She concluded the spurious letter by stating he was ending it all and would be waiting for Melissa in hell.

Sarah read it back to herself and smiled at her personal brilliance. Murdered bodies would lead to a meticulous and far-reaching investigation. On paper Maxwell was only renting this house off Sarah. It was impossible to completely mask her ties to this event, but the next best alternative was to bestow the cops with a straightforward plausible story as to why all this transpired. She had ventured to free herself from becoming a suspect. Any analysis of her connection to Roy or Maxwell could be extremely damaging.

She unplugged the keyboard, again covering her hands as she did so. Sarah replaced it with Zac's one. Now if they dusted the keypad for fingerprints or even checked for DNA matches, nothing would come back to her.

Maxwell was sitting in front of the oversized window when Sarah returned, opening the doors to release him. He refrained from turning his head round to look at her, instead preferring to survey the lake. He wondered if Zac's body was out there, frozen and lifeless within its murky depths. Sarah re-laced and tied her shoe, then called Maxwell to join her. She ushered him to the elevator, and they both stepped in. Maxwell weighed up the advantages in making a move for the gun. In such a tight space he was close enough to just snatch it, optimistic of beating her reactions. He speculated his superior strength would throw the odds in his favor, even if she was the one holding the weapon. Yet all too soon the doors reopened at the garage level and they stepped out. Sarah immediately regained a safe distance. Maxwell kicked himself inwardly, appreciating he had wavered on his best opportunity to recover from the situation.

"Come on, let's go, and you'd better hope Zac is dead," Sarah impatiently instructed, waving the gun back and forth. Before long they were outside, Maxwell quickly wished he had been permitted to take a coat. The unpleasantly cold conditions permeated his thin casual clothing, inundating his senses within seconds.

Sarah, looking equally affected by the acute climate, compelled Maxwell to continue and take the lead. She shivered behind him as they made their way down the driveway. Darkness had fallen over the entire area. The winter nights drew in fast and brought a renewed icy depth to the temperature. As they made their way down towards the road, both were completely oblivious that somewhere in the gloom and shadows, under the cover of the trees someone was there. Waiting, watching, ready to strike.

CHAPTER 42

Maxwell was first to reach the summit of the bank preceding the tranquil waters of the lake. The moon, no longer full, still cast sufficient light. Conversely to the few previous nights, sporadic clouds lingered in the sky. Maxwell realized that if one moved directly across the moon, in this environment unsullied by man-made light pollution, the effect would be to plunge the region into total darkness. If such an opportunity arose Maxwell knew he had to act without delay. Even if he just ran away as an alternative to confronting Sarah for control of the gun, it would reward him with an opening to redress the balance, or at least to consider his options without the threat of a gun pointed in his face.

Maxwell continued forward. He could see no sign of Zac's presence. Sarah was now over the pinnacle of the short hill and was able to see for herself. She looked directly down at the bench. It was difficult to make out, camouflaged in the dimness. However, its silhouette was discernable against the faint rippling moonlight reflection on the lake's surface. The bench was clearly unoccupied. Sarah's eyes scanned the whole area, searching for Zac or clues to his whereabouts, but to no avail. She half-heartedly concealed the gun, just in case Zac could see her. They reached the bench and the water's edge. There was no sign of another living soul, they were seemingly alone.

"I guess he's dead and gone," Maxwell suggested.

Sarah checked the ground around the bench for indications of any activities that might have occurred. No sign of anything out of place. "I'm not so sure. If he was going to swim out into the lake, don't you think he would have at least removed his shoes?" she remarked.

"It's hard to say for sure, somebody in that state is not

thinking logically. Besides which, who says he got in here? Maybe he walked around the banking and entered the lake further down."

Sarah reflected on the possibility, but it did not fit. This area was flat and easily accessible to the water's edge. Either side the bank steepened sharply, making it virtually impossible to walk along.

"Call out to him," she ordered.

"Zac!" Maxwell shouted loudly. They waited, but no response came. After both calling out several times, it became apparent he was not able to hear the shouted appeals.

"So how are we going to know if he drowned himself?" Sarah whispered, her voice tense, but muted. Although they were alone, it did not feel natural to say it out loud.

"I don't know," Maxwell shrugged. "We really need to wait for first light, maybe then we could see his body floating on the surface."

"Do you think it will float?"

"Dunno. I'm not really an expert in drowning people." Maxwell did not intend for the comment to sound sarcastic, but it did.

"So, it's possible even by morning we won't know for sure?" Acute frustration crept into her tone.

"Possible? I'd say unless we do find him alive it's almost assured."

Sarah became overwhelmed by antagonism. She needed confirmation, and soon. It would leave her free to shoot Maxwell and get the hell out of this ticking time bomb.

"There is another consideration," Maxwell added. "If Zac is alive and isn't stupid enough to be out here freezing his ass off in the dark, like us two, it probably means he's back at the house with your friend Ryan."

"No," Sarah snapped back. "We'd have noticed."

"You're sure? I'd say if he was back and heard a gunshot, he'd have kept his presence pretty quiet, don't you think? For all we know he could be calling the cops right now." Maxwell witnessed the panic filling Sarah's face as the idea hit home.

"Shit, we need to get back there, right now."

They both turned in unison and hurried back towards the house, climbing the gentle slope of the bank.

"Stop right there," a stranger's voice called out. Both Sarah and Maxwell froze in their tracks. They searched the shadows for the unperceivable source of the voice. Neither could locate anybody, but with many bushes and overgrowth ahead the perpetrator had his choice of hiding places. Maxwell could not categorize the owner of the voice but felt positive he recognized it from somewhere. It definitely did not belong to Zac.

"Who's there?" Sarah shouted out to the darkness.

"Throw your gun out in front of you," the voice commanded.

"No," Sarah shouted back adamantly.

It was answered by the sound of a gun being cocked penetrating out of the obscurity ahead. "Throw your gun out in front of you right now or I will take you down."

The instructions were clear. Sarah had no choice. She was unable to threaten back not knowing where the ambiguous assailant was positioned. Whoever he was, he had played the situation completely into his hands. Sarah threw both a sulky expression and the gun out in front of her as ordered.

"Now back up ten steps," the voice continued.

As they did so, Maxwell pinpointed who the voice belonged to. But it could not be. He must be mistaken.

"Roy?" he guardedly solicited. When they had reached a suitable distance away the darkened figure stepped out from his shadowy hideout. He walked forward and collected his prize of the forsaken gun. A few supplementary steps closer and Maxwell could see it was indeed Roy, large as life.

"Roy?" he stammered. "How can this be? You were dead."

"Well, obviously he's not," Sarah snapped scornfully at Maxwell before Roy could explain. "How the hell did you mess this up?"

"You took an overdose, I watched you."

"Well, Maxwell, in reality you watched me do what you wanted to see happen. Your willingness to believe made you easy to dupe."

It was a concept Maxwell was very familiar with, a particular weakness within the human mind, often exploited by con artists. It usually entailed fooling a mark into thinking they were about gain or win some easy money or valuable item, the too-good-to-be-true ruse. A third party with no association might well detect numerous warning signs that the scenario is all a scam, but the person involved is so obsessed with the prize they overlook anything else. Someone with blinkers on complying with the con artist's subterfuge is straightforward to trick for whatever gain the perpetrator wishes to take. It brutally aggravated Maxwell that he might have been deceived in such a fashion, but he still had no clue how Roy could have managed it.

"How?" Maxwell queried.

"Well, by sheer luck, the day before you showed up, I received a telephone call from Ryan."

"Shit! Ryan," Maxwell snapped.

"Ryan is now dead, and you will be joining him soon," Sarah blurted out, no longer able to curb her response.

"Jesus, Sarah, you're making this worse for us," Maxwell shouted back at her imprudent comment.

"Ryan is dead?" Roy gave the impression of distress at the news.

"Yeah, he came here earlier, just like you, wielding a gun, wanting to be the big hero. And just like him you're gonna end up dead," Sarah thundered with rage.

"Sarah, will you just shut up." Maxwell could not imagine why she wanted to fuel Roy's fire at the present time. This was a much more adverse situation than the earlier altercation with Ryan. Firstly, a dead body lay in the office. Any police involvement would without doubt result in himself spending the remnants of his life trapped behind bars with animals as his only company. Not the destiny he savored. Secondly the man now holding the gun, not counting the fact he was relatively annoyed, was a fully trained cop, practiced in dealing with such a dispute. Maxwell appreciated that, unlike Ryan, his chances of tricking Roy were slim to none. He would be a hard nut to crack.

"How did you do it?" he finally asked. Maxwell had to know how Roy had deceived him.

"First things first, Maxwell, where is Zac?"

"He's safe," Maxwell invented. He had to take the opportunity to buy them some more time, plus it probably would not go down too well if Maxwell told Roy he thought his son might be the latest piece of driftwood to settle in the lake. "It depends."

"Depends on what?" Roy returned.

"On how we undo this fix we're in."

Sarah at long last kept her hyperactive mouth closed. She could see Maxwell was trying to find a way out for them both. Of course, she had her own private line of attack should it be necessary, but for the time being she deemed it better to let Maxwell try it his way.

Roy looked around the lakeside.

"I don't buy it. You're out here looking for him."

"On the contrary, Roy, we came out here to discuss what we were going to do about Ryan. As Sarah has already filled you in, we were surprised by his visit and yes, regrettably we lost him, there was nothing we could so to save him. Naturally we now had a new problem to deal with, so we came out here to coordinate the adjustment to our plan."

"Maxwell, I still don't buy it. If you weren't looking for him, why have you both just spent the last two minutes calling out his name?"

Maxwell smiled and rubbed his chin. "Yeah, you got me," he laughed. "We were looking. As you can see for yourself, he's not here." Maxwell lifted his arms and candidly gestured all around to signify the point. Then he abruptly converted his tone and mannerisms to harsh and callous. "Roy, understand this, if he's not here and he's not in the house, of which you should be aware because I'm guessing you just watched us leave it, then it means he is in great danger." Maxwell told untruths like it was second nature.

"How so?" Roy asked, panic evident in his voice. "I already know your scheme involved killing him too."

"Ah yes, you're quite correct. But you don't know how, do you?" Maxwell enquired rhetorically. "At present I can reassure you he is alive and well, but after a few hours he is going to do something that will unwittingly lead to his certain death. If we can work this out, I will help you save your son." Maxwell was throwing as many lies at Roy as he could muster, in the hope something stuck. It did.

"What do you want to do?" enquired Roy, completely thwarted. For him this was not turning out in the way he had envisioned. He knew almost everything of the sick plan, but this one aspect he did not have all the pieces on. He just needed to establish Zac's location, from there it would all be promptly over. As with so much in Roy's last few years, sticking on the most crucial element was instigating his comprehensive downfall. Yet within Roy, a compelling energy of determination burned. This time he would not fail himself or Zac, at all costs.

"Give me your guns," Maxwell replied.

"No deal," Roy held firm. "Think of something else."

"Okay, explain to me how you're still alive and making my life harder than it needs to be?"

"We have time for this?"

"Yeah, we've got plenty for the moment," he lied again.

"Okay, as I said, Ryan contacted me. He divulged his function in the plan, to sleep with Melissa. Then he disclosed what he learned about the remainder of your scheme. He informed me you were going to force me to take my own life, and finally kill Zac, but he wasn't exactly sure how you were going to do it. I told that stupid kid to sit tight and wait for me to deal with it. I can't believe he was so unwise as to come back here."

"Yes, and unfortunately his stupidity ended up costing him his life. But how did you fake the suicide?" Maxwell wanted an answer, his conceited narcissism was injured.

"Once I knew what you were planning, I bought a bottle of vodka. I took it back to my apartment. I concealed a thimble full by the bath by sticking it under the soap dish. Then I emptied the bottle and refilled it with water. Before you ask, I poured the rest straight down the sink, I didn't drink a drop." In his mind for a split second, he relived pouring it away. This time it had not been a challenge, Roy had no temptation whatsoever to take a sip. In a defining moment, Roy had accomplished full control over his addiction. The authentic Roy had returned. "Next, I took a mountain of prescription tablet bottles I was using as a crutch and emptied them all in the bin. I located a back-street chemist and slipped him a few dollars to give me a range of different shaped placebos. I put them into the bottles and waited for your arrival. Sure enough, as predicted you came and forced me into taking my own life. Just for the record if I hadn't had the chance to prepare the subterfuge there's no way I would have agreed. Anyway, you witnessed me drink a liter of water and swallow god knows how many phony tablets. Just for authenticity, when you were distracted and not watching me, I pulled the thimble off the bottom of the soap dish and rubbed the vodka around my mouth and shirt. I must have stunk of the stuff, it worked like a charm."

"Ah, that's very good, Roy," Maxwell smiled.

"You're an idiot," Sarah whispered at Maxwell. Her face was seething.

"As for you, Sarah," Roy continued, "I knew there was more to this than just Maxwell. I had to get the full picture to bring this whole charade down. I spent the time after my bogus suicide extracting the truth. I know you're James Stoneman's twin sister. I accept full blame for his death. I would never try to make any excuses for what happened that fateful night. However, no matter how much I am culpable for taking your brother's life, it was never my intention. I did not set out at the beginning of that shift to kill a young child. What you're doing now is completely different. I know you're the instigator pulling Maxwell's strings to make your puppet dance to your tune. The difference between me and you are I accidentally killed James while drunk. You're damaging lives in a premeditated and purposeful manner. In my book that's far worse."

"Far worse?" she screamed back at him. "You have no idea what you did. You took my twin brother. That day, although I was only nine, half of me died a horrendous death."

"I do understand that, please don't think I'm making light of your loss, but no matter how terrible what I did was, it was an accident."

"I hate you so much I could tear your flesh away with my bare hands," Sarah spoke coldly, with no emotion.

Roy was taken aback; he had not anticipated the excessive intensity of dark thought and feelings ejecting from her mouth. Even Maxwell was surprised at the disproportionate aggression, despite recognizing her as a psychopath.

"Look Sarah, you want to hurt me and make me suffer, and that's fine. I understand your reasons. I just don't see why you would want to hurt Zac and then kill him too. He has done nothing whatsoever to you. He is completely innocent and yet you have destroyed his relationship with Melissa. Then followed my suicide with a letter from me telling him it was all his fault, and to top it off you want him dead too. I mean, for Christ's sake, where's your revengeful justice in that? You're sick and you need help. To be honest, I can't put into words how sorry I am to you for killing your brother, but for all the unnecessary pain you've inflicted on Zac, I ought to shoot you dead right now."

"Do it then," she roared. "You don't understand any of the implications of the shit you caused. After my brother died, my father's heart was forever broken. He had lost his only son and person he intended to take the reins of his empire. My father held old-fashioned beliefs. He viewed women as too soft and emotional to thrive in business. He was grooming James, even at that young age, to become a single-minded, cold-hearted captain of industry. After James died my father became paranoid his businesses would collapse when another finally took control. That other was me. As the only other heir, his daughter and in his eyes a soft woman, with a vulnerable susceptible persona would run the company into the ground or get walked over by the board. He never enlightened me about this, but I knew. Anyway, his health slowly deteriorated with stress after losing James. He just couldn't deal with it. He suffered terribly before he finally died five years after James. So now do you see, you killed my brother and tormented my father, until you took him as well. So yes, to get satisfactory revenge I wanted you dead, but I also sought to bring my father's suffering to Zac until it killed him too."

"Right, that's enough," Roy ordered. "I want to know where Zac is right now, or both of you start to lose body parts."

As Roy concluded his intimidating threat, one of the clouds Maxwell had been patiently waiting for moved across the moon. It conclusively eliminated any useful light, plunging the whole area into complete darkness. Maxwell, ready for the opportunity, ran at full sprint away from the other two. His heart immediately commenced pounding, pumping the adrenaline around his body. Sarah had also been waiting for an opening to exercise her own plan for escape. Although, unlike Maxwell, she had not foreseen this abrupt refuge of darkened camouflage, Sarah reacted just as swiftly. She grabbed the gun she had confiscated from Ryan and hidden in her jeans. Without hesitation she fired off three or four shots in Roy's general direction. Despite her blindness to his exact position, she heard him scream out in pain and fall to the floor. No shots were returned. Next, she turned her gun to where Maxwell had run off from and fired uncontrollably into the abyss in front of her.

Maxwell was already aware the opening batch of gunfire was aimed at Roy, but now anticipated some was to come his way next. He moved in a zigzag pattern hoping to increase his chances of avoiding a direct hit. The firing launched in his general direction and for a few moments Maxwell thought he was going to make it. Then on the fourth bang of the gun, purely by luck not judgment Sarah scored a direct hit. Maxwell was thrown to the floor with a smack. A seething red-hot pain burned and engulfed his entire back. It left the impression that his back was a raging blaze. Maxwell had been shot and he realized the injuries were critical. Yet even on the floor he continued to crawl, attempting to maintain his getaway. Soon after, as the moon returned from behind its cloud cover and restored light, the pain began to diminish. Sarah looked across at Maxwell, watching as he pathetically clambered along the stony cold ground. She turned her attention to Roy's location, but he was nowhere to be seen.

"Damn it," she whispered to herself, positive she had hit him. Obviously not well enough.

Maxwell, still crawling, was now coughing and choking on blood coming up from his lungs into his mouth. The functions of his body started to shut down, he was losing copious amounts blood at a profuse rate. Suddenly a foot flipped him over on his back. He was just able to make out Sarah looming over him, her gun extended out towards his head.

"It's time for you to cash your chips in, Maxwell," she unemotionally quipped. The final thing Maxwell saw was a single silent blinding flash. Then he felt no pain and saw no more.

CHAPTER 43

Sarah explored in vain for Roy. He had either hidden out of sight back in the shadows or run off completely. A new depth of anger stormed within her; all of this was for nothing if he wasn't dead. She was so compelled to finish him it hurt.

Sarah took stock. Out here she was completely exposed. Roy was still armed and just because she was unaware of his location, it did not mean he was unacquainted with hers, particularly as she was moving around in the open, looking for him, making herself a sitting duck. She was certain he would pursue her. As far as Roy was concerned, she could lead him back to Zac. Despite the fact that in reality she did not have the first clue where his son was.

Sarah reconciled her thoughts and decided to head back to the house. Roy would undeniably attempt to reacquire contact with her there, but in the house, she would have the advantage. Firstly, she knew the layout, and as far as she was aware Roy had never been in there. Secondly, if she were able to reach Maxwell's private office she could watch over every room in the house with the aid of the CCTV.

She ran. Her legs pumped as fast and as hard as she could humanly manage, like the pistons in a car engine. Throughout every second of her bolt for cover, Sarah waited in anticipation for the sound of a gun going off. She almost braced herself for the explosion of lethal pain throwing her to the ground. For all she knew, Roy could have positioned himself in the shade of the overgrowth surrounding the area simply waiting for her inevitably to pass by. She half scrambled and half fell down the steeper side of the embankment. No one was visible on the road, and before she knew it, she had made it halfway up the drive. By this point the adrenaline was falling short in supply and the fatigue of running at full sprint up the hill burned her calves. She was incapable of sucking in oxygen as speedily as her body commanded it. Everything hurt, but she did not relent her lightning pace. The knowledge that a loaded gun was possibly somewhere out there in the darkness, pointing directly at her head, motivated her performance to well beyond its normal confines.

The closer she got to the house, the stronger the fear of taking a hit became. By the time she had reached the garage door, a hysterical panic had devoured her, and she ran straight into the closed door itself, almost taking herself out. The impact had created an explosive clatter certain to reveal her present location to anybody in the vicinity. After a second or two she managed to compose herself enough to open the door. She stepped inside cautiously; her gun raised in expectation of the next encounter. She was continually regaining control of herself and now back in the place her relative familiarity against Roy the immediate threat level was rendered irrelevant, due to the obvious advantages in her favor.

She closed the door, but left it unlocked. The house was now her spider's web, equipped to trap Roy. Best not to lock him out of the one location she sought to hunt him out in. Her gun still raised, she allowed herself a quick perusal around the cars. No sign of anybody. Sarah crept over to a large red and chrome tool trolley positioned against the back wall. The trolley comprised sets of drawers all filled with spanners and the like. It encompassed a high wooden board bolted to its back for pinning up further selections of tools. Grabbing the trolley with both hands, she pulled with all her might, straining and grunting as the heavy metal compartment rolled out on its casters. The combined weight of tools made it cumbersome to maneuver. Eventually Sarah pulled it out, exposing a door concealed behind it. Sarah opened it and stepped into the back stairwell. It had been obscured from Zac and Melissa for the logical advantage it bestowed on the others when requiring, moving quickly around the house undetected. Now the same principle applied to Roy. Although on the inside she was unable to disguise the doorway entrance as it had been before, so instead she locked the door, assuming that Roy would choose the elevator over breaking down a locked door when the time came.

She raced up the stairs, taking three at a time, although now it was becoming a great deal more grueling to exert the effort necessary. Sarah was already exhausted from the sprint up the driveway and her legs felt like lead. She no longer had the incentive of conceivably being directly in the line of fire. By the time she had reached the door to Maxwell's quarters her bounding had transpired into large, labored steps, dependent on the aid of the handrail as a hoist for her upper body to facilitate movement.

Once inside, there was no time to catch her breath. Roy could not have failed to hear the crash as she stupidly blundered into the garage door. Sarah felt certain his wrath was on its way. Panting like an overwhelmed marathon runner she staggered over and clicked the monitors into life. Her chest was hurting badly. She began coughing, becoming conscious of the pain in her lungs caused not only by being overworked, but also from sucking in large quantities of freezing air from outside. Keeping her mind focused on the job in hand she flicked to the garage camera, but could see no one. Sarah was about to launch a search on the rest of the house, when the elevator information box in the corner of the screen reported that the elevator was moving down from the same level as she was on.

Was Roy in the elevator? The metal box was the one area inside the house without a camera, so Sarah was unable to confirm it was him. She asked herself how it was possible that Roy could have got here so promptly as to already have been up on the private quarters level and then to be leaving it. Sarah studied the elevator report box. It did not disclose which level it was requested to stop at. The only data presented was it was moving down. She already knew if it had been called by someone the box would display their location. That meant whoever had activated it had to be inside. She reasoned to herself it was feasible, if Roy had run straight back to the house the moment after she shot at him. She recapped the incident. She was sure she had shot him. He could not move that quickly if he was wounded, could he? The elevator had now passed the office level, its destination could now only be the garage or the pool.

Then a revelation came to her. The computer had an override control for the elevator. It could be used to stop it dead with the doors locked shut. It would provide the virtual web for Roy to become stuck within. Sarah desperately clicked on the elevator report with the cursor, instantly bring up a list of options. She dithered momentarily, not exactly sure how to do it. Her eyes flicked through the list of possible selections, but unfortunately for her not quickly enough. The elevator halted of its own accord at the garage floor and opened its doors. Sarah trying to catch up broke off the beleaguered operation and instead hurriedly clicked back on the camera access. The garage reappeared before her eyes. Yet it was not Roy who stepped out onto the concrete floor. It was Zac, accompanied by Buster.

"You're still alive?" she screamed at the monitor. Sarah could not believe it. After all the money, time and effort she had thrown into this elaborate vengeance, not to mention actually sleeping with Zac to accomplish the desired result, here before her was Zac alive and well, walking with her dog. Roy was still out there somewhere, playing commando. What a disaster. Apart from costing Zac a girlfriend the whole plan was a complete write-off. Sarah's fragile temper detonated. She exploded into a fit of rage, swinging her arms across the desk. She swept the computer, monitors, keyboard and anything else unlucky enough to be within reach off the control station, smashing it straight onto the hard tiled floor. Continuing her onslaught, she lifted the heavy wood and leather chair in front of the desk and inelegantly, but vigorously launched it across the room. It smashed into the wall, obliterating an expensive piece of artwork. Next Sarah grabbed a lamp off a stand. The body of it was made from heavy, thick ceramic. She hurled it into another wall annihilating it into thousands of minuscule pieces.

Emotion vented, she took Ryan's gun and headed back down the stairs. She was going to take out Zac herself, this time he would have no escape. She would kill him today if it killed her as well. A whole heap of drama and the intensive exertion was taking its toll on Sarah. Although her appearance was slim and athletic, her actual fitness level was a testament to not judging a book by its cover. Sarah had been gifted with what she referred to as "good genes." She had inherited the kind of figure most women would spend half of their waking lives attempting to achieve. Sarah did not eat right, she cherished junk food even if only in small portions. It was pretty much all she ate, not really caring for anything without a high cholesterol level. Her only saving grace was she could only manage a small portion at any single sitting. In a fast-food burger joint, which she habitually frequented, she never ordered the whole meal. It would be wasted. A solitary burger, burrito or chilidog was more than enough to satisfy her.

To complement her feeding habits, Sarah's lifestyle was deficient in meaningful exercise. Taking Buster for a walk was about all she could muster. She lacked the incentive to while away her life trapped on a treadmill, "power walking." What was the point when she was already so slim?

Now, though, rushing down the stairs took its inevitable consequence. A clouded, distant perception befell her senses. Her dexterity and coordination in negotiating the flights of stairs abruptly failed. In a single atrocious moment time seemed to freeze. It was at that instant the realization rushed through her – she was about to fall and was now at the point where nothing she could do was going to stop it from happening. Her hand still reached for the handrail in vain. It was too late. Sarah's body jutted forward leaning over the drop like a skydiver jumping from an airplane. Her head swapped places with her feet, her arms flailing about in a wild frenzy, attempting to control the unrelenting impacts to her body and head.

She reached the closing stages of the run of stairs in a

sickening fashion, before her body limply slammed into the back wall. She came to rest in a tangle of legs and arms. The gun lay innocently beside her like a pet lying quietly next to its sleeping master. Sarah remained motionless, knocked out cold by a violent impact to her head. Still alive, she was at least protected from her current vulnerability by the locked door. However, at present she was not able to do anything to stop Roy and Zac escaping to safety together.

CHAPTER 44

Zac wandered about aimlessly in the garage. Buster loyally followed him round. Zac did not have a clue what was going on. He had come close to taking that last fateful swim in the lake, but when it fundamentally came down to the point of executing it, he found himself unable to act. Not out of a sense of self preservation, but because of Melissa. Despite loathing the mistake she had made, deep down Zac conceded to himself that he still loved her more than anything else in his life, before or present. It had entailed reaching the precipice of taking his own life to achieve this awareness. Yet there it was, presented to him in a moment of transparency. He could not subject her to what his father had bestowed so cruelly on his shoulders. Taking his own life, without a letter publicizing his reasons would only bequeath her with the dire burden Zac currently carried. Melissa was unworthy of such a punishment, not for one single mistake.

Instead, Zac made a positive decision. He left the lakeside to return to the house and do what he should have done the moment he knew his father was dead – phone her. He wanted to confide in her, sharing his grief, but more significantly felt compelled to tell her he loved her and wanted to give their relationship another go. He would offer to quit his job and come home to be with her. With Melissa by his side, he could bury his father and try to put that ghost behind him, once and for all. He could fight to continue on in the face of adversity. Zac appreciated he could accomplish it, after all he had managed once before. A resurrection of his core essence ascended. He wanted to live and share his precious life with the one person who counted. Melissa. A partnership strong against whatever the world could throw at them. He hurried back to the house.

Once inside, just as he was entering the garage Zac was startled by a gunshot. It came from somewhere inside the house. Zac halted, listening. He did not know what to do. His first thought was not to use the elevator. Whoever fired the gun was highly likely to be a threat to his own life. Riding the elevator, yielding an easily perceivable noise as it traveled would alert the gun holder to his presence. Especially if it stopped on the same level as the unidentified perpetrator, leaving him trapped and totally exposed, like shooting fish in a barrel. Zac was thrown back to pondering the mystery of Lisa's disappearance. A lot more was occurring in this house than was apparent on the surface. Zac determined his best option was to take cover behind the furthest car from the elevator and the outside door. Then just wait it out and see what transpired.

It took a while and Zac began questioning whether it was in actuality a gunshot he had heard. His doubts evaporated instantly when he suddenly heard the elevator come to life. Zac braced himself and crouched a little lower behind his Aston Martin privacy screen. His breathing deepened, which in turn panicked him. It resonated so detectably in his ears Zac thought whoever was coming would hear it. He tried to breathe quietly. When the doors slid open, he was able to hear two sets of footsteps. From his squatted position he was unable to see who they belonged to. Zac summoned up some courage and risked a peek. There in front of him to his absolute bewilderment was Lisa. She was the one holding the gun. She demonstrated its presence aggressively at Maxwell. Zac could have gasped if he dared, but silence was his optimum objective in the current situation.

Then Lisa spoke words to Maxwell that Zac just could not believe he was hearing. "Come on, let's go. And you'd better hope Zac is dead." The thought slammed through his mind, what on earth did she mean by that? Why would Lisa want me dead? Zac was perplexed, but still aware enough to keep himself out of sight, at least until they had left the garage and had traveled some way down the drive.

Zac then turned his attentions to contacting Melissa. He quickly concluded in his current position it was not a priority. He could phone in a short while, once he had recovered to a safer location. Until then it would have to wait. Zac determined it would be in his best interests to leave the house completely. Then from a safe haven he could try to figure out what the hell was going on, without the concern of a gun being turned on him. Zac smirked at the irony, a short while ago he was earnestly deliberating the best way to end his life, but now here he was doing everything in his power to protect it. He could not leave Buster. Although he was Lisa's dog, Zac had formed quite a bond with the golden canine. It was risky to retrieve him, but it just did not seem right to abandon Buster here with all this going on.

Zac wasted no more time and jumped into the elevator. He opted to quickly stop off at the office. His thick winter coat was hanging up in there. It was vital to have it as Zac was unsure where he was going to go and how long it would take him to get there.

He stepped out onto the appropriate floor and walked down to the door. The house which had formerly appeared so contemporary now held a creepy sinister atmosphere. Something about it just did not feel right. He could not put his finger on it, whether he was experiencing a sixth sense perception, or just feedback from his currently over-heightened senses. Upon opening the office door, he quickly got his answer.

As the door swung open, Zac was instantly traumatized by the scene laid out in front of him. Despite hearing the gunshot, it did not occur to Zac that he might discover a dead body in the house, especially after witnessing Maxwell and Lisa leaving the house together. He could not think of anybody else likely to be in the house at that moment.

Nervously he stepped forward trying to establish the identity of the body. The head of the corpse was obscured from view by one of the empty workstations. Treading reluctantly forward Zac gained an enhanced perspective. He was appalled to observe half the back of the victim's head was missing, splattered out across the surrounding area. It was a revolting sight. Zac found it difficult to continue looking. Eventually Zac was able to determine the face, although it was blood soaked and askew on the floor. Zac immediately recognized the identity of the corpse.

"Alex," he whispered. For some time Zac just stood, staring at the body. Originally, he had to force himself to look to identify who it was, but now he had acquired that information, Zac was unable to turn away. Finally, he snapped out of his fleeting haze and reviewed his options. It was abundantly clear he could not overlook this. He had to contact the police right away and get out of the house before either Maxwell or Lisa returned.

"Could Lisa have done this?" he asked himself out loud. Just a short time ago Zac had feared for her life, now he had to contemplate that Lisa herself was a dangerous killer. Whether she was or not, Zac now had the clarity of vision to see he only wanted Melissa. He would not care if he never spoke to Lisa again.

Zac had two valid options open to him. Either he could get Buster, grab his cell phone and make a run for it, hoping somewhere down the road he would be able to find a signal. Or secondly, he could contact the cops now from the house and then make a run for it. He categorically required police assistance. He really did not relish the prospect of not being able to locate any signal, so he opted for the second choice. The moment Zac made this decision, panic began to boil and splutter within. He became very conscious of the time, he had to be quick. He grabbed a phone and dialed 911. It connected, but just rang and rang. Within thirty seconds Zac was perspiring heavily and breathing erratically. The panic had combined with frustration. Every second that passed seemed an eternity. His thoughts prompting him with the warning that every second he wasted here was a second less he had to escape to safety. His mind struck a chord when it reached the theory that if he left it too late, he might end up looking just like Alex.

In an attempt to remove some of the eggs from his solitary

basket he elected to use his computer to contact the emergency services, using both mediums in unison until one connected. With the phone still to his ear he rushed over to his desk and flicked it off standby. The monitor glowed back to life revealing yet another bombshell to Zac. On the screen, the application had been left open and Zac shuddered as he discovered a letter apparently from himself. A letter he had no knowledge of, let alone wrote. His pace quickened with his heart pounding like a drum inside his ribcage. It was a suicide note. Zac could only stare in bewilderment. How could this have appeared? he thought to himself. Who would write such a thing? It disturbed him further to consider whoever wrote it must have been anticipating he would take his own life, attempting to use it for their personal gain. Maxwell sprang to his mind. It was his file on Zac's state of mind concerning the reproach of Roy's suicide that had tipped Zac over the edge. How convenient he should leave out such a document, in such a place where he was likely to find it.

However, blaming Maxwell left large gaps. The suicide letter on Zac's computer gave a fictitious confession of the murders of Ryan and Maxwell. He could not think who Ryan was, but the detail seemed insignificant when compared to the big picture. On that consideration, one agenda of the letter became clear. He realized if he had ended it all, the onus of Alex's murder and whatever was going to happen to Maxwell would be easily attributed to him, thus leaving the real perpetrator to walk away above suspicion. From the indication in the letter a similar fate awaited Maxwell, which as a consequence only left one person, the same person who just led Maxwell away at gunpoint – Lisa.

"911 Emergency, what service?" the telephone suddenly responded. It startled Zac. He jumped and almost dropped the phone. Being so distracted by the letter on the screen Zac had practically forgotten he was phoning the emergency services.

"911 Emergency, what service do you require?" The voice on the other end of the telephone re-asked. Zac debated whether it was a beneficial objective to get the police involved at this point in time. He had no clue what or why things were occurring as they were, but before he involved outsiders who would be looking for a culprit, he had to ascertain why someone was trying to frame him. He conjectured Lisa was behind this and now he could fight back after not committing suicide. Now he knew about the murdered body and the counterfeited note, but the question begged, what else had been planted to trap him? If he involved the cops now, he might well be effectively tying his own noose. He had to find out more first. Zac did not want to hang himself. He ended the call without word.

Zac got up, grabbed his coat from the back of the door and left the office. He could not stand to be in the same room as the corpse any longer in any case. Once outside he took some time and a few deep breaths to compose himself. What now? More investigation was required, but at the same time lingering around the house was just as dangerous as remaining uninformed. Zac recognized that if Lisa found him in the house, he would be the next target. He reached a prudent resolution. He would grab Buster and a flashlight then head down to the boatshed. He could focus his initial investigation there, searching for clues in relative safety. He would be hidden away from the house and if anybody did come it would be easy to run and hide in the surrounding trees.

Without squandering a further moment Zac jumped into the elevator and headed up to his private quarters. Once he arrived at his door, Zac slid the key in the lock as silently as possible. He could not be sure if anybody was skulking around inside. Zac was unable to be sure of anything at the present time. He stealthily turned the key bringing about an audible click as the lock moved open. A noise he had never observed in the past, but now the sound emerged in a plain and evident resonance. It forced Zac to stop for a second. He listened against the door. Nothing but silence. Finally, Zac acquired the confidence to push the door open. He awaited it to creak loudly totally exposing his covert entrance, but it mercifully preserved the silence.

The entrance hall was in darkness. Zac peered in, looking through to the living room. He couldn't really perceive anything as the dimness thwarted his endeavor. Every shadow could have been a threat loitering, waiting to strike. The inclination to resolve this dilemma by switching on a light prevailed. He would either know instantly of any jeopardy or if he was safe to advance. However, implementation of this act would categorically substantiate his presence. Whatever the outcome, the conclusion would be rapid. Not as now, all drawn out and suspenseful. Zac repositioned his hand onto the light switch, but just as he was about to flip it down, he perceived a sound from within. It gave the impression of originating in an area off the living room, possibly the bedroom or bathroom.

Zac froze like a statue, not sure what to do next. Before he had the opportunity to make that decision, he heard more noises, a fast-moving pattering sound. It was getting closer all the time, still out of sight, but now in the lounge. Finally, the mystery perpetrator drew into view. It was Buster. Zac smiled at his foolishness. He gave Buster a welcoming embrace. At least he retained one friend in the current situation. He wisely grabbed a jumper and dressed his coat over it, priming himself for the wintry jaunt. Next Zac rummaged around the cupboards to acquire a tool suitable for breaking into the boatshed. At that point the uplifting thought of Gene arriving in the near future comforted Zac. He did not know when Gene would arrive, but Zac was confident he would conclude this nightmare. He decided it was best to wait in the refuge of the boatshed until he heard a vehicle pass by. Once in contact with Gene, Zac believed he would take control. Peering into the cupboard under the sink he discovered a broad-shafted heavy-duty screwdriver.

"Perfect," Zac told Buster. He slipped it into the deep pocket of his winter coat and rushed out, dog by his side, to the elevator.

Whilst riding down to the garage, Zac's diminished dread once again began to intensify. The contemplation of Lisa waiting for him at the bottom raised his paranoia to an unparalleled level. Visualizing the elevator doors sliding open to reveal her standing before him with gun outstretched set to bring his status to that of Alex petrified him. Before Zac could think of anything he could do to prevent such vulnerability the bell pinged with is standard audible resonance, signifying it had reached its destination. Zac winced as the door protracted back into the wall with an excruciatingly slow pace. However, to his relief, only a garage free from apparent threat was exposed. Zac blew out a sigh of relief and hurriedly stepped out into the open.

Crouching slightly, he cautiously advanced forward, conscious that somebody could be hiding behind any of the sumptuous individual motor vehicles dotted around the room, much like he had done himself just a short while ago. Nothing untoward appeared, until Zac detected a tool trolley was pulled out of place, breaking its uniformity with the others. Stepping closer he could see it had been pulled out from the wall and unceremoniously dumped a few yards out from its conventional home. As he approached it his eyes were drawn to the additional feature replacing it. Now laid bare was an unspecified doorway. Zac could not help but become intrigued by the latest revelation. A door unknown to him, purposely concealed. A single question circled around his head, where did it lead to?

Common sense demanded that Zac get the hell out of there, to stick to the original plan and go straight to the safe house that was the boatshed. Yet curiosity fought back. Zac pondered on the doorway, could it lead to further answers? At present Zac was only confident about the fact somebody was trying to frame him for murder. Not having the slightest idea about any other aspect of the events occurring around the house would make this very complicated to explain to the cops, or even Gene. Even more so as Zac remembered something his father had told him many years ago when he was still a cop.

"In a homicide, the first suspect is always the person who discovers the body, and with good reason," he had commented. The snippet of knowledge had remained with Zac and now surfaced to taunt him. Zac elected to investigate behind the door.

Stupid or not, he needed to attempt to understand something, anything, about what was happening. If his future actions would lead to him becoming the prime suspect, Zac knew enough about the cops to realize he had to fight his own corner.

For the briefest moment Zac legitimately wished his father was there with him. Not just because he was dead and he wanted him back, but for the first time in years Zac accepted the only person who could help him now was his pa. Zac swallowed hard. He was abandoned and forsaken. He had to handle it alone. Nervously he crept up to the door. Buster followed, projecting disappointment that they were not heading for the outside door. Zac reached out and extended a trembling hand to try the handle. It was locked. Zac was ready to feel disappointed at this apparent dead end, but something quickly took that sensation away. He was able to hear a distant vague crashing from somewhere beyond the door. However, his curiosity evaporated like the steam from a kettle, replaced by terror like the raging and bubbling, boiling water inside.

Zac leapt back from the door, but his erratic movement spooked the dog. Zac instantly recognized Buster was shaping up to discharge an alarmed bark. In lightning flash speed Zac whipped down to the defensive pooch and wrapped his hand around Buster's mouth

"Buster no. Quiet," Zac as much pleaded as commanded. Luck was on Zac's side. Buster seemed to understand and relinquished his effort to give them both away. Again, Zac blew out in relief. "Come on, boy, let's get out of here."

Grabbing Buster's collar, and remaining half crouched Zac led his companion towards the outside door and what he prayed was freedom. Yet just a couple of paces shy of his escape everything changed. To Zac's complete horror the door handle of the outside door in front of him began to move. Someone was outside the door, making their way in. Zac did not have the additional time to jump into hiding. Buster and he were trapped in the open, completely exposed and defenseless. All Zac managed to do was brace himself as if he had just stepped out in the path of a moving car and wait for the inevitable impact.

The door swung open to reveal someone other than the threat of Lisa or even Maxwell, but instead a person who Zac would have given anything to be at his side at this moment in time – his father. Of course, being of the belief he was already dead, this came as some shock to Zac. He jumped back, falling to the floor, the whole time maintaining a fixed stupid-looking stare at the man who had returned from the grave.

"Pa?" Zac spluttered as Roy gleefully approached the son he loved so dearly. Before Zac could even actively embark on taking any of this in Roy grabbed him off the floor and hugged his son with all his might. The liberation to discover his son alive and well was an unsurpassed moment in Roy's contentious lifetime. It took all the torture and anguish of fighting his way back from the gutter and validated it. This was his repayment, to be granted this awesome high of emancipation. In the moment that followed, Roy had his epiphany. The road ahead was in that instant laid out straight and clear for him. The wrong turns of the future journey were plainly marked out now. Roy vowed never to take another as he lovingly embraced his son.

"Pa, you're alive," Zac resonantly claimed, joining his father in the over-exuberant embrace. Relief and confusion rushed through his body.

"I'm so sorry, son. I didn't mean to let you think I was dead. I should have got here sooner. I wanted to, I never wished for you to think I was gone." Roy's apology was sincere and heartfelt.

"Where is Gene? He told me you were dead, and he was coming to get me."

"Yes, I made Gene tell you that. I know it seems an awful thing to do, but your life was, and still is, in danger. I tried to get here before the suicide note reached you, but I couldn't make it in time. If you had known I was still alive after the letter you would be dead by now. I had to let you think it, just to buy some more time. I'm so sorry, son."

"It's okay, Pa. I understand." It did not matter to Zac

anymore, his father was here, alive and well. He had come when Zac really needed him. This time he had not let his son down. For a period, Zac entirely lost sight of the danger they were currently in. The overflowing respite consumed everything. However, Roy soon regained and maintained his vigilance.

"Zac, do you know where Sarah is?" he enquired searching the garage area with his eyes, whilst his arms continued to clamp lovingly around his son's torso.

"Who?"

"Sarah. Sorry – you know her as Lisa."

"Sarah?" Zac asked, before he continued without waiting for an answer. "No, I don't know. I think she killed someone."

"Yeah, she did," Roy confirmed.

"Sarah?" Zac could not understand where this other name had appeared from.

"Yeah. Look, I don't have time to go into it in detail at the moment, but I'll explain it all to you later. All you need to know at the moment is that this is all a set-up. We were set up, nothing you know about Maxwell or Sarah is true. She's the sister of James Stoneman, the boy I killed. She is out for revenge and has used Maxwell to engineer everything that has happened. That's why the suicide note I left blamed you, because I was made to write it. I don't blame you for anything, you know that, don't you, son?"

"Yeah, Pa, I do," Zac smiled as he answered.

"I'm certain Melissa was played into doing what she did, and the grand finale was for you to end up dead. Maxwell is dead now and Sarah is the killer. She's around here somewhere and now she's after us."

Maxwell's death failed to register in Zac's mind. This was not the time to consider the implications of others. At present his thoughts were simplified, concentrated and streamlined to one effect, self preservation. That was Zac's primary motivation, all other factors blended into the background.

"I heard banging behind that door," Zac informed him, pointing with his eyes. Roy looked over at the door with a stern determination fixed on his face. He rose, breaking himself from their reunion embrace. Roy pulled out his gun and reengaged his focus to ending this. As he stood up, Zac became aware of a disconcerting bright red contaminate on his hands and arms. He studied his father's body, suddenly noticing blood all over him.

"Shit, Pa, you're bleeding."

"Yeah, I'm shot," he answered casually.

"Christ! Are you okay?" Zac cried, panicking.

"Yeah, don't worry, son, it's not as bad as it looks," Roy lied. "I've already had some dealings with Sarah tonight, as you can see. Don't worry about it though, I'll patch myself up as soon as I can." With a purposeful stride, Roy walked over to the door and placed his ear against it. He could hear nothing, only silence. He tried the handle, but as with Zac, he only found it locked. He considered trying to kick it down, but the door opened into the garage. Attempting to force it open the other way would be a futile effort. Besides which, Roy understood he was hurt far more severely than he had divulged to Zac. He was in no condition to go about forcing doors open. Instead, Roy searched for an alternative.

As their current location was a tool-laden garage, Roy quickly found his "Plan B." On the board next to the door was a tire lever. He grabbed it and without delay slid it between the door and its frame.

"Pa, please be careful," Zac warned, not sure what else to say.

"It's okay, son. This will soon be over," he replied, applying strength to the level of his voice. The sound of wood splintering and straining was clearly audible, yet the door did not give. Roy placed the gun on the trolley to free up his other hand in the hope of exacting greater leverage on the tool. After repositioning it slightly he pulled with all his might.

CHAPTER 45

Meanwhile, on the other side of the door Sarah had regained consciousness. Every part of her body ached from her dramatic tumble down the unforgiving stairway. Her head was throbbing the worst, hurting so acutely she could vomit. However, much like Roy, her determination to finish this prevailed over her injuries. The pain was considerable, but her resolve was dominant. She stood awkwardly before the door, gun cocked and aimed. Listening to the splintering as the door progressively gave way.

In an abrupt action the door finally lost its battle and rapidly sprang open with accelerated venom. The tire lever flew though the air, spiraling wildly before crashing to the floor with a penetrating reverberation. Roy immediately found himself staring down the barrel of Sarah's second gun, his own just out of reach on the trolley. He stood motionless, knowing he was trapped. Sarah could not help herself and threw a sarcastic smile at Roy.

"Checkmate," she whispered triumphantly, before pulling the trigger. "Click" went the gun, but nothing else, the Magnum being exhausted of bullets during her undisciplined shooting spree outside. In the split-second preceding Sarah's next move, she cursed herself for being so stupid. How could she not have checked? Now she had to react fast, Roy was already stepping back towards the trolley. Sarah become conscious he was reaching out for something. Looking ahead of his moving hand she realized it was his gun.

Without any further delay she leapt forward, screaming aggressively. As Roy wrapped his hand around the weapon, he was impelled from his feet with an almighty thud. Sarah had crashed directly into him. The impact was sufficient to take Roy down to the ground, weak from his previous gunshot injury, impairing his ability to withstand such a physical attack. Holding onto the shaft of the gun they both crashed to the floor. To make matters worse for Roy the solid concrete winded him badly. Immediately Sarah tried to grab the gun and turn it towards Roy. By gripping the shaft, he managed to maintain its direction pointed more toward her than himself but had no opportunity to make contact with the trigger and neutralize his opponent.

Zac jumped up, trying to aid his beleaguered father, but with the gun flailing about wildly he had to be careful to avoid catching a wayward bullet. It forced Zac to maintain a distance for the short term.

Buster, however, had no such respect or fear of guns. To him Roy was the danger. Sarah was his owner and in trouble, so he did what any virtuous dog would do and jumped into the mêlée trying to force Roy to back off. Zac observed in horror as his father, Sarah and Buster wrestled it out for dominance. With the gun still moving uncontrollably he was unable to advance in. Roy had maintained his control of the shaft, but Sarah now had her finger up against the trigger and could fire whenever she desired. Zac ducked and dived several times as the path of the gun passed through where he stood. Buster had hold of Roy's arm, growling loudly as he slowly increased the pressure on his bite. Eventually the load became too much for Roy to take and he let out a deafening scream. Moments later a gunshot rattled out around the glorified car park.

Buster yelped as if he had been shot himself. He jumped away and scampered to a safer distance. The severity of the bang had startled him, but Buster was fortunate only to suffer a shock, not the deadly wrath of the weapon.

The struggle between Sarah and Roy slowed to a bloody conclusion. Roy scanned Sarah's beautiful blue eyes. His mind was transported back to the day he last looked into his late wife Amy's eyes. They had met him with precisely the same manifestation – cold, barren and empty. Her lifeless eyes staring back, without anything behind them.

Sarah was dead. The bullet had fired straight through her detached unloving heart, stopping it instantly. In a moment of pure irony, Sarah had pulled the trigger just as the gun was pointing at herself. Zac ran over and pulled her limp lifeless body off his struggling father. It was evident the brutal conflict had amplified the rate at which Roy was losing blood. The sickly red essential life provider was now streaming out from under his coat. Zac studied his father's face. All the color had drained from his skin and Roy was fighting to remain conscious.

"Pa, no, stay with me, please don't die. I need you. Please don't leave me," Zac wholeheartedly begged, holding his father in his arms.

"Son, I love you. I'm so sorry for all the pain I've caused. This time I managed to be the father you needed, but now it's up to you. Phone Gene before the police, his number's in my cell. I collected evidence against Sarah and Maxwell, and Gene is fully aware of their plan. He'll help you explain all this to the cops." Roy paused while he caught his breath. Even talking was becoming a strain. "Go be the man you can be. You have another chance, please do it for Ma and me," he panted, fighting the onslaught of invading darkness.

"Pa, no!" his desperate son wailed.

"You're a man now, Zac. I'm so proud of who you've become. Keep hold of that dog, he'll help you through the hard times ahead. And do me one other favor – talk to Melissa. She was played the same as us, they tricked her. I know there's no real excuse for what she did, but Melissa was coerced into it. Maybe you could find it in your heart to forgive her. I'm sure she's learnt her lesson." Roy's voice was becoming fainter.

"I will, Pa. I love her." Zac was unsure what to do. He wanted to get help but was reluctant to leave his father. "I should phone for an ambulance," he sobbed.

"I love you, Zac." Roy struggled to get the words out along with his last breath. Zac could feel his body let go. It became limp and heavy.

"Pa! Pa!" he shouted at the unresponsive body in his arms. But Zac knew he had gone. He descended into uncontainable emotion. Irrepressible tears flooded his eyes, running down his angelic face in a torrent. They splashed down onto his father's head as he pulled it up to his own. "I love you, Pa, I love you so much," he told him as he continued to rain tears down on his father's lifeless face.

Buster trotted back over to Zac; now confident the danger had passed. He sat next to Zac and pressed his head against his side.

"Go and be with Ma," Zac whispered into Roy's ear then gently placed his head back onto the ground. "Go and find her. You've paid your penance, now be free."

Printed in Great Britain
by Amazon

58611424R00154